AUTHOR

MASTBAUM, B.

CLASS

F

TITLE Clay's way

Clay's Way

Clay's Way

Blair Mastbaum

alyson books
los angeles

© 2004 BY BLAIR MASTBAUM. ALL RIGHTS RESERVED.

MANUFACTURED IN THE UNITED STATES OF AMERICA.

THIS TRADE PAPERBACK ORIGINAL IS PUBLISHED BY ALYSON PUBLICATIONS,
P.O. BOX 4371, LOS ANGELES, CALIFORNIA 90078-4371.
DISTRIBUTION IN THE UNITED KINGDOM BY TURNAROUND PUBLISHER SERVICES LTD.,
UNIT 3, OLYMPIA TRADING ESTATE, COBURG ROAD, WOOD GREEN,
LONDON N22 6TZ ENGLAND.

FIRST EDITION: JULY 2004

04 05 06 07 08 a 10 9 8 7 6 5 4 3 2 1

ISBN 1-55583-819-7

LIBRARY OF CONGRESS CATALOGING-IN-PUBLICATION DATA
MASTBAUM, BLAIR.
   CLAY'S WAY / BLAIR MASTBAUM.—1ST ED.
   ISBN 1-55583-819-7 (PBK.)
      1. GAY YOUTH—FICTION. 2. PUNK CULTURE—FICTION. 3. TEENAGE BOYS—
FICTION. 4. SUBURBAN LIFE—FICTION. I. TITLE.
PS3613.A8196C58 2004
813'.6—DC22   2004043878

CREDITS
COVER PHOTOGRAPHY BY SCOTT COFFEY.
COVER DESIGN BY MATT SAMS.

FROM MY HEART, TO SCOTT

Part One

1

Alone in my room
Island storm shower passes,
Raindrops = company.

I wake up. Aloha. I have to piss really bad. I stretch, stand up on my bed, and pee out my window. Blue sky, fluffy clouds, golden sunlight, a soft breeze, exotic birds chirping, and the scent of plumeria flowers in the air—another fucking beautiful day on Oahu. I flop back down on my uncomfortably hot bed and trace crisscrossed lines on my chest from sleeping on my bunched-up sheets. I jump down to the floor—to the scratchy sea-grass rug my mom made me get last year because the carpet was so wrecked from hair dye—crawl over piles of haiku I wrote last night, and look around for something to wear. All my cool punk clothes are dirty-and not like worn only once and then thrown into a pile. I wore them probably ten times each 'cause I've only got a limited number of T-shirts and shorts and pants that are cool and make me look like me instead of some young Republican fashion victim, my mom's dream.

I crawl around naked, smelling T-shirts till I find one that's not so bad, then climb to my feet and rub my eyes. I look in the mirror, which is half-covered with my best haiku from the last year all taped up around the edges, and mess up my bright-blue spiky hair—to make it punk—and hold my arms behind my head and pose like a model. I'm trying to look sexy or whatever. It doesn't work. My arms look like twigs, and my ribs stick out like a stray dog's. I rub the hair in my armpits and smell my hand. It smells good. It reminds me of having fun. I pull on the thin line of hairs below my bellybutton. It's the only new part of me that I actually think looks kind of cool. I flex my arm muscles in the mirror, then pull down my T-shirt, which has this cartoon of a couple on the front. The couple holds on to their knives and forks in front of a dead pig with an apple shoved in its mouth. Above and below them, in little-kid handwriting, it says: STOP THE LUAUS! STOP THE INSANITY!

I like it 'cause it pisses people off.

I shove my bare feet into black suede Etnies and step into a pair of long camo shorts. I jump up on my bed and throw my skateboard—and my green backpack that has my haiku notebook, a banged-up carton of cigarettes, surf shorts, skate tools and some other junk—out the window and jump out after them. I can't take the front door 'cause I don't want to see my parents and explain where I'm going or any bullshit like that. I try to miss the brown patch of grass caused from pissing out the window all the time, but wind up landing right in the wet spot where I just peed.

I strap my backpack on, drop my board on the street, and skate off, passing houses like a bullet. People couldn't see me if they tried. I'm just a blur. I don't want people thinking that they understand me or can get a handle on me from what I'm wearing or my haircut or anything like that.

The sky is light blue with dense, wet clouds sticking to the sides of the Koolaus, sharp green mountains lined up like a huge eroded dinosaur spine that divides the island in two. A giant cloud-dagger slices into one of the mountains. A waterfall cascades down its sheer cliff like blood from a gash into a narrow valley where the rusty twisted pieces of a crashed Japanese Zero still lie.

Cars drive by me. A couple Hawaiian guys in a brown pickup truck screech past, honking and staring just to act tough. They make me feel like I shouldn't be here, which really sucks 'cause I already have a hard enough time leaving the house without being totally stoned.

I look away from the mountains down to my board, which is slowly veering onto the road. "Fuck." I jump off. Just two more revolutions of my skateboard wheels and I'd have been dead meat, a smashed-up pile of roadkill. When my board stops, I watch the passing traffic and I feel insecure immediately. I pull my shirt down and notice there's a streak of dried come across the bottom. I scrape some off with my fingernail. I spit on it and rub it in. My camo shorts have blue splattered all over them. I lean down and sniff it. I think it's from when I dyed my hair Bright Aqua Ocean Mist—at least that's what the Krazy Kolorz jar said—a couple weeks ago. I'm so trapped inside my mind I didn't even notice this shit all over me.

I skate up to the pizza place to meet Jared to buy pot. I'm nervous 'cause I don't want to have any uncomfortable conversation with some stupid surfer to get it. I wish there was a drive-through where you could just hand the twenty to the guy and get the pot in a paper bag.

Jared's sitting on a picnic table out front with a triangle of cartoon-looking pepperoni pizza in front of him. His floppy black hair is parted in the middle like curtains and his thin eyes are squinted so they look like cuts.

I look inside at all the pizza guys holding big wooden trays with uncooked pizzas on them. They're all blond and tan and great surfers, and they have this way about them, like amazing confidence and egos that I hate, but at the same time they turn me on.

It's pretty fucked. I hate those dudes.

"Aloha, J-boy." I say "aloha" all the time, but not like a normal haole-Hawaii boy would say it. I say it with satire—one of my secret weapons hardly anyone my age gets. I think it's lame, so I say it even more than someone who really does speak Hawaiian.

"What's up?" Jared shoves his soda over to me. "Want some?"

"Sure." I take a big drink. "Sucky day, huh?" I prop my board on the table.

Jared laughs. "You're so pessimistic." He loves it here. He likes sunny days, swaying palm trees, stupid white sailboats on the horizon, and beautiful sunsets. He's so lame sometimes it kills me. He's my best friend, and we waste a lot of time together, but it's like we're holding on to some fragment of friendship from when we were young, like fourteen.

"Listen to these, man. I wrote them last night." I unzip my backpack and get my haiku journal, a black old-fashioned French notebook my aunt sent me from Paris. I read purposely loud so all these Hawaii-lovers can hear. "Hot sand invasion. The people love skin cancer. Rats love SUVs."

Jared looks around to make sure no local boy is paying attention because I'm defying the "aloha spirit," which is what everyone here calls being nice and respecting the islands and all that crap.

"Haole surfer-boy. Unintelligent islands. Local just means dumb."

A girl gives me a dirty look, so I read another: "Brown roaches arrive. Centipedes in shoes...

"You're so predictable."

"No, you are—I knew you'd say that." I look across the street at the skateboard shop. It's called Board of Hawaii, named for how I feel living here.

Board intimidates me. Most skaters are assholes. They think they're the center of the world. I do too, I guess. But the skaters are cooler than everyone else at least. Every other dude on the island is a surfer, and they all act like they're so in touch with the island, with the waves, the tides, the moon, and the culture, and it's such bullshit. They don't know any more about this place than I do.

I take a huge drink of Jared's soda, and it drips down my chin.

A woman watches me as I wipe it up with my sleeve. She gives me the same kind look she'd give someone who was mentally challenged.

I take another messy drink. "How do you know this guy?" I don't trust Jared—he has the potential to really dork out, like he doesn't understand the social order—and I don't want to go in there unless this is a sure deal.

"Don't worry. My sister knows him."

"What do we have to do?"

"Just ask him, I guess."

"Is it that guy—Marcus?" I picture this cooler than cool guy who owns the shop. He's slick and handsome and Japanese and super low-key and he looks like he's flying when he skates or even when he walks across the room. I don't want to have to ask him for anything.

"No, dude. Quit freaking out."

For Jared to tell me to stop freaking out is pretty major. He's always the one who's spinning out of control about something—he has too much energy for one skinny Asian kid. The closer I get to sixteen, the more neurotic I get. I zip my backpack and strap in.

We skate across the street and up onto the shopping-center sidewalk, passing the video store, the Hawaiian candy shop, and a NO SKATEBOARDING sign that's been scraped-up with knives and pelted with rocks and covered with stickers. It looks like the target for aggression of every skater on Oahu. I jump off my board a couple storefronts before the skate shop 'cause I don't want anyone to see me fall on my face trying to kick-flip on the Board sidewalk. To be safe, I punch the tail and carry it by the truck.

"How do you know he'll have it?"

Jared tries to ollie up onto the sidewalk and his skateboard slams into the glass door. Bang!

"Nice, stupid."

"Cut it out, dude. You're paranoid."

"I'm not paranoid. You almost broke the door."

Jared flings the door open and walks in.

I look at myself in the glass over a bunch of taped-up punk fly-ers and mess my hair up so I look like I've been skating for hours.

We walk in and the electronic eye counts me and dings. I immediately notice a security camera pointing down at us from the ceiling. I duck my head, afraid of having my insecurity recorded.

Jared nods to the guy behind the side counter, then goes over to a rack of T-shirts. I hurry over to him and hide behind the rack like a rat scurrying from bright light. It's pathetic.

"Where's the guy?"

"Over there."

I look at him through the tops of T-shirt hangers. *Oh, fuck. It's Clay.* He must have just started working here. He shouldn't be here. He's a surfer. He should hate it here with all the little skate-rat boys. He must be friends with Marcus, so he puts up with us for the money and prestige of having a bunch of skater boys think he's god.

I sort of knew Clay a couple of years ago, but he wouldn't remember. Our dads were friends for a while—actually, his pancho-wearing, goateed, cult-leader-looking surfer-dude dad worked for my dad—but Clay's dad totally dumped mine after he divorced Clay's mom and moved to the Mainland. I went to Clay's house, though, one time when I was like eleven, and we hung out in his room. He had pot, even though he was only thirteen, so we got really stoned and I ended up hugging him and hallucinating, and he didn't make me feel stupid. I'd never smoked before, but I didn't tell him. He was wearing a karate robe, and he was talking like crazy. He had just started surfing, and he told tell me all these stories about having a really hard time and being made fun of for being a skinny little Portugee cockroach—the term used for young surfers in Hawaii. And Portugees get a bad deal in Hawaii. They're like this race that's between haole—white—and Hawaiian. Dark-complexioned and black-haired, they originally came to the islands to harvest sugar cane—basically slave labor—and now they get teased for talking too much and bailing the hardest while surfing, which, of course, isn't true—sometimes.

When I reenter the real world, Jared is staring at me. My hands are rubbing some girly pink T-shirt.

"Man, what are you on?"

"Shut up." I lick my hand and rub it all over my face to look like I'm sweating, pull the neck hole of my T-shirt open to show some of my chest, pull my shorts down low, and squeeze my hands together to make it look like I have some muscles in my arms. I'm afraid to talk to Clay or even look at him. I've beaten off to him more times than I can count.

He'll be able to tell.

He sits behind the glass counter case with his feet up. Skate videos are stacked behind him, and he's watching one on an old TV. His arms are behind his head and his stool's tipped back so far it looks like he's going to fall. His left arm's in a cast with a whole bunch of shit written on it. Above the cast, there's a tattoo shaped like Oahu with a plumeria where Kailua is. He's tan and has black buzz-cut hair. The veins in his forearms stick out, like he's just been surfing or something. His red T-shirt fits perfectly. He's skinny, but with muscles, like the perfect amount—not from working out, but from surfing. They're real muscles, not decoration. He's got to be almost eighteen by now, and he looks better than ever. He grew up to be a real ripped little Portugee boy. I heard he dropped out of school, but whatever. School's a waste of time anyway—especially in Hawaii, where the teachers are dumber than the students.

I can't take my eyes off him. My hands move the T-shirts on their hangers, but it's just some rodent instinct. I couldn't care less about them.

Jared nudges my shoulder. "Go ask him."

"You fucking ask him. He's *your* sister's friend."

"OK, but come with me."

I follow him out from behind the T-shirts and up to Clay's counter.

Clay finishes watching for a second, then reaches for the remote, and pushes pause. "Eh, braddahs. Howzit?"

Jared nods like he's cool, which he isn't. "Nothing much. Just hanging."

I can't take the awkwardness of small talk. I look up at the TV. It's frozen on a dude sliding a monster handrail.

Jared leans over the counter. "Do you know where we could get some pot?" He says it way too loud.

"Fuck, you guys, chill." Clay looks to see if Marcus heard, but he's still on the phone talking about kegs for a party.

My skateboard slips from my sweaty hand and shoots into the counter, making a hairline crack in the glass. The fluorescent light inside the case makes it obvious. "Sorry."

Clay looks me straight in the eye. He leans down to investigate the crack.

I lean down on the other side.

We trace the crack on opposite sides of the barrier. Our fingers are only centimeters apart.

I feel embarrassed by the intimacy of my soft touch on the glass. When I look at him I feel such a strong connection, like something just clicked that's been missing my whole life. Clay stares at me, then stops moving for a second. He's like a rare captive reptile in a glass tank. I want to free him.

I want to kiss him.

"No worries, brah." He stands back up and holds out his hand to shake. "I'm Clay."

I jump up like an overeager dork, practically throwing my hand at him, but our hands sort of fumble against each other because he does some kind of complicated cool-boy surfer hand-shake. I have no idea how to do it, even though I've seen guys do it all my life.

"I'm Jared."

Clay and I look over at Jared.

Jared reaches his hand out to Clay and does the whole routine perfectly. Then he looks at me like he's a cool Asian boy or some-thing, which he's not.

"How much you guys interested in?"

I look at Jared, whose face is blanker than I've ever seen it. He doesn't even know the proper measurements to say.

"Not much," I say. "Like, maybe enough for a couple joints."

Clay laughs. "I'll smoke a joint with you guys." He pulls out this little BACK IN sign that's a clock with the circled "A" for anarchy drawn in the face. He sets the plastic clock hand to fifteen minutes.

I was hoping he'd set it to four hours or maybe there's a switch you can flip to make it say ETERNITY—and make everyone else freeze so we could be alone together. I'd be the only human left moving, so he'd have to like me.

2

Monster waves
Back on his surfboard,
the flying boy.

We follow Clay out the back door through the dark storeroom filled with stacks of skate decks. He smells like a mixture of salt-water, sweat, and trees.

We go through the back door out into a closed-off alley with a couple Dumpsters and a NO PARKING sign covered with so many skate stickers you can't see the yellow. The gnarly ripped-up asphalt is littered with cigarette butts. An old couch with a couple issues of *Surfer* magazine on it props open the back door.

Clay tries to reach into his pocket with his casted arm. It's hard for him to twist his shoulder in the right direction to wedge his hand in. He finally brings out a film canister of weed and some rolling papers. I zone out watching him as he rolls a joint like an expert.

He holds the joint up to my mouth.

I can't breathe.

Don't panic. You have to calm down.

I take it between my lips.

He pulls a lighter out of his pocket and lights me up.

I take a big hit and start coughing. I feel really stupid, but I can't help it. It's stronger pot than I've ever smoked. I pass the joint back to Clay. Our hands rub up against each other as I let go of it.

He takes a big hit. His chest puffs out as he holds it in. He leans back and his T-shirt rides up on his stomach.

My eyes are pulled to his bare skin. It's smooth and tan, and there's a thin trail of hair from his belly button to the waistband of his boxers.

Clay looks down to his stomach where I'm staring, then up to me, like he felt my eyes on his skin.

Jared reaches for the joint. Clay gives it to him. He takes a huge hit and winds up coughing worse than I did.

Clay looks stoned. His face softens and his eyes turn slightly pink. An alligator smirk curls his lips up a little. He looks back at me, then down my torso.

I focus my mind and send him a telepathic message:

Ask me to hang out with you.

Remember me from when I was in your room.

Ask me to be your best friend and go away with you to be naked.

I'll just take what I've got in my pack.

That's all I need.

"So, where do you guys skate?"

Jared hands me the joint. "The old folks' home behind McPoison's."

I give the joint back to Clay, trying again to feel the heat from his hand on mine. "Keolu School, when it's not crowded. They've got a great railing and some steps."

Marcus sticks his head out the door. "Bro, you gotta phone call."

"Thanks man." Clay gives him a shaka hand sign. He looks funny and stoned and I can tell that if we were alone, we could laugh and hang out and have a great time together. He hands me the joint and punches me lightly on the shoulder. "Keep it, brah. I've got my own supply."

"Thanks."

Don't go. Don't go. This is the most fun I've had in years, maybe ever, the most stimulated I've been in my whole life. I feel like climbing the nearest telephone pole and cutting the wires.

"Yup. Laterz. See you aroundz." He turns and just stares at me—maybe because he's so stoned.

I stare back. "OK…aloha."

Something flies in the air between us that I've never experienced before-like waves of nuclear electricity. It's powerful. I'm amazed I can't see it. If the energy was harnessed, it could power all of Tokyo. It's a universal force. Stronger than anything I've ever felt. He karate-chops the air, then runs inside, almost tripping on a board that's lying on the floor in the back room.

"He's cool. I told you."

Jared's so naive sometimes. Cool isn't half of it.

"I gotta go, man. I have to mow my parents' lawn." I'm lying so I can have some time alone to think about Clay.

"I thought we were gonna get stoned."

"We're already stoned."

Jared's useless now.

I miss Clay already. I skate home as fast as I can, anxious to run to my room and come while thinking of him. At the front door I reach into my pocket for my key. "Fuck." I must've lost it again. I walk around the house and check all the doors and windows. No luck. Like we've got anything good to steal anyway.

My fucking parents keep locking my window like they're these robots that do nothing else but lock. They know I use it more than the front door. For a while I look for a hidden key that has never existed, fooling myself into thinking it's still possible.

Next I walk around the house to the back porch—which is green with moss because it never dries—and drag a chair into the lawn so I can lie in the sun. I'll get a little tan so I look better the next time I see Clay. Maybe I'll fall asleep and dream about him. I see my mom's bright-orange cat behind my reflection in the dining room window. He's rubbing against the glass all cat-like, like he's stoked to get some action. It's gross. I hate the sexuality of cats.

I walk up to the window, like there's any chance in hell he could actually help me. "Get the fucking key, you dumb-ass cat." I flick the glass and he runs away.

I throw my backpack down and go back and lie down in my mom's chaise longue. The sun's really hot. I sweat and smell myself, and I think about the same kind of smells on Clay's body—which really makes me want to jerk off. I stand up and walk to my next-door neighbor's shed thinking like a criminal, controlled by his dick. The door's open. Cool.

I walk in and pull my shorts down. They bunch up around my knees, and my dick pops out and points up at my face. I picture Clay leaning back on his stool at Board, with his arms back behind his head, with his dragon tattoo showing under his sleeve, the strip of skin exposed above his waistband, the scar on his forehead, the place where his hair meets the nape of his neck. I imagine how rad it'd be to touch him all over his body, and for his hands to be on me.

I start beating off. My hand becomes Clay's in my imagination. My dick surges upward, and I shoot on my neighbor's workbench. It's more come than I've ever shot before. I guess I was never really turned-on looking at skate magazines and local ads for surf shorts. Beating off to those doesn't even compare. My come looks anarchic all over power tools and screwdrivers. Biological vandalism. I light up a cigarette. I love Clay. He's the best. I look out the shed's dusty window at my house.

Fuck. My mom's home and she's spraying some wilting Mainland flowers that my dad planted yesterday. They're daisies and pansies and all these faggy-sounding flowers that don't belong on this tropical island anyway. No wonder they're dying already.

She's wearing her work clothes: a boring dark-blue business pantsuit thing, a string of pearls, and blinding-white canvas boating sneakers that make her look good and conservative. It's all wrong for what she's doing. She should be wearing shorts and a T-shirt, like every other mother would on this island.

I sneak out of the shed, close the door, and run around the house, then back down the side yard to make her think I'm just coming home from skating.

The hose slips from her hand and flies wildly around like an attacking snake. Water shoots everywhere. It splashes the cat and it runs under the neighbor's fence. Water shoots my mom's face and soaks her pantsuit so the fabric sticks to her legs. Her white shirt gets drenched too, and I can see her bra and the shape of her breasts.

I caused this. My ejaculation was so powerful it fucked with our whole plane of existence.

I grab my backpack and slip in through the now-unlocked back door just off the kitchen. I grab a soda and go to my room and close the door. I kick off my shoes, take my shirt off, and throw my skateboard on the bed. I throw my pack down and stand in front of the full-length mirror. I look cooler for some reason. My neck looks thicker. I practice making cool faces like Clay makes. "Eh, brah. What's up?" I suck my cheeks in and pucker my lips out. "Hey, Clay. You wanna hang out? Cool." I'm such a dork. I'm not even close to being as cool as he is. I don't know what to do. I need to learn how to surf. Maybe I can go over to Waikiki and join one of those tourist classes. I should get a tattoo, but what? A dragon. That would be copying. He'll be freaked out. A tiger? A Hawaiian flag? No way, I'd get my haole ass kicked.

I shake myself, start over. "OK, here goes."

Sam, just be yourself. "Hey. What's up?"

That was okay.

I jump on my bed for a while, trying to make as many punk rock sounds and grunts as I can—for practice—watching the earth go by as my view out the window comes and goes, up and down, up, down. It's medicinal. I stop and look at my room. I hate the stupid soccer trophy still sitting on my desk from when I was eight and the model boats my dad used to help me make and my dumb clothes and piles of stupid haiku. I need a change.

I get a beer from my mini-refrigerator. I know, I'll dye my hair again. I get some dark-red vegetable hair-coloring, rub it all over my head, and wipe the rest on my shorts. My hair turns violet—the red mixing with the blue. My hands stain in seconds. This shit doesn't wash off. I lie on the floor and stare at this mobile of our solar system I've had forever. It twists and jerks in the afternoon breeze. I take a big gulp of beer and burp. I reach for a model of a 747 and fly it around the room. It has the old paint scheme of United. It takes off, levels off after a sharp turn to the left, and flies from my chest to my bed with a stop off at my desk for re-fueling.

I close my eyes and listen to neighborhood sounds: cars driving at their conservative neighborhood speed, strollers rolling on the sidewalk, a roving pack of ten-year-olds who found someone's cigarettes.

I have to call him. I dig the Yellow Pages out from beneath the pile of old haikus under my bed. I find Board of Hawaii and grab the phone and dial. It rings and my heartbeat multiplies.

"Hello? Board." The voice is scratchy and cool sounding. I listen as hard as I can to see if I can tell if it's him. I hear him breathing.

"Hello?"

I clear my throat and deepen my voice. "Aloha, is Clay there?"

"Yeah, hold on. Clay, phone call." The phone gets thrown down on the counter.

I hear some rattling and fidgeting with the receiver.

"Clay here, for all your skating needs and more." He sounds way better than I even remember, and I remember him being perfect.

"Hello?"

I don't know what to say. Just having him on the line is enough. I quietly tear the page out and shove it in my pack.

My door flings open. "Sam?"

Fuck. I hang up as fast as possible. I hope he didn't hear that. Just the sound of my Mom's voice would make him run. "Can't you knock?"

"Sorry. I didn't know you were home. I was coming in here to check something."

"So, you were just gonna come in my room?"

"It's about your birthday, honey." Her voice is halfway between sweet and bitchy.

I want to tell her she shouldn't even bother with my birthday. I don't give a shit about it. It means nothing to me. "Don't get me anything. Money would be good."

"I'm not giving you money. It's too impersonal."

"I don't care. I like it."

She looks around the room. "It's a mess in here. How can you live like this?"

"I'm an animal."

"Why are you dying your hair again? Your natural color is so nice."

"Why'd you lock my window? I couldn't get in."

"Carry your key. Someone's going to break in."

"Who, like the natives? Hawaiians in loincloths are going to steal our television?"

"OK, Sam, very funny. Where's your key?"

"I lost it."

"How many keys have you lost?"

"Eighty." I laugh. "Now leave. Aloha, Mom."

"I don't want stains all over the bathtub when you rinse your hair. Scrub the tub and don't use our towels." She leaves and closes my door behind her.

Not that I liked her before, but she's meaningless now that I have Clay. I don't even need food or air anymore.

3

It's birthday 16:
Flowers outside my window
I feel...average.

It's 12:38 P.M. and now I'm sixteen, which means nothing. My parents won't let me drive till I'm seventeen. I can't buy beer or even cigarettes.

Clay doesn't know it's my birthday.

It's Sunday. I peek out my door. My parents are doing their normal afternoon nonsense on the back patio. They refused to acknowledge my fifteenth birthday because when I turned fourteen I told them I hated them. I never thought they'd really go through with it, but they did, and actually it was sort of a relief—but this year I can tell my mom's gonna try and turn over a new leaf or whatever and make me feel like an idiot birthday boy again. You know, with candles and all that.

Last year, Jared came over with a huge chocolate cake with a plastic skateboard ramp and skater on top. It was impressive. My mom looked guilty in a gnarly way when he came through the front door, and I loved it. Her plan to make my birthday suck failed miserably, and the cake was so good, like bakery good, much better than some dried up carcass she could have made. So this year, she's doing the typical shit: sneaking in my room, getting my sizes for all the preppy clothes she'll buy that I'll never wear. She's gonna sing to me soon. She'll be making up for last year's birthday. I'm dreading it. I hate opening presents in front of people and being the center of attention.

I think it's disgusting that I'm related to them. They envy dudes that own yachts but don't have any books on the shelves. They talk about money all the time, and they think welfare should be ripped from the poor. They like white clothes and play tennis and think skaters are rats who don't deserve to be treated with respect. If they weren't my parents, I'd flip them off on the street, key their cars as I walked by, and shit like that.

I look in the mirror first thing to see if I look any different. My hair looks cool purple. I look around my room. It looks too young for a sixteen-year-old. An award hangs on the wall from a middle-school spelling bee. Framed photos from when I played fucking tee-ball are sitting on my desk. I can't believe I lived with all this claustrophobic shit around and didn't go crazy and end up hanging myself. I throw my stuffed animals to the top shelf of my closet to get them out of the way. They look really dumb. Most of them fall back down on me, which feels good. They're light and soft and fluffy and they smell like my bed. I lie down in a big pile of them.

Footsteps come down the hall and stop outside my door.

I don't know if it's my mom or my dad, but I think they're spying. "Aloha! I can hear you. Who's out there?"

"Good morning, sweetie. Happy birthday." My mom opens my door and sees me lying shirtless in my underwear in a pile of stuffed animals. She stares at me like I'm a freak of nature. Her eyes wander up and down my body. "You haven't grown up so much after all."

I cover myself up with a big stuffed giraffe. "Shut up, Mom." I put on a T-shirt that says PARENTS SUCK and make my hair really messy and spiky with Elmer's glue. I have a need to freak them out, but it's getting harder and harder, because I've already done almost everything they ever dreaded—like smoking pot, getting drunk, staying out too late, dying my hair green and blue and white and black, and being honest enough to tell them to fuck off when they should. I walk down the hall, dreading the formalities ahead.

Mom and Dad sit at the kitchen table reading the Sunday paper. Mom sort of smiles when she sees me, but I can tell she's dreading this as much as I am. She's afraid I'm going to tell them I hate them again or something. She gets up, reaches into the oven, and gets out a big pancake with sixteen candles stuck in it.

I can't fucking believe this. A *pancake* that my mom probably fried up like five hours ago. It looks pathetic. It's greasy and flat and huge. I could never eat it, but I guess I'm going to have to take a couple bites or something, so they don't think I'm completely unappreciative.

Dad folds the business section down dramatically and looks at me over his glasses. "Jesus Christ, you look like drug addict."

"Aloha to you too, Dad." I sit at the table.

"Robert, it's his birthday. Come on." She tries to light the candles but it looks like she's never used a lighter before.

I take it and light the candles.

She sets the flaming pancake in front of me. "Make a wish."

OK. Make Clay fall in love with me and ask me to move in with him in a cool house on the North Shore with tons of pot plants. And a personal chef and a big lock on the gate so no one can get in, ever, and make him naked all the time, just walking around the house and being happy and smiling with lots of boners and lots of money and drugs and no school...

"OK, honey, blow out the candles."

"OK, Mom." I guess I was taking too long. I blow out the candles.

Wax drips all over the pancake.

"Sweet sixteen." She reaches underneath the table and pulls out a wrapped, long, weird-shaped thing with a card on the top. She hands it to me.

It's heavy. It's a skateboard. At least they tried.

"Read the card first," Mom orders.

I look at the yellow envelope and set it back down on the table, unopened—then I grab the board. It's wrapped in paper that has little baseballs and mitts on it. I think it's some sort of comment on what I'm not. I get sort of stoned looking at it.

"Open it," my dad orders, pointing to the skateboard, like he's ready to get this over with and go golfing, like he does every Sunday.

I pull the stupid paper back. It's cool. It's a Blind board. The picture on the bottom is a little kid with a huge head and an all-knowing smirk. It probably reminds them of me, an evil little shit. I set it on the table and spin the wheels. "Cool, guys. I like it. Thank you."

My mom leans over and kisses me. "So it's the right one?"

"Yeah, it's excellent."

"OK…" She reaches under the table for another gift with a big red bow on it. It's a dorky white helmet with PRO-EXTREME written on the side.

"I don't need a helmet, Mom."

"Yes, you do, and I want to see you wearing it."

I examine the helmet, acting like I'm checking it out and that I like it and all that. The gift tag's on the inside. It reads BOARD OF HAWAII. This has to be a sign.

She's fulfilling my destiny without even knowing it.

I picture her buying the helmet from Clay. Terror rushes through my chest. Did she talk to him? I don't want him to know I have such an idiot mom.

Dad gets up and goes into the garage, probably to polish up his golf clubs.

Mom clears the table. "I'll put this in the refrigerator. It'll be great cold, for later. Don't forget the card." She hands me the yellow envelope.

"Thanks Mom. I love you."

For giving me an excuse to see Clay. You did something a hell of a lot cooler than you think you did.

A crackle of lightning shoots through the sky followed by booming thunder with a slight electric roughness at the end. I can see rain coming out over the jagged Koolaus. A heavy shower sweeps in and pounds the house with huge raindrops. Maybe the streets will flood and turn into rivers. Clay could paddle in and save me.

I go into my room and set the new skateboard on the floor and step up onto my top bunk. I stand on the edge of the mattress and aim for the center of the board. I jump. I land right in the middle, but it flies out from under me and slams into my closet door. It breaks a couple louvers near the bottom. I fall on my ass, making a loud thud on the floor. The rain's pretty loud, so maybe they didn't hear. I roll the board to the center of the room and jump up and down on it. I sneak out to the garage with the board under my arm.

As soon as the door closes behind me, my mom opens it again, pops her head out, and sees me opening the garage door. It's pouring outside.

"Where are you going? You'll fall and break something."

"I'm just gonna try it out. Is Dad gone?"

"Yeah, he went to the golf course to wait out the rain." Her head pops back into the door and it closes.

I look through my dad's toolboxes. There's lots of wrenches and hammers and a whole bunch of other weird shit.

I set the board down, wheels facing up, in a big iron vice grip thing and turn the knob till it's held in tight. I grab a huge rusty plumber's wrench and hit the back truck and wheels as hard as I can. They snap off. A wheel goes bouncing around the cement floor. The wood splinters, revealing the white inner layers of the deck's construction. It looks sort of realistic, I think, though I've never skated hard enough or weighed enough to really break a board.

4

*Reflections off
waves he rides,
the one I love.*

I ride my bike through the pouring rain, holding the fucked-up board under my arm. Giant drops pelt my face so it's hard to see. My backpack is getting soaked, probably ruining my cigarettes. Halfway down my street, the rain stops-the sky turns clear and blue and the pavement is dry and hot. I look back to where it's raining. Fifty feet behind me, it's cloudy and gray. The road steams as water evaporates off the pavement.

A perfect rainbow crosses the sky, which makes me feel lame, like I'm on the front of a greeting card. *I love you, son. You're my world.* Fuck. I forgot to open my mom's card.

I'm soaking wet, but I ride all the way to Board of Hawaii before I stop. I park my bike at the far end of the parking lot, because it's a lame kid's bike that I'm still riding since the one I got last year for Christmas got stolen, and I can't tell my dad I need a new one 'cause he'll be really pissed off. I wring out my shirt. Bluish-red dye runs down my face and my hands are stained red from yesterday. I duck down and look in the window between a flier for the "Big *Mele*," a punk rock show in this pasture valley, and an ad for a skate demo that's going to be here in the parking lot next week. My breath fogs up the glass.

I see Clay standing at the back counter, concentrating on screwing a truck on a board. I walk in, hiding the broken end of my board under my arm in case I chicken out. I sneak a look at Clay.

He looks up, sort of happy to see me, I think. Maybe it's more of a confused expression. "Eh, brah. What's up? Why you all wet?"

"Hey, man. Aloha. It's raining in my hood." I try to sound cool, unaffected, not nervous as fuck. I start to walk over to him and notice myself in a mirror mounted on the wall. I'm soaking wet on a sunny day. I look like such a weirdo.

"Hey." Clay looks up at me.

"Hey."

"Like your hair."

"Thanks."

"Did you just do it?"

I look at my red-stained hands. "Yeah. Part of it." *Oh, my God. We're talking. A normal conversation. This is too cool. I'm going to pass out. I wish I could, so he'd have to give me mouth-to-mouth.* I stare at him and my mind goes blank. My only instinct is reptilian. I want to pounce on him. I can't look away. I'm amazed at how beautiful he is.

"So what's up?"

I snap out of my daze and look down. "Nothing."

"Want some more weed or something?"

"Uh…no." I lower my voice. "I need a truck for my board." I bring it out from under my arm and put it on the counter, wheels up, like it needs surgery. This is so transparent. It totally looks like I just bashed it on the curb or something.

He has to know I faked this. I would've had to drop in from a seventy-foot ramp onto concrete to break the truck totally off like I did. He's gonna see through my whole act, figure out that I broke my board to have an excuse to see him. This could be a huge catastrophe if I don't play it cool. "That's brand-new, dude.

What happened?" He sounds impressed. He doesn't know. Maybe, he thinks I'm an excellent skater that can do 900s on the ramp. "Some lady bought it yesterday. I put it together myself." He looks me straight in the eye. "Was that your mom?"

"Oh, yeah, guess so. Birthday present." I feel really stupid for saying "birthday," like I'm a little kid.

"No fuck? Happy birthday." He leans over the counter and punches me in the shoulder. "How old are you?"

"Sixteen." I feel so incredibly stupid. A lisp came out of nowhere when I said it.

"Sweet sixteen." He pinches my cheek. "Dude, why aren't you wearing the new helmet?"

"'Cause I'm not a huge fucking dork."

He reaches into the glass case and pulls out two cool-looking wheels and a really expensive truck, looks around to make sure no one's watching, and hands them to me. "Put these in your pack, quick."

I feel his warm breath on my face as he whispers it. I want to dive over the counter and attack him and strip his clothes off. I take the wheels and truck from him, feeling as much of his hand as I can, and shove them in my pack. "Thanks." I look him in the eye, and we get sort of stuck together through our eyes. It's totally inspiring and sexy and embarrassing at the same time.

He looks away, and his face goes blank, like he just came out of a trance. "Happy birthday." He reaches for his anarchy clock and sets the dial to morning. He grabs his keys and twirls them around his finger. His key chain is a small green lizard. "Marcus, I'm outta here, man. See you tonight?"

Marcus looks up from his phone conversation. "Clay, it's only five."

"Cover for me, brah." He flips him off jokingly. Clay gets what he wants when he wants it.

I need him. I can't walk another step or take another breath without him. I'm addicted. I'll need methadone when we have to separate.

"Come on." He walks to the door and I follow him outside holding my broken board and my pack.

"Uh…so, thanks again. That's cool of you." I shift my weight back and forth and play with my balls through my pocket without thinking about it.

Clay casts his eyes down to where my hand is still bouncing my balls up and down, then he gets in his truck—a gray Toyota pickup that's all dented up and dirty, like he'd driven it through the Sahara and back and never washed it. I take my hand out immediately, and I don't know what to do with it. I shove it in my armpit and pull on the hairs.

He rolls down the window. "You wanna smoke a joint?"

OK, something's not right. Things never go this good for me. This is a setup.

He leans over and unlocks the passenger door. "Get in, brah."

I walk around the back of the truck, so he doesn't have a chance to really look at me and decide I'm just a stupid little sixteen-year-old loser. I throw my broken board in the back and open the door. It smells like sand, sweat, and dirty clothes. The floor is covered with old fast-food cups, empty cigarette packs, torn-up surf magazines, a couple of video boxes, and the T-shirt I saw him wearing the other day at the shop—a green one with a flaming volcano on the front. I want to smell it.

I throw my pack on the floor and almost reach for the seat belt, but decide that's not very cool. I look forward and take deep breaths to calm myself down. I'm afraid to look over at him. I might not be able to control myself. I'll blurt out, *I love you.* There's a dried gourd head hanging from the rear-view mirror.

"Weed and papers are in the glove box."

I open it and a load of tape cases and tapes and a chunk of sand-encrusted surf wax fall out onto the floor and into my lap. I find the pot and papers in a little cloth bag.

"Roll one, brah."

I don't know how to roll a joint, but I try. I grab a video box to use for a flat surface and pour a little weed out on it and break it up with my fingers. I pull a paper out of the case and attempt to roll a joint. Some pot spills as we turn a corner.

I manage to roll something that looks vaguely like a joint. "How'd you break your arm?"

"Playing football. We were playing on my friend's roof this one night and it was raining. I went out for the ball and ran off the edge."

This is so fun and easy after hanging out with Jared the genius for so long.

Clay looks over at me, and stares hard into my eyes at a red light. "It's not funny, man." He punches me in the shoulder. "Just kidding, brah. The cast's ready to come off. My arm's good as new under here. Hey, where do you live?"

"Haiku Village." *Fuck*.

"You got a saw there?"

"I think so…why? You gonna hack me up?"

He holds up his cast as he takes a corner really fast. "Where's that joint?"

I hand him the joint. It's pathetic, sort of like a skinny worm.

Clay looks at it and laughs, then lights it up. He takes a big hit and exhales. It fills the cabin with yellowish haze, lit by the sunlight, and streaming out his open window. He drives like a fucking maniac, passing cars on the wrong side, double the speed limit. It's sexy.

He hands me the joint, half-gone.

"I'm dying to surf. I've been tying plastic bags around this thing with rubber bands, but it gets soggy and sick-ass rank."

"Turn left here."

Please don't be home, Mom and Dad. Do me this one favor, if you ever do me one again. I secretly hold my hands together and pray to Kamehameha's spirit or whatever to make them leave if they're home or stay gone for hours if they aren't. I hope there's nothing embarrassing lying around my house. *Oh, fuck.* My bedroom floor's covered with stuffed animals, and the phone book's lying open to the ripped-out Board of Hawaii page. He'll think I'm a stalker out to invade his life with baby food and stuffed giraffes.

We pull into Haiku Village. The iron letters are inset into two stone walls that mark the entrance to my neighborhood. "Turn here."

He turns hard, almost making a screech, and speeds up to forty-five, which seems really fast in my boring neighborhood. There's not much room for rebellion in the confines of rows of houses, only built in about ten different models from the late '70s. We approach my house.

My heart rate speeds up and my hands start to sweat. "That's my house right there." I point to it. My voice cracked like when I had to give a speech at school. Fuck. I've done it. I've made myself real.

He's going to see it all: my boring fucking life, my lame room, my stupid house, the meaninglessness of my existence. I have to get out of this. I could say my parents beat me and he's not allowed inside. I could say I have severe dyslexia or amnesia and I can't remember where I live.

"What's wrong?"

"Oh, it's just…my parents suck. We should hurry before they get home."

He pulls in the driveway, which I know will piss Mom off if she comes home and doesn't have her parking space, but I don't want to tell him not to.

I get out, holding my backpack, and Clay follows me up to the house. I try the front door knob and check my pocket. "Oh, fuck. I don't have my key. Hold on." I run around to my window. "Please. Please be unlocked." I reach up and slide it open. "Yes!" I climb in and jump from my bed to the floor. I throw my sheets over the bed and try to hide the dumb stuffed animals. I look at myself in the mirror and unstrap my pack and throw it on my bed. I frantically take my shirt off and dry my armpits with it. I throw it down and grab another one, shake it out, and pull it on, then I stack up my haikus, which are scattered all over the floor, and throw them on my little boy desk. I run down the hall and fling the front door open. I feel stupid, like I should say "welcome" or something. Clay's standing there all proud-looking, holding my broken board. "You forgot this."

"Thanks." I take it from him and lean it against the coat closet door. The house is dim and cool and quiet and peaceful compared to the hot, sunny day.

He walks in and looks around. His presence, confidence, and rawness make the house seem petty, overly decorated, fake.

"Changed shirts?" He takes his slippers off by the front door and flops down on the couch.

I'm stoked he noticed that—even though I feel stupid about it. My ears are ringing. I pace back and forth in front of him, straightening up the house, trying to hold my chest out, and clenching up my stomach to make it look muscular. I'm making casual look painful. I don't know how to seem normal. I need a prop. I should offer him some beer or get an ashtray, even though my parents would flip if someone smoked in the house. It's worth it. "You want some vodka or something?"

He looks at me like I just said something ridiculous. "That's cool, brah." He sits way back on the couch with his legs spread far apart and his hands over his crotch. He breathes and sighs, like it feels good to sit in this peaceful room that no one in my family ever uses.

I get two cans of Coke from the kitchen and walk back in. "Here. They were out of liquor." I hand one to him, roughly, so he doesn't think I'm willing to kiss his ass, and sit down next to him, barely on the edge of the couch. I stare at his neck, and the veins running through it down into the collar of his red T-shirt. I get a whiff of the laundry soap his mom uses. I can't stop my legs from fidgeting on the floor. It's making the whole house shake, and rattling a cabinet across the room.

"So, what do you wanna do?" I say, way too fast, so it sounds like some corporate slogan or something. I go to take a swig of my Coke, but I miss my mouth and it spills down my chin onto the front of my T-shirt. I want to take it off, and just be shirtless with him, but I'm too skinny and white.

We either have to fight or jerk off, because I can't take this tension much longer.

"Let's get that saw, brah."

"OK." He saved me. Something to do. I let out the air I've been holding in my lungs this whole time and feel my chest deflate.

Clay stands up and looks around. He walks down the hall. "That your den?"

Fuck. He's seen my freak cave—the place where I beat off, stare at myself in the mirror for hours, and examine every part of my body like I'm a monkey.

He's gonna sense the weirdness and run out screaming.

I practically run after him down the hall. "Uh, yeah, I'm just getting around to throwing some old shit away."

He hands me the joint, and I relight it and take a hit. "I'll take your hit. Blow it in my face."

I blow the smoke in his mouth. Our lips touch and surges of electricity bounce between us. It's the closest we've ever been. I hand the joint to him. He takes a hit and blows his smoke down my throat. A bubble of heat surrounds us in the hallway. He looks back at me like we're sneaking through somewhere we shouldn't be. "*Iruka binbinkuru karupisu.*"

"Japanese, right? What's that mean?"

"Let's chop this shit off my arm." He holds up his cast.

"OK," I say. I guess he's not going to tell me what he said. We walk past the never-used living room. The couch is messed up and wrinkled from where we were sitting. It looks like we had sex on it. "Come on."

He follows me out the back door toward the neighbor's toolshed.

I leave a trail of pheromones behind me. I hope they're influencing him, secretly influencing him to kiss me in the shed. I check the neighbor's driveway to see if they're home. One car with its trunk open. I can't tell him we can't go back there just because I'm afraid they'll catch us. He'll think I'm a wimp with no sense of adventure. He surfs fifteen-foot waves.

We sneak up to the door. The dog behind my house sees us and starts barking, shoving its nose under the fence. I open the plywood door and jump in.

Clay crouches down, sneaks in behind me, and closes the door.

The shed still feels like desperate sexuality. I move the tools around on the workbench to lighten the vibe a little. I hide a wrench that I came on the other day below some sandpaper.

He hands me a saw. "This is perfect," he whispers. I think he's impressed that I can get my hands on all these tools. It's totally masculine.

Clay rests his arm on the wooden workbench. "OK, cut away, little brah."

I grab his upper arm, over his tattoo, to steady it for cutting, and hold the blade over his cast. My boner pokes at the workbench. It's beginning to hurt. If it touches him, even by accident, through two layers of fabric—my shorts and his—I think I'll come. Sweat drips down my armpit and down the side of my torso. The blade looks dangerous against his cast.

He grasps the back of my neck with his free hand. His palm feels like it's burning through my skin, revealing the innermost parts of me. "It's okay, dude. You won't hurt me. I'm invincible." He winks and makes a sort of superhero smile and cocks his head.

I saw back and forth, quickly. The blade gets close to his skin, where the plaster stops and cotton bandages start.

"Ah! Stop!" He yanks his arm up and it breaks the bare light bulb hanging from the ceiling. The shed goes dim and slivers of glass rain down on us. The vibe is romantic and moody, with just a little spurt of yellow filtering through the canvas covering the small window.

"Sorry. Did I cut you?" My words sound too intimate in the darkness, like couples in movies lying in bed together late at night after sex, next to a crackling fire in the fireplace, so I add, "dude."

"No, but you looked insane, little man. I didn't think you were gonna stop."

"I wouldn't hurt you." *Oh, God. That was so obvious.* I open the shed door and light pours in. Clay pulls and rips through the rest of the layers of his cast and throws it into the trash can, which I have to remember to get out later. He rubs his white, newly exposed skin over his mouth and nose. "Fuck, it smells like a moldy dog."

It smells strong and rank, but kind of turns me on. It's a strong variation of what he smells like, like what would happen if he didn't take a bath for months. I inhale as much as I can. The molecules that carry the scent are part of him. I'll never be the same. This base-level information will take my brain weeks to analyze. "Don't you wanna keep it?"

"Nah."

I look down at the cast and examine the pen-and-ink drawings of sharks and Hawaiian tikis. "Those drawings are cool."

"My friend drew those. I've got lots of his work."

I'm jealous. Who is this friend? Does he like him?

We walk out of the shed through my backyard.

I see a couple flakes of white frosted glass in his hair. "You've got some lightbulb in your hair." I reach up to his head.

He stops and leans over.

I brush it off, feeling electrical charges beam off him.

He gets a chill and shakes. He feels it too. "Wanna come to this party tonight? It should be pretty rad."

Oh, my fucking God. I feel my mouth turn up and smile. I wish I had a mirror so I could adjust my expression to not look as stupidly happy as I do now and come off like some sort of eager little boy who wants to be cool.

We walk into my kitchen and he hops up onto the counter.

I can't formulate a *yes* without sounding like an overeager idiot. I feel like I'm standing with a blank look on my face and my mouth dropped open like in cartoons.

Mom honks her horn outside.

"Oh, fuck." Clay's truck is in the driveway. I look down and realize I still have the saw in my hand. I shove it in the oven and grab the garage door opener from the stupid wicker basket on the table by the back door. I push the button and stick my head out the door leading from the kitchen to the garage to scream at my mom out front. "Hold on!" I slam the door behind me and run around the kitchen like a maniac making sure no evidence is lying around, checking every surface.

I tell Clay, "Go out the back door."

"What's up? Does she beat you?"

"Uh, no. She's just weird. I don't know."

"Fuck that." He walks out of the kitchen, then out the garage door toward her car.

I want to scream *stop* and tackle him to the ground, but I can't move or speak. Two completely different worlds are colliding and I feel helpless. A warm fuzziness makes my stomach feel weird. It's like I'm being cared for. He's forging my way for me.

He leans down into the Volvo's driver's side window. "Hey, I remember you. I sold you the skateboard. I'm Clay. Need me to move my ride?"

"Yes, Clay, that would be nice." Mom sounds bitchy. She stares at his tattoos like they're leprosy.

Clay struts over to his truck. "So, you wanna come or not, brah?"

Mom pulls the Volvo into the driveway and pops her trunk. Groceries fill it to the brim.

Don't be a dork. Stay calm. Don't act like it's the best thing you've ever heard. I take a deep breath. "Yeah." I wave him closer. "On the corner, okay?" I point up the street.

He nods and winks at me, like it's funny that I had to say that all secretly. "I'll pick you up at seven. Cool, brah. Laterz."

"Bye." I wanna say "I love you" and blow him a kiss. I want to make him sign a written agreement to confirm that he'll show up.

He gets in his truck and revs the engine. He peels off, making a loud screech, a thin trail of smoke, and a black mark on the street.

I can't take this. I want to run after the truck like a dog. I stare into the street, imagining what his truck looked like in our driveway with him sitting inside it, paying attention to me, talking to me. I think about his face and try to plant the image in my mind forever.

"Are you going to help me with these bags?"

"Why are you such a bitch?"

"God damn it, I had three open houses today and I'm tired. Don't be a brat. Who was that boy?"

He's my fuel for survival, the reason I'm alive. How can she not sense that? "He told you—Clay. You met him, remember? He's my friend."

"Well, you're not getting in that truck with him, so don't bother asking. He drives like a maniac." She points down the street where Clay just drove off. "There's no reason for that kind of showing off."

A good sign, I think. Maybe she feels like he'll take me away, steal away her baby, violate her sense of family, affect me in ways that I never thought of.

I hope so.

I grab a bag of groceries, walk into the house, throw them on the kitchen counter, and sneak out the back door to the toolshed to get Clay's discarded cast. I shove it under my shirt and run to my room. I lie back on my bed and stare at it and smell it.

5

Brisk walk, crisp spring day.
Hoping for cherry blossoms
sticking to my feet.

I shut my door—so my parents won't know I'm gone—and climb out my window into the warm, still evening. The streets are empty. There's the savory smell of hamburgers cooking on barbecues, which makes me hungry. I'm missing dinner by leaving early to meet Clay so I can have some time to cool off and so I don't come off as too excited about a party he probably thinks is no big deal. I walk down to the end of my street, where the road and driveways are paved and the streetlights have been put in, but the houses aren't built yet.

I sit down on the curb in front of a big hole in the ground, dug for the foundation of a new house. I wait, trying to look normal, leaning back, not too upright, not too reclined. I take some deep breaths to calm myself, then I stare at my arms and flex my biceps to try to make it look like I'm all cut. I lean back and look at the world upside-down. I've been waiting for at least fifteen minutes and I'm starting to think he's not going to show up, which would fling me right back into my life before him—pretty fucking boring stuff. If I had a watch, I'd check it over and over again, like some Republican waiting for a late private jet, who was about to miss out on some third-world real estate development deal. "Fuck!" He's not coming. I'll never get to be so close to him again. I get really sad, like real gnarly depressed. I could cry or hit something hard that would rip my fist. I look up at the sky. "Fuck you, sunset."

Clay pulls up. He nods and just sits in his truck—doesn't motion for me to get in or wave, or anything.

I don't know what to do. Time is moving extremely fast now, almost canceling out the whole time I waited, which must have been like half an hour. I wish I had instructions or something. I stand up, open the door, and jump in. "Aloha." I slam the door.

"Careful, brah. Almost spilled the shit." He has an open baggy of white powder in his hand. "I got some coke. Do you want some?"

"Uh…maybe later."

"Sure? It's good shit."

I love when he calls me that, even though I don't feel like his brah. "OK, sure."

He peels off like in movies. We whirl past half-built houses laid out along paved streets. The newness of the unbuilt neighborhood turns me on in a way. Everything's possible at this point. This neighborhood could turn out to be a luxurious retreat with looping driveways or a slum with cars up on cement blocks and boat parts scattered through the lawns.

We stop abruptly, and he turns the truck off.

Everything goes quiet. It's the loudest, most obnoxious silence I've ever heard. It's unbearable. I feel like kicking and screaming to break the spell.

"OK, man, you done this before?" He looks serious.

My heart beats faster. "Yeah."

"No, you haven't."

"No, I haven't."

He can read my mind. We're meant for each other. "Dude, find something to make lines on. I think there's a CD case or something on the floor."

The black shirt he had on yesterday is on the seat between us. I want to steal it to smell and beat off with. "I don't see anything." I reach up to the rearview mirror and try to snap it off. "I think these come off." It breaks off in my hand.

"Oh, great, you broke it, you little punk." He looks at me with intensity.

"Sorry."

He smiles. "No worries." He was joking, thank God. He pours a small pile of coke from the plastic bag onto the mirror and divides it into two equal rows with his driver's license.

I lean my head to see the photo. He had dreadlocks then, down to his shoulders. I'm glad he cut it. He looked like a hippie.

"OK, man." He rolls up a twenty. "Here you go."

Adrenaline floods through my veins. There'll be a TV movie of the week about me—the sixteen-year-old coke addict living in paradise. "You go first."

"OK." He leans down over the mirror, within inches of my crotch, and snorts. He looks experienced and confident, like one of those kids in an antidrug commercial, rebellious and dangerous and cool.

My turn to snort.

I hope I don't fuck this up. I can handle this.

He holds the mirror to my face.

I lean down and bump it with the rolled-up bill. Some powders my lap and dusts my T-shirt with whiteness. He's gonna be pissed. I'm such an idiot.

"Careful, brah."

I'm doing everything wrong. This is like relearning how to be cool. "Sorry." I lean down and snort up what remains of my line. It burns my sinuses.

He accidentally scrapes over my crotch with his license and pushes the spilled coke onto the mirror.

My dick gets hard from feeling him touch me, even though it's only a driver's license. I act like I'm readjusting myself or whatever, and pull my shirt down to cover it. I feel great, like a perfect machine.

We get out and walk over to a dugout hole in the ground with a wood-framed skeleton of a house built on top of it. The dirt is layered, like an earth-science model, all different shades of yellow, orange, and red. The colors of clay.

He pulls his little BMX bike from the back of his truck, and rides into the dirt yard and slams on his brakes. His wheel spins out to the side, spraying clumps of dirt into the air. In one solid motion, he stands up smoothly and scrunches up his T-shirt sleeves. He looks powerful and amazing, like a wild wolf superhero, all jumped-up on coke and proud of his perfect skid.

I jump down into the pit, getting my Etnies all orange with dirt. He rides down the incline into the pit after me, and kamikaze-falls off his bike, leaving it to crash into the other side of the pit. He rolls on the ground and comes to a stop on his back. His shirt pulls up and I can see his side corrugated with the impression of his ribs. The fall knocks the wind out of him. He looks vulnerable.

The streetlamp flips on. The light has a strange sort of yellow buzz to it, and the colors of the dirt and his hair and skin look more intense.

It turned on for us. There's no one else around, and no one lives here to need it. It turned on to help me see Clay, to help me stare at him. He's one of the wonders of the world, along with Halong Bay and the Great Wall of China.

He catches his breath and gets up. He tries to look tough and unaffected by wiping the sweat off his forehead with his sleeve and then scrunching it up again above his shoulder. "It's all about knowing how to take a fall. Wanna learn the best move ever for defending yourself?"

"Sure."

He stands behind me and holds my arms out. The heat from his body radiates through his clothes and warms my skin. His chest muscles flex and tighten against my back. "OK, bring this hand up. Stand up straight. Stomach in, shoulders back. Think of your head being pulled to the sky."

I let my body go as he directs me.

"Good." He pulls my arm back. "Now, bring this forward and slice the air here." He pushes my arm forward, slicing through the still air. "Like that."

It feels good and powerful and efficient, like a strong punch and at the same time, a beautiful, artistic stroke.

"Now, try it alone." He walks in front of me and folds his arms.

I feel like I'm auditioning for him. I raise my arm and as hard as I can, bring it forward though the air. I lose my footing and fall onto my back with a thud. It's horrible, the most uncoordinated stupid thing I could do. I feel my face turn red.

He leans down and looks me over. "All right?" He examines my face. "There's something in your eye."

I want to reach up and kiss him.

Supporting himself with one arm, Clay rubs a piece of grit from my eye. "You'll get it. That's the most important movement in karate." His eyes dart and move around my face.

"I like it, though. It's cool. It's like art."

He sits down and looks into the sky. "Exactly, man. That's what people don't get. It's art…it's beautiful." He looks at me in a long, strange moment of quiet. A bird chirps overhead and breaks it. "Oh, man, this party. We have to motor."

We get into the truck. He turns the radio on to some punk rock song and cranks the volume up high. He lights up a cigarette.

I drop my lighter, and it hits my knee and bounces to his side of the floor, near his feet and the gas pedal. I lean over to get it and smell him on the way down.

We turn a corner, and I see the party. It's totally wild. Cars are parked all over the place. Kids are scattered through the yard. A guy carries a keg on his shoulders onto the front porch. The house is built on stilts and it looks like it might fall down from all the people bursting out the front door. A guy and a girl are on top of each other, making out under the house. I feel a wave of insecurity. I don't know if I'm cool enough for this. I'm afraid I'm not going to be able to talk.

Clay pulls into the front yard and turns off his truck. He shoves his bag of coke and his lighter and cigarettes into his pocket.

I get nervous instantly and my boner goes away.

A guy walks up to us. In the headlights his eyes sparkle like a dog's. He has lots of tattoos, and he's wearing a black T-shirt with the sleeves cut off. His arms are muscular and his complexion makes him look like he has a thin coating of oil all over him, like a car mechanic. He's tough-looking but skinny, like a bull dog puppy. He has two black pit bulls on leashes.

"Miller's here. Rad." Clay jumps out and runs over to the guy and throws his arms around him. "Aloha, brah! Welcome back. How was Guam?"

"It sucked, brah. Tree snakes everywhere."

I get out of the truck, feeling stupid that I don't know anyone. My outfit isn't near punk enough for this party. I nod to the guy, and Clay looks over at me, like he forgot I was here.

"Miller, brah, this is my boy Sam."

I nod to him, trying to seem tough. "Aloha."

"Aloha, dude. Howzit?" He gives me a warm smile, which feels good, like soft warm sunlight on my face.

I follow him and Clay up to the house. On the front porch, kids hang out on old couches and chairs. A guy with a green Mohawk barbecues on a greasy grill. Beer cans and plastic cups are thrown everywhere. A burned-up mattress is discarded by the side of the house. It's cool, a whole new world I didn't even know existed. It's anarchistic. It's crazy. It's like the kind of place where you can do anything.

We go inside the trashed house. There are lots of couches, extension cords everywhere, empty beer bottles all over the floor, and a pile of skateboards by the front door. Huge speakers scream out NOFX and Rancid and all the music I really like. Surf posters cover the walls and a goat skull hangs above the stereo system, which looks like the most expensive thing in the room. Groups of short-haired, tanned, skinny, muscular dudes walk in wearing skateboard T-shirts and cutoff cargo pants. Girls with dyed black hair hang out and laugh. They all seem cool but intimidating, partly because they're all older than me.

I look like I live with my overly protective parents. I sit on the couch, which is coated with dog hair.

Clay flops down on a chair across from me, right next to the keg. He nods to the music and bangs the drumbeat on the arm of the chair. "Better than middle-school birthday parties, eh, brah?" He looks fucked-up. His pupils are huge, and he has a grin that's halfway between scared and ecstatic.

I get up for a beer. "I'm sixteen, dude." I punch him lightly on the arm. Too lightly. I hope I didn't seem like I just wanted to touch him.

"I *know*, brah. Just playing with you." He pumps the air pressure thing on the keg for me while I fill my plastic cup.

I'm being too literal. This always happens to me when I get nervous and feel like I have to prove myself.

A guy walks into the room.

Clay jumps up. "Frankie-boy! Howzit?" They hug each other, then Clay looks at me. "Frankie, this is Sam. He looks like he could use some weed."

I smile. "Hey." I'm buzzed already. I hope I don't end up puking tonight.

Frank hands me some pot and papers. "Roll one, brah?"

"Uh, sure." I can't believe how cool this world is. Guys hug each other. People just hand you pot. Everyone's drunk and cool and old enough to do what they want to do. I wanna grow up so bad. "Smells like good shit." I hope they think I know what I'm talking about.

Clay smiles approvingly and goes off upstairs with Frank, to do more coke, I think.

I sit down and try to seem high and out of it so that I don't have to talk to any strangers. I'm horrible at it. I lose my personality completely when I'm forced to be entertaining or interesting. I don't think these dudes, except for Clay, would like me if they really knew me. I write haiku. I don't surf. I hate the sun.

They think I'm like Clay because he brought me. They think guys who think like I do are fags.

"Little Sammy turned into a joint-rolling slave," a girl's voice says. Someone taps my shoulder.

I flinch and look up.

It's Kendra. Jared's sister. She looks older and cool, sort of relaxed in a totally mellow way.

Instantly, I remember lip-synching fake Joni Mitchell concerts in her bedroom, baking cookies with rum and vodka and anything else we could find to put in them. One New Year's Eve, when we stole liquor from her parents, we shot off a huge M-80 Super-Rocket, and it misfired and burned down her shed. They're all embarrassing things in the context of being at this party. Majorly lightweight shit. I smile. My stomach's flying.

She leans down to hug me, but someone calls her to the

kitchen. "Hold on, Sammy. I really want to talk to you." Her hair tickles my face.

Her gardenia perfume brings back another time like magic.

I was waiting for Jared in his room. He was in his family's living room, being yelled at by his parents. We'd made too much noise the night before camping in a tent in his backyard. We were playing strip poker with this weird girl, Lisa, from down the street. I was getting pretty turned on or whatever the day before because Jared had this calendar with surfers on it up on the wall, and I couldn't stop looking at it as we were watching horror movies and talking about where to get pot or beer. When he left the room, I locked the door and found this movie I knew called *Space Camp.* I fast-forwarded to this part I like, with this boy in one of the bunk beds at the camp. I paused the tape at the moment when he sort of sat up, shirtless, to turn his light out. I got a boner and started to jerk off. Just as I was getting really into it and concentrating, I heard a bump and the door flew open.

Kendra stood there, tall in the doorway, and looked between me and the TV screen. She quickly turned away, like she accidentally walked into the wrong room and didn't even notice me.

I freaked out and escaped through Jared's window, which was the first time I used a window as a door. The next day when I saw Jared at school, I told him I felt sick and had to go. I don't think Kendra ever told him, but since then I've only seen her from a distance. I was fourteen and a half, and I've avoided her since.

She walks back in. I'm freaked out now, thinking about her expression that day. She sits on the arm of my chair and puts her legs up on top of me.

I jerk away as she puts her hand on my shoulder.

"Oh, my God, Sammy, relax. Are you okay?" She laughs.

"Uhh...no...fucked-up." That sounded stupid and I can't get this joint to resemble a joint.

"Me too. Let me help you with that." She takes the pot and the papers. "God, I haven't seen you in like two years. You haven't changed a bit. Well, except you're taller, and your hair is…purple?" She laughs. "What are you doing here?"

"You know Clay?"

"Oh, yeah." She's saying something about him with her tone and I don't like it. Did they fuck or something?

"We're friends. He brought me."

"He's cute, don't you think?" She nudges my side, like she's kidding me.

"Whatever."

"He won't even talk to me. Not nearly the gentleman you are, Sammy." She makes me feel too handsome and polite. "Jared was talking about you the other day. I asked about you. You guys need to come over to my apartment and hang out. I'll buy you beer. Gotta girlfriend, Sammy?"

"Uh…no, not now. I was going out with Cynthia for a while." I shouldn't have lied.

"Swinging bachelor."

I smile, but inside I'm grossed out at being thought of as a bachelor.

Is Kendra a spy? She rubs my head. "You've got a beautiful head. Are you coked up? You're grinding your teeth like crazy." She finishes the joint with a lick. Her tongue's moist and plump.

"Yeah, sure am. Me and Clay did some on the way over."

"Never thought I'd see you on coke." She lights up the joint and takes a big hit. She makes it look elegant.

"Wow, I feel old. You did it with Clay?"

I wish, meaning, did it, like sex.

She hands me the joint. "He turns wild on that shit." She tilts her head at me, like she just remembered what I said about doing it with Clay. She looks out the front door. "Fuck!"

I lean forward on the couch to see what she's looking at. A couple guys are relighting the burnt-up mattress. The flames grow huge in seconds.

She gets up and runs to the front door and I follow her. "You guys! The cops are gonna come and take our keg away!"

I lean out the front door. A guy with a Mohawk lies on the grass looking at the sky and a blond guy with no shirt on jumps up and down smoking a joint on one end of the burning mattress, which is only, like, a foot from the front porch. A girl tries to melt a beer can on a fire in the barbecue. Dogs are everywhere running and play-fighting. It's like a whole new society with no rules. I wanna go wild. I wanna strip my clothes off and run around the yard.

Everyone starts to pour beer on the fire. White smoke flies up into the night sky.

We walk back inside and Kendra starts talking to a big dude with tattoos, the guy who gave me the pot and papers. It seems like she wants to fuck him. She looks really pretty. Her red hair is long and tied back. Her skin is smooth and shiny, and she's still wearing all black, like I remember.

The pot guy looks at me. "Where's my joint, dude?"

Me? I look down and notice the half-smoked joint in my hand. I'd forgotten about it. "Here, thanks."

"Wanna go upstairs, or take a walk or something?" the guy asks Kendra. He looks away, trying to seem aloof.

"I don't think so, Mark."

Mark reaches down the front of his jeans, and Kendra rolls her eyes.

"Quit scratching your balls. It's gross."

"Know where the bathroom is?" I get up, embarrassed to watch Kendra with this dude. "I have to piss super-bad."

"Yeah, I think there's one upstairs."

"OK, cool seeing you."

"OK, Sammy." She pinches my cheek. "You look happier, or something. I knew my mom was wrong about you. Just kidding." She rubs my head. "Give me a kiss, cutie. I'm in a little argument with my boyfriend. Come save me later."

I kiss her and smile. I wanna find Clay. I walk off, trying to act like I don't have to piss worse than I ever have. I climb the stairs. The carpet's destroyed and has burn holes all over it. I spot the bathroom ahead. The door's open.

I hear someone taking a shower—the sound of water hitting a plastic curtain. I'm not sure if I should go in. I stand in the doorway. *Fuck it,* I tell myself. *It's cool. This party's pretty mellow like that.* I walk in and take a deep breath. I hold my dick out over the dirty toilet and piss. Relief.

"Frankie?" Clay screams from the shower.

"No, it's Sam." I'm jealous. Why would Frank be in the bathroom when Clay's taking a shower?

"Oh, Sam, hey. Can you close the door, brah? It's cold."

I look in the mirror to make sure I look okay, then peek around the corner. I see his shoulder, his calf, and his hip—all flush up against the clear plastic curtain.

"You still in here?"

"Yeah. Why're you taking a shower?"

"I don't know. Felt like it. Where have you been?"

"Talking to that Kendra girl."

"Think she's hot?"

"I guess."

"I guess?"

"Uh…I mean…she's my best friend's sister."

"So?" He's quiet for a second. "Dude, come here." He sounds like he's scheming. The adventure in his voice inspires me.

I walk over to the shower. I feel the humidity and heat, like from a rain forest, drifting out from around and over the curtain, which is dirty with mold at the bottom.

Clay rips aside the curtain. He stands naked in a stream of hot water with a goofy smile. "Get in."

I freeze and absorb flashes of him like photos: Dark pubic hair. His dick, not much bigger than mine. The hair on his legs. His torso.

I have no control over myself. I step into the shower. Instantly, I'm warm and wet. My clothes get heavy. Bluish-red hair dye runs down my neck and chest and T-shirt. My camo shorts turn warm and stick to my legs and hang down low. My shoes get soggy and squishy. It's like some sort of fucked-up womb. There's no better place to be in the world than this tiny wet, warm, steamy space. The smack of the water hitting my clothes is deafening. I look down at the streams running off my T-shirt, then up to Clay. I stare at him in the filtered light shining through the curtain. We're only inches apart.

"You have all your clothes on."

I don't know what to say. I'm pathetic, desperate, turned on.

"I feel like God!"

My dick's the hardest it's ever been. I need to touch him. I have no control over myself. I reach out for his chest. My hand clenches up before it makes it there. I sort of hit him, my hand fumbling on his bare chest, then falling to my side. He looks at me, saying nothing.

Please kiss me.

He jumps out of the shower. His balls bounce as he jumps. He turns and looks right at me, rubbing his chest with his hand. "I love you, man." He says it like he's talking to a dog.

Involuntarily, my hand goes to my dick—but I can't jerk off here.

Clay dries himself with a dirty towel and steps into some cutoff army pants. He looks at me and smiles. "Taking a shower with your clothes on. That's pretty punk."

"Uh…yeah."

He runs out, leaving the door open.

For no good reason, I feel like I should cry—maybe because I don't know what to do after this. Everything else will be a disappointment.

I rinse out my mouth and let water hit my eyes so they get more red. It'll make me seem more out if it. I turn the water off. That was the coolest and weirdest thing that's ever happened to me. I get up and walk out of the shower and wipe the fog off the mirror. I'm dripping with color and water. I see this shocked happiness in my face. I stare at the veins in my forearms. They're sticking out almost as much as Clay's.

I have to find him. I walk down the hall leaving wet footprints in the carpet. I look through a half-open door.

Clay's sitting on the floor. He looks calm. The carved wooden plaque on the door says *STEVE*.

I see the guy who's probably Steve.

He looks at home in the room.

I walk in, holding my breath, dripping, and shivering a little. Inside Steve's room, it's much quieter than the rest of the house. A dim lamp is on. The floor's covered with dirty brown shag carpeting, and there's lots of ancient-looking records, bongs filled with dirty water, the smell of a million smoked joints, two ashtrays, and cool posters of surfing and bands I've heard of, but don't know much about—the Beatles, the Clash, and Led Zeppelin. It's cozy in here, my mom would say, except they're smoking pot and fucked-up. That would ruin it for her.

I walk in, dripping big drops of water onto the carpet.

Clay's lying on his back with his wet armpits open proudly.

Steve sits on his bed, a futon on the floor. He leans over his two-foot long bong, holding on with both hands, and takes a huge hit that makes his cheeks go all Skeletor. He looks about twenty-one, and he has brown hair and a chipped front tooth. Trippy music comes from his big, old speakers.

"You took a shower with your clothes on? I've done that." He laughs. "You want some dry clothes, little bro?"

I sense this open way about him. "Sure, man. Thanks."

He reaches behind himself on the bed and throws me some flowered surf shorts plus an old David Bowie T-shirt that smells like his room.

Clay watches me while I change.

All I can see is my limp, cold water-shrunk dick and these ugly-looking hairs that have just begun to grow on my inner thighs. I take my wet underwear off and walk into the shorts as fast as I can, catching my pubic hair on the zipper. I pull the T-shirt on.

Clay laughs and smiles at me. He looks really fucked-up. "That's a trip, man. You look like Steve."

"You think?" I straighten out the T-shirt on my shoulders.

Steve looks at me and sits up straight. "I'm pretty cute." He says this in a goofy way, then turns around to change the record.

Clay lies back, looks at the ceiling, and rubs his chest.

I watch Steve put the needle down. The record scratches.

I lie back.

"This has been Steve's room since the fourth grade." Clay looks around at all the posters.

"I never had the same room for more than two years," I say. "My mom likes moving."

"Oh, Sammy, you poor little gypsy."

"Shut up."

Steve hands me his huge bong. You wanna hit?"

"Sure." I lean over the huge green see-through tube and suck in part of a big hit and am instantly and totally stoned. I'm almost scared because now I can't stop thinking that I'm sitting in a room with two dudes I don't know—and one of them I'm in love with, and if he finds out, he could be really freaked. I look around the room to avoid having to make eye contact with Clay or Steve. "This room has a lot of history in it."

Steve takes the bong from me and tweaks up his lighter flame. "There's no such thing as history, dude. It's always now." He hunches over the bong and sucks in another huge hit.

"No, it's not...it's right...now. I just left you behind." Clay grabs the bong from Steve, takes a huge gulp of smoke, and lies back. "Nature is unknowable.... Surfing is the only time I'm whole...the only time I'm...at peace." He turns around and looks at me, waiting for a response.

The only thing I can think of to say is this haiku I wrote: "Unknowable waves, wake a lonely dog to bark, remind him it's winter."

Clay lifts his head. "You've got it, man." He looks over at Steve, who's totally passed out. He moves the bong under Steve's desk and lies flat on his back on the floor with his head on the mattress just inches from Steve's feet. He closes his eyes.

I'm gonna be in trouble because my parents don't know where I am. I wish I lived here. I lift my head to look at Clay's smooth stomach and the line of hair above his shorts.

The next song starts playing. It seems like it was made for little kids or stoners. I crawl over and get the album cover. It's super trippy. All the Beatles dudes are dressed up as different fuzzy animals. I reach up and turn the light out.

Clay's passed out with his head on Steve's futon.

I guess I'm sleeping in here too. *Cool.*

The Beatle dudes chant, "Smoke pot, smoke pot. Everybody smoke pot, smoke pot." I fall asleep, slightly spinning from the beer and pot.

I wake up. It's still dark. I don't know where I am. I lift my

head. I can't believe I'm here. The record is over and I can hear the
needle scraping softly at the end of the record. This is the coolest
thing I've ever done. I look at Clay. He's sleeping. How could I
have been sleeping here for so long and not enjoying it? What a
waste. I look at the clock. It's 3:43. A couple hours have passed, I
think. I whisper, "Clay?"

He doesn't wake up.

I lie beside him with my head on Steve's mattress and softly—
like it's a spiritual experience—touch his chest. Chemicals rush
through my body. I wish I could jack off, but it's too risky.

Still, he shows no sign of waking.

I move my hand slowly down his chest, feeling the curves of his
muscles. I trace around his nipples. He's hot and a little damp.

He reacts with almost imperceptibly slow movements.

I sit up and hold my face only inches from his skin above his
underwear waistband. I inhale deeply. It's perfect, warm Clay-
filled air. I slide my hand as softly as I can down his stomach,
and I lift up his underwear waistband a tiny bit. I push my finger
in and feel the top of his pubic hair.

He thrusts forward barely an inch and takes a deep breath.

Someone pounds on the door. *Fuck.* I jerk my hand away and
curl up as fast as I can on the carpet to fake being asleep. I squint
my eyes so they look closed, but I can still see. I'm shaking.

Clay and Steve don't move.

Kendra peeks in and takes a photo with flash, then ducks out
and closes the door.

Cool. Now this is recorded. It's permanent. It's real. I wish that
photo were mine.

Steve moans and flops around on his bed.

I nuzzle into Clay's side, where his ribs make little ridges under
his skin, but he rolls over away from me, still sleeping.

Downstairs, the party rages on.

6

Fresh summer Sake,
evening turned fast to morning
What a hangover.

I have a horrible hangover in the morning and I think Clay does too by the look of him. His eyes are swollen, and he's walking like he'd do anything to prevent his head from moving too quickly. I grab my clothes off Steve's floor. They're still soaking wet, dripping all over his records and everything. I check to make sure he doesn't notice. Luckily, he's still unconscious.

Clay and I walk out over all the passed-out bodies and get into his truck. Everything outside looks boring. It's back to the real world again, with adult rules and standards about what's appropriate and all that. We drive out of the neighborhood and down the road back to Kailua.

Clay looks dazed.

I feel so stupid. I wouldn't have been so daring last night if I wasn't drunk and stoned. I stare straight ahead, so he doesn't have to have uncomfortable eye contact with me. I watch two girls biking down the street with their surfboards. They obviously went to bed a lot earlier than we did. I don't want to demand any attention. I want him to think I'm cool on my own—in my own head—and that the party was no big deal.

He turns a corner like a maniac and shifts to fourth.

I look around the inside of the truck, which reeks of smoke and sweat so bad it makes me want to hurl. The brown dashboard's sticky and dusty and has all kinds of broken tape cases thrown all around it. There's a rash guard with a big rip in it on the floor under my feet. The back windows rattle like crazy when we drive over any sort of bump and one panel is patched with a broke-off piece of an old skateboard. I watch out the window as we drive through downtown Kailua, basically a couple strip malls and some plate-lunch restaurants with local dudes hanging out in front, eating. As we wait at a stoplight, a girl that sort of looks like Kendra pulls out of Pali Bottle Shoppe, a liquor store where it's easy to buy alcohol for underage kids.

Clay puts his hand on my shoulder, and I flinch. "Calm down, dude."

I settle back into the seat.

He doesn't move his hand off my shoulder.

My hand starts to shake. I have to think about breathing so I don't hyperventilate. I can't move, even an inch, or his hand might slip away. I brace myself as we turn again and go over a bumpy section of road where the pipes underneath are being replaced.

He moves his hand off my shoulder.

I want to grab it and put it back.

He traces over my collarbone with his finger and scrapes along my chest and stomach, down to my lap, where my hip bone sticks out. He doesn't look at me, but he slows down and turns a corner more carefully.

I try to situate myself so I can look casual and calm, but it's hard. My foot's tapping the floor like crazy and I can't stop it. It's expressing all the panic and lust and anxiety and joy in my whole body.

He moves his hand to the top of my leg and rubs down to my knee, with pressure and forcefulness.

My dick grows in Steve's shorts and almost pokes straight out the fly.

He's gonna feel it if he goes any closer with his hand. He moves his hand over to the center of my lap and takes my boner in his hand through my shorts.

A high-pitched ring takes over in my ears, and instantly it feels 200 degrees in the truck. I want look at him, but it's too risky. I'm afraid he'll have a horrible frown on his face, or maybe he's teasing me to see if I'll go along with it, then ditch me. I have to see. I look over at him through my eyelashes.

He looks back, not embarrassed. He has my boner in his hand and he's looking at me. This is insane.

I almost can't handle this. I'm gonna pass out.

His face looks charged and strong, flushed almost pink. His eyes look watery and deep, like a Native American's. I can see a vein in his neck pumping blood through in pulses. He looks so alive. It's like we're meeting each other for the first time.

Everything outside the truck windows turns into meaningless blurs.

I can't believe he can still drive. "Hi," I say, without thinking.

"Hey," he says back—with a hint of fear on his lips.

I grasp his wrist.

"Fuck!" He rips his hand away from my crotch.

I did something wrong. *What did I do wrong?*

He looks in his side-view mirror. "I think your mom's behind us."

I turn my head around to see. "Shit."

She waves to me with a mean look on her face. She's taking away my freedom, just when I finally felt some, at the high point of my life. It must be some sort of motherly instinct to destroy her kid's life.

Clay pulls over in front of my house.

I want to say, *I love you, I need you, I want you,* but I don't know how he'd take it. I want to make sure we can do this again. I have to plan a meeting site, or save money to rent a hotel room. *Something.*

I can't go on if there's no chance of this ever happening again.

He looks straight ahead and shifts the truck into neutral.

I don't know what to do. "Cool, thanks." I grab my pile of wet clothes.

"*De nada.*"

I jump out. "Aloha." I run up to the front door.

Clay drives off.

I watch his truck as it rounds the curve out to the rest of the world. Understanding the world felt so close and manageable just minutes ago. It's miles away now. It's tied to the back of his truck with wires.

My mom pulls into the driveway, and stalks me. "Where've you been?"

I hold the sopping clothes in front of my crotch so she can't see my boner. "I spent the night at Clay's. I was too tired to come home."

She looks disgusted. "I told you I didn't want you riding with him. Don't leave your room until your dad gets home."

I storm off. "Screw you."

"Don't drip that on the carpet."

I slam the front door on my way in. I'm on a mission. All I want to do is beat off. I go into my room and lock the door.

Jared is lying on my bed reading a skateboard magazine.

Fuck. Everyone's against me. No one wants me to come while thinking of the boy I'm in love with. This is a horrible conspiracy. It's just gonna build up inside me till I burst. "What are you doing here?" I throw my wet clothes on the floor.

He sits up and throws the mag on the floor. "'Don't leave your room until your dad gets home.'"

"Shut up."

"Why are you so sweaty?" He stands up with his skinny arms swinging beside him, and the veins in his temples popped out.

"'Cause it's hot."

"You're breathing heavy."

"No, I'm not… So? At least I don't look like the Asian son of Frankenstein."

He walks across the room toward me, like he's a sleepwalking monster. He corners me against my closet. The back of my head hits the closet door. "So, you're an old man now?"

"Yeah."

He looks at me, closely. "What's up with you? You look different."

"Well, my hair's purple, duh."

"My sister said she saw you at Steve's party."

"Yeah, I was there. Clay took me."

He's jealous. I can tell because he won't look me in the eyes. "Was it cool?"

I try to be all mellow about it, like it's nothing new for me. I nod.

"Aren't all those dudes like big assholes?"

"You know, man, they're cool once you get to know them."

Why did I say that?

"Did you do drugs?"

"The drugs were unbelievable, coke, pot, hash, whatever you want—name it, it was there."

"You should have told me about it."

"Well, you know, you sorta have to know someone." Instantly, I feel bad for saying this.

"Whatever, man."

"You sorta have to know someone"—he knows I'm just acting big.

"Wanna see my new drawing?"

"Sure."

He pulls a rolled-up piece of paper from his backpack and

unfurls it on my bed. It's a huge, half-finished ink drawing of a shark underwater biting a surfboard and a surfer in half. There's a little boat with a bunch of kids hanging out in it smoking pot. They just sit there, stoned, and watch their friend get eaten. Body parts and organs float around the boat and one kid catches a liver or something on a weighed-down fishing pole.

"Dude, that's cool." Jared always impresses me, just when I think I'm totally bored with him. "Actually, those guys at the party *were* kind of assholes."

Jared lights up. "I knew you thought they were." He looks at his drawing, admiring it.

"I mean, Clay's cool—you know him—and this guy, Steve. He's pretty mellow. That was so weird seeing your sister, I felt like…uhh…well, remember when you and I used to sneak out and spy on those parties? We used to think it would be so cool to be there. It was weird, once I was there. I didn't really even have fun, except with Clay."

"I've been telling you that for like a year." He looks at me like he admires me. It's a familiar expression. I'm always the one who tries things first.

"It's still cool you went, though. The drugs sound cool."

"They were. I was so fucked-up."

Jared laughs in his goofy way, like an old man, and cocks his head sideways. He leans in close to me and whispers, "My sister has some acid if you want to do it soon."

"That'd be cool." I'm lying. I'd only do it with Clay. I walk over to my door and start to open it.

"I'll take the window." He's trying to be cool. He used to always make fun of me for using it. He climbs out, and his shoelace gets caught on the sill. He almost falls on his face. "Fuck!"

"Later, Jared." I'm happy he left. He's cool, but he doesn't understand love yet, and I do.

I find some clay-colored Krazy Kolorz dye called Southern Sunset and rub it in my hair. The blue and red are almost washed out anyway leaving my blond underneath. I trace a "C" and "L" and "A" and "Y" on my chest after I coat my head. It looks so cool. I lie back on my bed, thinking about touching him, and fall asleep.

The sound of my parents arguing in the other room wakes me up.

The dye dried in my hair and it feels like plastic. The CLAY I wrote on my chest is stained and darker orange than when I put it on. The room looks like a murder site, reddish dye on my bed and pillows. I open my door and slink down the hall to the bathroom to rinse my hair. The rest of the house is cooler than my room. I turn the water on hard and lean down to rinse. The dye looks trippy going down the drain. I sneak back to my room, like a spy, hiding in afternoon shadows.

I hear a loud explosion from some stupid action movie my parents are watching.

I lock the door and look in the mirror. I like it. It's the color of clay. I drop the towel that's wrapped around my waist and stare at my body, the body Clay was touching. My dick surges up and gets hard. I close my eyes and concentrate on him and me in his truck, trying to re-create the whole thing in my head. I get a little depressed and confused because I don't know if it will even happen again. I'm not exactly sure what caused him to want to touch me all of a sudden.

7

Cusp of monsoon rains
Tadpoles: fast shrinking puddle
Things are looking up.

Feeling anarchic and revitalized from what I think a shrink would call "healthy dreams," I roll off the side of my bed, reach for the phone book underneath, and flip through it for Clay's number so I can get his address. I feel like a stalker, but I can't help it. I find five Anderson's on the windward side. Moki, Leilani, Kam, Kyoko, and Susan. I think it's pretty safe to assume it's Susan. Clay's a Portugee boy, not Hawaiian or Japanese. I dial the number.

A machine picks up. It's Clay's voice. "Hey, if you wanna talk to me or Susan, leave a message—but don't make it too long 'cause you suck. Aloha!" He laughs, and it cuts off after some static.

I hang up and tear out the page with his street listed on it. I strap on my pack, jump out my bedroom window, and hop on my bike 'cause I haven't fixed my board yet. I ride out of our stupid neighborhood and down the narrow Kam Highway. Cars fly past me with huge gusts. It's hard to keep my balance. I turn onto Clay's street, and ride my hardest up the tree-covered hill. The houses are built on poles, and most of the driveways are dirt. Huge banyans and tall coconut palms sway in the breeze. Behind the neighborhood, there's a sheer cliff, tall and eroded, with waterfalls splashing down through the green. The air smells fresh, like just after a huge rain. I stand up to pedal harder.

A pickup truck pulls up beside me, and a big Samoan surfer guy sticks his head out the window. "Hey, you fucking haole. What you doing here?"

I lose my balance a little and almost fall.

"What the fuck happened to your hair?" He wings a coconut at me.

I duck and it whisks by my head, but I lose my balance and crash into the gravel on the side of the road. My bike lands on top of me. I throw it off and give the guy the bird but he's way down the road already.

"What the fuck's wrong with you people?" My knee's bleeding and my elbows are skinned. The chain lies in a pile like a snake and I don't know how to put it back on. I pick it up, wrap it around the pedal and walk it up the hill. I get grease all over my hands. This shit wouldn't happen if Clay was with me. The locals hate me, even though I'm local too. They think of me as not belonging here 'cause I'm white. I'm a haole. I'm shark bait. I'm shit. My ancestors took over their islands.

Pushing my fucked-up bike along, the chain dragging on the pavement, I search around for Clay's house. The house numbers don't seem to mean much in the neighborhood. The order of houses is off and between some houses, two hundred numbers skip. I turn right and see a house, sitting back from the others. The numbers are carved out of orange wood. It's Clay's house. I slowly walk closer, ducking behind trees and sheds on the way, so he can't see me coming and escape out the back. I hide behind a lauhala tree across the street and spy.

The house is low and long and old and grown over with ferns and trees.

I don't see his truck. I dump my bike on the grass, light up a cigarette, and lean on a fire hydrant across the street. I could wait here all night. A dog barks from inside his house.

A Toyota drives past me and pulls into Clay's driveway. A woman with long dark hair—the same color as Clay's—gets out and goes to check her mailbox, which is right in front of me. She's wearing a muumuu, and she has big jade beads around her neck and wrists. She's a hippie and she looks naturally happy, over a layer of like, "I've seen it all." She's totally interesting, much more comfortable in her own skin than my mom. I bet she smokes weed.

I freeze. I don't know what to say. I must look like a stalker.

She looks at me, as I sit on the fire hydrant and watch her.

"Hi," she says.

I act like I'm just hanging out here, like I hang here all the time and she's just never noticed. "Hi."

She looks over at me again.

I have to say something. She'll think I'm scoping her house out for a crime or something. "Are you Mrs. Anderson?"

She nods and closes the mailbox.

"I'm a friend of Clay's. I was just riding around, and I thought I'd stop by and see if he's home."

She looks into the carport. "Oh, Clay's not here. He's probably still at work. He usually gets home about now. What's your name?"

"Sam."

"Your hair's an amazing color. I should try that."

"Thanks. It's called Southern Sunset."

She looks down at my bleeding knee. "What happened to your leg?"

"Nothing much. Fell off my bike."

"Come inside. We'll put some Bacitracin on it and you can wait for Clay. Help me with the groceries?"

"Sure." I grab a bag of strange-looking vegetables and fruits my mom would never buy, and follow her in. The dog jumps up on me and I almost drop the bag of greens.

"That's Sharky, Clay's dog. Sharky, meet Sam, and get down." The dog walks into the living room and plops on the couch.

The house is full of plants, hanging from macramé holders made from lime-green, brown, and orange yarn. The living room has a low couch and a glass coffee table that looks like a sculpture. We go into the kitchen. It has teak cabinets and brown tiles, the same color as '70s coffee mugs. I put the bag of greens on the counter next to a huge fern that drapes down into the sink.

"Sit down. Put your leg up." She gets a paper towel and a tube of anti-bacterial cream from the cabinet.

I set my pack on the floor and put my leg up on the table. I feel self-conscious about the hair on my calves. I haven't had a real relationship with an adult since I've had hair on my legs and my armpits. I pull my long shorts up so my knee's exposed. It has pebbles and dirt mixed with loose skin and dark red blood. She sits down next to me and wipes my scrapes with a wet paper towel, then rubs the cream on gently. I feel a warm buzz in my stomach from being cared for. It's a great feeling that I haven't felt in a long time. Ever since my mom started being selfish and bought a new Volvo, she stopped most of her mothering and started yelling at me.

"Here, put this on." She hands me a big Band-Aid. "Would you like a guava juice?" She walks over to the refrigerator.

"Uh, no, thanks…well, sure."

She grabs two cans, and hands one to me. She takes a big slurp out of her can, then grabs a glass and opens the freezer to get some ice.

I spot a photo on the freezer door held up with a Hawaiian tiki magnet. It's Clay standing in front of the Makapu lighthouse, shirtless, with a pink lei around his neck. His arm's around a blond girl in a tank top. She has big white teeth. I'm jealous immediately.

Mrs. Anderson closes the freezer, and I get up to analyze the photo up close. She stands next to me with her shoulder pressed to mine. "That's Tammy." She takes a drink of her guava juice, the ice rattling in the glass.

I look away and stare at a kooky '60s abstract print in a frame. It's blue circles expanding outward till they turn into specks, like dust. That's how my brain feels seeing Clay with his arm around this girl, this girl that has a name. "Family?" I sit down again. My knee hurts.

"No." She takes another drink of her guava and holds her finger up telling me to wait a second.

This is horrible. This is the worst thing I could possibly see, ever, and it's in Clay's kitchen. I thought I'd find only good clues here, more evidence to lead me into utter love and devotion.

"It was taken about a year ago, just before Tammy left for school. Oh, God. Clay and I got in a terrible fight right after we dropped her off." She pushes her hair back and closes her eyes for a second.

"Is she Clay's girlfriend?"

The front door flies open, and the dog jumps off the couch to investigate the noise. "What's up with all the traffic on the Pali? Hey, Sharky-boy." Clay takes his shoes off and throws them down in the entryway. "Whose bike is that in the front yard?" He walks into the kitchen. Then he sees me. He looks over to his mom standing by the freezer then back to me, like we're planning an evil scheme to overthrow his power.

"It's mine. Aloha."

He sits on the countertop, acting like it's no big deal I'm here, even though he never told me where he lives. "Hey. What's goin' on?" He looks comfortable and relaxed in the environment of his own house. He makes it seem like a crash pad, somewhere he's so comfortable he doesn't look around anymore.

"I was just riding around. Thought I'd stop over and see what you were doing."

He gives me a long, measured look. "That's cool. Your hair looks punk."

"Thanks."

His mom smiles and breaks the uncomfortable slow pace we have with each other. "You guys want tuna sandwiches? Hammerhead, you hungry?" She calls him "Hammerhead." That's hilarious.

I hope he's embarrassed.

He pauses for a second. "Yeah, sure."

I look at him for approval and then feel stupid for doing it. "Sure, if it's not too much trouble, Mrs. Anderson."

"Ugh. Don't call me that. Susan's fine." She gets a jar of mayonnaise out of the refrigerator. "Did you hear about the tiger shark they caught in Kailua yesterday?"

Clay perks up. "How big?"

"Sixteen feet."

"No way. That's almost as big as my dick."

"Clay!" His mom whips a kitchen towel at him.

He laughs and looks at me.

"You wish," I say, but I'm totally embarrassed.

Susan laughs and Clay watches her, making sure she doesn't pick up on our intimacy. "Is Tammy coming home for summer break?" she asks.

He stands up from the table. "Yeah. Sam, wanna hang out in my room?" He doesn't want to talk about her. That must mean something.

"Sure, but..." I look at his mom making sandwiches.

"We'll eat those later, Mom. I wanna play some music for the little brah." He takes off down the hall and I follow with my pack, admiring his macho strut that I could never emulate exactly.

I follow him to his room, and I wonder if I'll remember anything from when I was eleven. My heart beats superfast. I walk through the door and I feel like I never left, though he's never mentioned I've been here before, which is totally weird, but I'm not going to say anything. He has a way of forgetting things, maybe because he smokes a lot of weed, or maybe because he wants to.

The bed is messed up, and the pillows are folded into balls and strange shapes, suited for him sleeping and hanging out and beating off. There's a whole wall full of shelves with videos and some books on them, just slightly more full than I remember. The walls are covered in wood paneling and the same surfing posters. Shirtless guys with deep-looking eyes pose on waves with emblems below. A huge *Apocalypse Now* poster that was always there hangs above his bed. It shows a bright-orange sunset over a meandering river. Ashtrays and half-smoked joints all over the carpet are new because he used to have to hide it all. The carpet is scattered with T-shirts and slippers and skate shoes and surf wax. I add my backpack to the mess.

A neon-green chameleon sits on a dead branch inside a glass terrarium. It looks tripped-out and mellow. He didn't have a lizard before. It's a full-on trend now. If you think you're all tough and you're a surfer-boy on Oahu, you have a lizard. I don't get it, but it's true.

I walk in, almost tripping over a pair of plaid boxers.

Clay turns on a lamp without a shade. He's in silhouette, like a ghost haunting the room.

I can see his shape, but not his face.

He can see all of me, like I'm being questioned by spies. He lifts his arm to scratch the back of his neck, and his shirtsleeve falls up so light filters through the thin cotton. His hair looks golden from backlighting.

I look back and forth between him and the pair of boxers on the floor.

He gets something from his dresser drawer and flops down on his bed. "Look at this pot." He opens a film canister stuffed full of strong-smelling weed.

I look to the floor at his boxers again and picture how cool he'd look in them. I sit down next to him on the bed. I'm afraid I won't be able to control myself and I'll attack him. I can't believe we're on his bed together. If I move, he moves from the vibrations. I lean over to be closer to him and look at the pot. "That looks like good shit."

I have no idea what good shit looks like.

"That's $800 worth. I'm gonna buy this camera—the Arriflex SR2, and I'm gonna make a punk rock, science-fiction, surf road movie. It's gonna be insane." He stands up on his bed in front of the old *Apocalypse Now* poster and waves his arms as he talks. He had the same poster for like five years. He's loved that movie since he was twelve. The lamp on his nightstand casts his shadow on the poster, but huge, behind him. "I'm gonna fill it with blood and sex and horror, brah. I'm gonna run my truck off the Pali lookout and film it from the bottom. I hope it explodes. That would be so cool. This chick, Lisa, already said she'd get naked. It's gonna be…audacious!" He sticks out his tongue and makes rock-and-roll hand signs out to his sides. He stands above me on the bed. Fuck, it's so weird. I remember him talking about this same movie when we were kids.

"When's that Tammy girl coming?"

Clay jumps off the bed to the floor. "Tomorrow, I think. She's from here." He takes a cricket out of a small cardboard box and throws it into the terrarium.

"Oh." I roll over facedown. I hate her already.

"What?"

"Nothing."

The phone rings. The eyes of a frog-shaped phone on Clay's shelf light up, and the ring sounds like a frog's ribbit. I remember it from years ago; I always wanted one 'cause he made it seem cool.

He ignores the frog phone and stares at me. "What?"

"Nothing."

"Hammerhead! Phone!" his mom calls from the other room.

He walks to his phone, sits on the floor with his back to me, and picks it up. He holds it gently, like it's fragile, close to his face. "Hey…just hanging out." He lowers his voice. "What are you talking about? I am too… Yes, I can't wait… I am not… Yeah. I'll pick you up… No, I want to… Did you tell Susan the flight? Okay, me too… Yeah! Me too… Why are you acting like this? What? No. I'm not mad… I'll see you tomorrow." He hangs up quickly.

That was undeniably the sound of a boy talking to his girl-friend. There's no other way to interpret it. I feel sick. I think this is what betrayal feels like. I want to cry, but I can't in front of him. He'll think I'm a pussy.

He looks at me defensively, his chest out, like I'm just one of his surfing brahs hanging out in his room and he's afraid I'm gonna make fun of him for taking shit from his girlfriend. "What?"

"You sound different when you talk to her. Kinda fake. Like a kiss-ass."

"Fuck you. I already have one bitch nagging me."

"Fuck you, asshole. You don't have to be a dick."

"Then don't be such an annoying little shit."

I get up off the bed and throw his pot canister across the room as hard as I can.

He jumps up, and slams me into the wall. He shoves my shoulders up against a poster of a guy surfing a huge wave.

He stares into my eyes. His face is red, and his eyes are watery. I can feel his breath on my face. What if he's a psychopath? I picture him methodically cleaning up my guts.

The veins in his temples are pulsing. A layer of sweat coats his skin. His eyes look like they're going to pop out. "Fuck you," he whispers. "Don't do this to me." He drops his head and stares at the ground. His face softens and his eyes fill with tears. Tiny hairs on his arms stand up and he starts sobbing. He squeezes me close and tight to his body. He rubs his nose and chin and cheeks against mine. The stubble on his chin rubs against my lips.

I push back into him, trying to feel all the resistance I can, the pressure of him on my body. He rubs his mouth along my cheek and across my lips. He kisses me and sticks his tongue in my mouth. A rush of adrenaline surges through me and I start sweating. My body is going to melt in his arms.

Clay slides his hands down my shoulders and arms and pulls my T-shirt up over my head. It pulls on my ears and makes them feel hot.

I can smell my sweaty skin, exposed at last. For once, I'm not embarrassed by how skinny I am. It doesn't matter. This is more intense than anything I've ever done. Nothing else will ever compare. My ribs rise and fall as I breathe. The hair on my legs looks sexual. I feel like I'm floating above the bed, unable to feel all of this.

He pulls off his T-shirt. He looks like an amazing sculpture, like the one in Waikiki of Duke Kahanamoku, the first modern surfer. His blue boxer's waistband rides a couple inches above his shorts, which tent up in front.

I can't believe I'm allowed to touch him. I lick his chest and I can taste his skin, still salty from surfing.

He pushes me onto the bed.

8

Gusty cold storm winds
blow off the remaining buds
Summer's spell is sweet

Clay rolls off me, smiles, and rests his head on the pillow. "I'm sorry I hit you." He closes his eyes like he's going to sleep.

I crawl up in his bed, under the covers, into his warm, sleepy world. I hear a strong gust of wind. Leaves fly into the screen on the window and I smell the healthy scent of oncoming rain. The rain excites me. "Clay?"

He moves a little and pulls the pillow over his head. "Huh?"

"What's going on? What are you thinking?"

"I'm tired." He tells me this like nothing happened between us. "OK."

I get up, try to put my shorts on, and fall on my face.

"Dumb shit." Clay laughs and goes under the covers.

I walk over to his lizard's terrarium. It's a Jackson chameleon—neon-green with huge eyes, a permanent smile, and a broken tail. They live in the wet parts of the island. Clay probably caught it himself while hiking the Koolaus. The lizard's face looks like Clay's when he sleeps. I walk over to the dresser where there's a photo of Tammy. I flip her off and put the photo facedown. Next to it, I find a photo of Tammy and Clay. He's shirtless in front of a waterfall.

I stick it in my pocket.

Lightning crackles in the distance, followed by booming thunder far away.

"I gotta go. I gotta mow my yard."

He sticks his hand out from the covers and gives me a shaka sign.

I was hoping for *I love you. Let's kill everyone so it's just us and hide away together and have sex and stare at each other till we die.*

But, hey, at least he acknowledged me.

I strap my pack on and take a skateboard from out front of Clay's house and throw my bike in his carport. I have to leave something here as proof that today happened. I throw the old, beat-up board down on the street, take a couple steps back, then run forward and jump on the board, flying down the hill faster than I've ever dared to before. I'm out of control, and I don't care. Clay's protecting me now. I look straight up as I roll down the hill. The sky is getting darker. It's going to rain soon. I skate home down the centerline of the Kamehameha Highway. Cars honk and barrel around me, but I'm not scared.

I get home and start mowing the backyard. My dad's inside doing a crossword puzzle and watching some crap financial news show about how to get richer by fucking over poor people. I mow Clay's name into the grass, repeating the letters over and over again.

My dad walks out the back door and looks at the yard with totally exaggerated disgust. "You're going to have to do a better job than that if you want to get paid."

"I'm not finished. God!" I scream over the roaring mower. "Don't watch me, or I'm gonna chop my foot off."

I finish up the lawn, then go to my room. I jump up and down on the bed and leap over to Clay's skateboard. I skate around my room, from my bed to the wall, falling off and making black marks on the baseboards, using all the energy I can. It gets my blood pumping and

I sweat a little. Clay's smell is still on my skin. I take off my shirt, and look in the mirror. Who's this skinny little boy? This is so embarrassing. And Clay saw me like this? I drop to the floor and do push-ups till my arms are tired, then do sit-ups till my stomach hurts. I open my closet door, hang on to the top of it, and do pull-ups—fourteen of them. Not bad. My veins stick out. My skin is damp and shiny. I look in the mirror again. I look good, I guess—OK, anyway.

Clay likes the way I look, and he's the best-looking person I've ever seen.

I sit on the floor and lean on my bed and take out the photo I have of Clay, shirtless and wet in front of the waterfall. It's bent-up and warm from being in my pocket. Tammy. I have to get her out of here. I can't believe she's in my room. I get scissors from my stupid little kid desk and cut her out so Clay stands alone. I spit on her till her face and body comes off the paper when I rub it. I mangle her face and rip her arms and legs and breasts off. Then I light a match and burn her.

She melts and sizzles.

"Are you smoking in there?" my mom screams from the other room.

"No! I'm melting wax for an art project." I lie back in my pile of stuffed animals, grab my notebook from my backpack, and write a haiku: *Clay's bed, summer, afternoon sweat is love, riding home smiling.*

My door flies open, and Jared walks in. "Man, you smell like shit."

"Can't you knock?" I hide my notebook in my pack.

He walks over to me and takes a deep smell.

I lift my armpit. "I've been working out." I raise my eyebrows.

"Oh, yeah, I can tell. You must be up to ninety pounds. Where were you earlier? I came by—no Sam-boy home."

"Smokin' some weed with Clay."

He looks jealous. "You'd sort of have to be stoned to be friends with him, huh? He *is* a dealer."

"Well, then I'll stay stoned all the time."

Jared looks totally confused. To him, Clay's a drug dealer, a dumb-ass loser surfer not worthy of our attention because everyone else gives him too much already. He must sort of know somewhere in his brain that I like Clay or something, because I usually hate these kinds of guys as much as he does. He has to know I'm gay, but I never brought it up. I don't think he'd mind even, but that's just not the sort of thing we talk about. He never mentions what girls give him a hard-on, so why should I, I figure. He's cool, though, and his parents are liberal, and his uncle's gay and they hang out all the time, so I know he wouldn't care if I told him.

When we were younger, I would sneak out, lie, steal money, or anything to spend the night at his house, to see him lie in bed with no shirt on, to watch him sleep. I used to suggest we go swimming way more than a normal amount at beaches where I knew no other kids would be, but that's all faded. Anyway, I used to fall for almost every good-looking boy, so having a crush on Jared's not saying much, especially back then.

"Well, I'm on my way to my drawing class. Guess I better go." He smiles at me, and there's a sadness in his eyes—not like the kind of sadness when a friend gets murdered or something, but the kind of sadness when a pet dies. I watch him walk out into the very beginning of a thunderstorm.

Big dark storm clouds cover the sun and make my room go dim. The air smells fresher. The storm makes some ions exchange, from the earth to the sky, and back again.

I sit with my elbows on the windowsill looking out. The wind cleans my face. The house creaks in the wind. Tears build up in my eyes and blur my vision, but they don't run down my face. I liked hanging out with Jared. Now, I'm lonely. It's a risk letting him

leave, letting him in on my new life. I need to hang out with someone, be with someone to share opinions, smoke together, be brothers. I'll call Clay.

He has to be up by now.

I dial and it rings.

"Hello?" It's his mom.

"Hi…Susan?" I feel weird calling her by her name. "It's Sam."

"Hi, sweetie." She talks to me the same way she talks to
Tammy. I feel like part of a fucking harem.

"Clay up?"

"He had to go back in to work. Marcus broke his leg skating a
ramp, so he's covering for him."

"OK, thanks." I dive out my window and ride to the skate
shop. I don't know if it's a mixture of love, happiness, or sadness,
but I feel really lonely and, if I'd stayed home alone, I'd have been
crying, and I didn't want to feel that pathetic.

I lean my board outside and walk into the shop.

Some guy is sorting random skate shoes on the floor, and a couple
other guys I've never seen before are building boards on the counter.

I walk right up to Clay. "Aloha. What's up?" I feel like it's been
forever since I've seen him, but it's only been like three hours.

"Hey," he says in a monotone.

Is he bored with me already? What did I do wrong?

"What're you doing tonight?"

"Picking Tammy up at the airport, and she'll probably want to
hang out with Maya and Becky." He looks over at the guys to see
if they're listening.

"So, why don't you get someone else to pick her up? We could
go to the look out and smoke pot or ride bikes or play video games
or walk around Waikiki and check out the prostitutes or harass
tourists at Ala Moana or…"

He looks around the shop and gets really mad. "Dude," he says

with his teeth clenched, "I'm picking Tammy up. Lay off, brah."
He relaxes and leans closer to me, monitoring everyone else in the
store over my shoulder. "Don't come over when Tammy's here,"
he says in his surfer cool-boy accent, like that's supposed to make
it okay. He looks me right in the eye. "Got it?"

"No."

He ignores me and starts locking up his display cases.

It starts pouring outside. The storm's here. I'm heartbroken. I
need to cry or hit him. I need to hit myself for being stupid enough
to think we were best friends out of the blue. I knew something
was coming like this. It was too good to last-not with my luck.

"I'm closing up."

"No shit."

I hate you, you asshole prick fake.

"You wanna ride? I can swing you by on my way home." He
acts like everything's okay.

What a liar.

I bolt and slam through the door. As I skate home though the
rain, I think I'm having a nervous breakdown. My insides are
melting into an indecipherable mess. I wanna ride in front of traffic and kill myself. That would show him.

He'll be sorry when I'm gone.

I climb in the window of my room and lie on my bed and cry.
My stomach feels tight and sore. My eyes burn. I hate being sixteen. Everything's changing and getting more confusing than I
ever thought it could. I'm all alone, and just hours ago I felt so
cared for, I felt so alive, I felt like I'd never have to be lonely again.
I think of a line from the movie *Apocalypse Now* that Clay has
the poster for: "I was going to the worst place in the world, and I
didn't even know it yet."

Part Two

9

Late spring ice storm
broke the promise of fresh
blooms and horny boys.

Walking around on Wednesday evening, the clouds form animals in the sky. I usually see them only when I'm high, which I am.

My pot-consumption level has risen dramatically, from getting high whenever to getting high at least four times a day. I hang out at home a lot more, taking photos—of myself mostly, because my art teacher, Ms. Yamamoto, said it will help me discover my inner soul or whatever. The four joints a day are provided by Clay on short stopovers he makes on his way to other pot deliveries.

He doesn't talk much. He never mentions that I stormed out of the skate shop crying. He's nice and friendly, but he fakes being busier than he is. All I get is, "Cool, brah. Laterz. I'll call you." He never does. It's been like this between us for at least two long weeks. His pot-delivery service is very successful. He got to quit working so much for the skate shop, and he's got more time to surf, and he's going to be able to buy that 16-mm camera he needs to make that stupid movie he's been talking about since he was eleven.

Smoking pot all the time has its drawbacks. It gets me really paranoid. I imagine I hear my parents come in when I'm jacking off. It's terrifying to picture them walking in, eyes and mouths gaping wide, and seeing my boner, which looks a lot more grown-up than the rest of me. Letting them see that side of me would let them in on a lot more than I ever want them to know. I smoke yet another bowl out of some hippie pipe I found out skating and I'm way too stoned to stay inside. My room starts to feel like a teenage prison.

I walk up the hill to Clay's house, and my backpack feels too heavy—too many haikus, I guess. I'm sure he won't be there, but I just wanna see his house and think about how fun it was to hang out with him there. I might stop in to say hi to his mom, but I figure she probably doesn't like me anyway.

The shadows on Clay's street are long in the afternoon sun. I see a kid I had art class with last year leaning out his window, shirtless, waiting for someone, probably for Clay, to come by with his weed. I walk around the corner and see Clay's house up ahead. His truck's not there. Susan's blue Toyota is parked in front and a car I've never seen before is parked beside hers—in Clay's spot. The car is annoying-looking. It's too sensible. It looks like a car that a nurse or social worker would drive.

It's Tammy's.

I tiptoe up to the driveway to look into the car. Kleenexes, coins, a pink swimsuit on the passenger seat. I pace around the street and light up a cigarette. I want to storm into the house and demand an explanation. My mouth turns dry, and my armpits sweaty. I sneak up the side of Clay's house and crouch by a tree stump.

I have a perfect view into the family room. The TV's off and the stereo's on, which means socializing, talking, trying to spend quality time, whatever that is. I can hear some sort of jazz, the kind of music someone puts on when a guest is over and they wanna drink wine and talk about boring shit. The doorway to the kitchen is lit. An occasional silhouette walks by the opening, cooking or carrying things from the refrigerator.

The family room light flips on. I almost jump up and run away, but all my fear just stays in my chest, and I wonder if this is how a heart attack would feel.

Susan walks in and fluffs the pillows on the couch and chairs. She sits down on the sofa and looks out the window, right into my eyes.

I wave, without thinking.

She doesn't respond. She looks into the glass and pushes her dark brown hair back. She's only seeing her reflection.

My body unclenches. Thank fucking God. She would have thought I was some freak, stalking her and Clay.

Tammy walks in.

Her hair's straight and blond—like in the photos—and she's incredibly suntanned and pretty, in that local haole-girl sort of way. She's wearing an open white blouse with a couple gold chains underneath, probably holding heart lockets or some other little nursery charms. She sits down on the couch with Susan. They smile at each other and talk with so many expressions of interest and humor that this can't be real unless they are the two most oblivious people in the world. I can tell a fake expression anywhere.

I hear a car drive up.

The headlights spotlight the house next door as it turns into the driveway. It's Clay's truck. I can tell by the sound of the engine.

Clay's dog barks.

"It's only Clay, Sharky!" his mom screams.

Clay rips through the front door and slams it behind him. He walks straight to the family room, where Susan and Tammy impersonate having a nice time. He walks over to Tammy, leans down, and gives her a kiss somewhere between the mouth and her cheek.

My angle's wrong to see exactly.

Tammy grabs his hand and doesn't let go. She rubs it while he talks to his mom.

I can see their mouths moving, but I can't hear the words through the glass.

Clay told me not to be around when Tammy is. If he loves her, I'll kill her, knock her off, drop some poison in her drink. I need to go inside. I'm not going to let him get away with this so easily. I'll act like I'm just stopping over to drop in—some casual "I was just in the neighborhood" bullshit. I look down at myself to see what they'll think of me when they open the front door. T-shirt, dirty shorts, muddy sneakers, insecure posture, shaky hands, stoned for days. I'm so pissed off and nervous, my teeth are chattering. I walk to the front door and check the knob. It's unlocked. I slink in and run down the hall, quickly and precisely, into Clay's room. I can hear my heart beating.

His room's cleaned up a little. I flip off the photo of Tammy. I know it doesn't do any good or anything—it's not a voodoo photo, but it's still fun. I hear Susan walking into the kitchen.

"I think I smell something burning."

I tiptoe down the hall toward the kitchen and slink past the doorway before his mom gets there. Sharky looks at me and cocks his head, then barks, but just once. I slide across the tile and almost hit the washing machine. I can see down the hall, all the way into the den.

The back of Clay's head sticks up above the back of the sofa.

I want to shoot him with a tranquilizer gun, distract Tammy, shoot her with a real bullet, lock Susan in a closet, and take Clay's body into my room and add him to my pile of stuffed animals. I crawl down the hall on my hands and knees and up behind the sofa where Clay and Tammy are sitting. I take a deep breath and sneak underneath the end table. I have a filtered view of their faces though a gauzy, Hawaiian tapa-print tablecloth.

"What's your mom doing in there?" Tammy sounds like such a bitch.

"I don't know, making dinner or whatever."

He said "whatever." He had to have picked that up from me. *I'm influencing him, affecting him. This is good.*

Tammy's voice is like a little girl's, begging the daddy that spoiled her for attention. "I thought we were going to go out for dinner."

"What?" He's totally confused.

"I wanted to be alone with you, honey."

He looks away as if missing the punch line of a joke. "I love my mom's food."

"Oh, Clay…" she says, like he needs to grow up or something.

I hate listening to her talk down to him like this. All's wrong in the universe when he's being treated badly. I lean forward on my elbows so I can see Clay's face. Sharky stares at me from his place on the carpet. This is so fucking weird. What am I doing in here? Loving Clay has made me insane.

"You're such a mama's boy," Tammy says.

Clay just stares at the TV. He doesn't understand what a shallow bitch she is. He doesn't understand how disconnected they are, because he doesn't understand girls, except his mom, and she treats him like a surfer-boy king.

I feel sorry for him, but I can't do anything, and I hate it. I feel like I haven't taken a breath in five minutes.

"Clay, let's go to Baci. I haven't had their ravioli in ages. Go in there and tell her we're going." She looks at her upper legs and strokes them.

"OK…God." He starts to get mad, but then he makes a really innocent little-boy face and smiles at her. He gets up and walks within an inch of stepping on my fingers—there's sand on his feet from the beach. "Mom, I think we're gonna go out for dinner."

"Why? Hammerhead, I made your favorite—penne arrabiata."

He whispers, "Tammy wants to go out—*be alone.*"

"Clay, I've been cooking for three hours. Talk to her."

He shrugs his shoulders and walks back into the family room.

Tammy waits with a mean look on her face, probably because Clay didn't ask her to marry him or something stupid like that. That's the kind of girl Tammy is. I can tell. She wants to trap him in legal papers and screaming brats.

It's horrible to see Clay be made into a puppet by a girl who's projecting her own insecurities on him by blaming him for everything that's wrong with her. I know Jared would agree, and his dad's a psychiatrist. I wish I could jump out from under the table, hug him, tell him how cool he is, and take him away from her, but he wouldn't go.

He's into this for some reason. He thinks that his life will be *perfectly fine* if he works at some stupid place, marries Tammy, and continues to dream about making movies and fooling around with boys.

That's so depressing. I thought Clay had it all figured out, but I'd never seen him kiss Tammy's ass before. I roll out from under the table, all military style, and crawl down the hall. When I'm out of sight, I stand up and run into Clay's room. It smells like pot and dirty socks. I hear footsteps. Fuck, they're following me. I run over to the closet and dive inside and take my backpack off slowly and quietly. I tense up and stop breathing. I have a narrow view through the crack.

Tammy walks in and Clay follows her. "Why did you drag me in here?" She's as whiny as ever.

"Tammy, you're being mean to my mom." He looks away at his television, which isn't on.

"That's not true. We were talking before you got here. Your mom fucking loves me."

I slowly sit down on a pile of Clay's skateboarding shoes. I can see the bend in Clay's arm, and Tammy's mouth. I lean forward to get a better view. Clay doesn't know how to respond. He just looks at his hand.

"Just leave her, Clay…tell her to fuck off," I whisper.

He looks at the closet.

I make eye contact with him, but I'm pretty sure he can't see me. He'd say something right away. I wave to make sure. He just stares into the darkness of the crack. I think he wishes he could just jump in and hide from Tammy and all her demands.

"What are you looking at?"

"I thought I heard someone talking."

"Quit trying to avoid looking me in the eye, Clay."

He sighs. "I'm not. Okay? Wanna go? My mom's gonna invite her friend over to eat, so it's fine." He sits down on his bed.

He's lying.

I feel sorry for Susan. All her years of being a great mother wiped out by one rude demand.

"In a minute, Clay. Hold on." Tammy sits down on the bed and reaches over to Clay's chest and feels around inside his shirt, rubbing his chest. She slides her hand down his stomach and onto his crotch.

His legs open slightly wider and he raises his T-shirt a little at the bottom, so there's an opening between his shorts and his shirt.

My stomach burns. I need a cigarette, ten cigarettes. The veins in my temples are pulsing hard with blood and chemicals. My eyes have no need to blink. My heart races faster than I've ever felt it. My impulse is to jump out if the closet, rip that girl's hand off Clay, throw her across the room, and mutilate her. I want this girl out of here and back into the part of my brain that only dreaded this actually happening. I want her fucking hands off Clay before I go insane.

Get away from him, you slut!

She works her hand into Clay's pants. The waistband of his underwear holds her wrist like a bracelet. Clay just sits there, her hand on his dick. It better not be hard.

She reaches deeper into his pants and starts jacking him off fast, like total hamster-speed.

He thrusts slightly into her hand.

I lean forward to see his face better. My head presses against the door.

His head's back and his eyes are closed. His neck looks sexy, sinewy, shiny with sweat. Maybe he's thinking about me.

He had his eyes open when we were doing shit.

Tammy moves her hand up and down and pulls down the front of his shorts. Her hand's on his boner. Light tan, peach-colored, perfect, smooth skin and his dark pubic hair.

I can't breathe.

She looks like she's doing some sort of nursing procedure. It looks like porn. A weird mix of sexuality and disinterested ritual.

I get a hard-on. It confuses me. I'm full of so much feeling. Turned on, fucked over, jealous enough to murder. A rich lady would take a Valium now. I need heroin.

Tammy unbuttons her shirt and keeps jerking off Clay with her other hand. Her pale tits plop out. Clay doesn't look at them. Tammy slides her hand down her body and lifts her skirt above her waist. She slides her hand into her underwear.

Clay comes. I see it shoot up a little and run down Tammy's knuckles.

She keeps jerking him off, though. "Fuck me, Clay."

He looks like he's in pain. His lips are snarled up, and his eyes are wide.

She's abusing him, exploiting him. She should treat him like a fucking prince.

This bitch doesn't know that it fucking hurts to jerk off after you've already come.

"Tammy, sweetie, I came." He says this with an odd mix of affection and disbelief, but not anger, as I hoped.

"Oh…fuck…oh…oh, Clay, baby…. Oh, God…fuck me…" She's totally acting like she's in a porno movie, like everything she knows she learned from watching one. A thin layer of sweat coats her skin. Clay looks into her eyes as she's coming, or giving birth, or whatever the fuck she's doing. He laughs when she's done—a sort of small, affectionate laugh.

"Why are you laughing?"

"Because you looked cute"—he wipes his nose with his arm—"and because you're so dramatic."

"Nice—the first time we even do anything in like…months, and you don't even fuck me."

Hearing this makes me feel gross. I've got to get out of here. It's not right to be spying on this shit. I won't be able to be pissed off at him later if I hear all this. I already feel too sorry for him.

"OK, Tammy, let's just go. I don't want to argue. Let's go eat." I can hear anger buried deep in his voice.

Tammy gets up off the bed, adjusts her skirt, and walks to the door. She opens it and leaves. "I'll meet you outside."

He takes a last look around the room and gets his wallet from the top of his dresser. He picks a T-shirt up from the floor and smells it. He puts it on, then leans down and picks up a chunk of green surf wax. He rubs it hard and then beams it at the wall. It takes a chunk out of the paint where it hits. His lizard jumps in its cage. Clay walks over to him. "Sorry, bro." He walks out, closing the door behind him.

The room has a deafening buzz, like their energy is still here, still battling. At least Tammy's gone, even if Clay had to leave to get rid of her.

She's horrible. My worst fears are confirmed.

Clay not only still wants to be with Tammy, he'll do it even when she's treating him like shit. His feelings about her are convoluted and fucked-up. How can he be so stupid? How can he not see what's going on?

I get up and stretch my legs. I open my pack and steal some pot from his dealer-boy drawer and take a couple of his wife-beaters and a pair of his boxers, just in case I never see him again and he gets stolen into Tammy World for all eternity. I smell his mom's cooking and instantly get really hungry, like totally, completely hungry—on the verge of passing out Sahara Desert–style.

She turns the stereo on. Joni Mitchell's high-pitched voice echoes down the hall.

I zip my pack and lie back on Clay's bed, the place where the horrible coupling took place. I don't smell Tammy, but I do smell Clay. I can't believe the bed's not tainted by her. Lying here seems to calm me, but it's deceiving. She was here.

I hear Susan on the phone. "OK, Linda. Sure. No problem. I've been looking forward to a night alone anyway. I can get some painting done. Right. Okay, talk to you later. Night." She turns up the music.

I'm not sure what to do, how to get out of here. I have nothing to do tonight. I walk over to Clay's window. It looks easy to escape, but I'm sure he never had to do it. My window's practically a door, I use it so much. I feel the screen. It looks easy to take out. I unscrew the dusty aluminum screws and the screen falls out onto a shrub. I strap my pack on and jump out and squeeze awkwardly between the sill and the top of the window, which won't open very high for some reason. I land on the screen, which makes the other side pop up and hit my leg. It stings. I trip over a wooden stake—a support for a young tree—and land sideways in the wet dirt.

This is pathetic. I lie in the mud outside Clay's window in the dark while he and Tammy drive to some fancy dinner with candles and wine. I look up into the night sky. The moon shines down on me through high clouds, and the breeze makes my dirty shirt sway across my chest. The big, puffy clouds are being swept away by a high-pressure center or maybe a distant hurricane. I can hear the music when the breeze blows a certain way.

A young hippie-sounding girl sings about being in love and not being loved back.

I cry. All this thinking is doing me no good. I feel a huge emptiness in my chest. I want to destroy something. I can't stop crying. Why does love have to make me feel so terrible? I wonder if Clay knows what he's doing to me. If he doesn't, I'm even worse off. I feel so alone. I want to fly away. I want to die. I want to be romantic with someone. And look at me—pathetic. Everyone else is with the person they love—kissing, hanging out, smoking weed—and I'm crying alone in the grass in front of some guy's house, trying to be quiet so no one notices me. This fucked-up haiku comes into my head: *Lonely boy tears, mixing with raindrops, can't tell the difference.*

There has to be more. I feel a frown on my face that I have no control over. I press my ear to the ground. I can hear something— like vibrations. Maybe it's highway noises from far away, maybe cars screeching around corners, or a distant earthquake, but I'd like to think it's the earth. It makes me feel less alone to know that the earth lives and breathes and feels things like I do. I hate to be like this, so hippie-boy.

I get up and brush off leaves and dirt from my shorts and T-shirt. I spit on my hands, rub them together till they look clean, and wipe them on the grass. I walk around to the front of the house. The door is still cracked open.

10

Lonely moon night sky
can't console the hard aching:
teenage boyhood soul.

My knuckles make a rattly, tinny sort of knock on the flimsy aluminum screen door.

Susan doesn't answer, but Sharky comes running up, barking.

"Hello? Hi, boy."

"Hello?" Susan yells over the music.

"Uhh...hi. It's Sam."

"Sam?" She walks up holding an almost empty wineglass, and smiling. "Hey, handsome. You scared me." That's nice of her to say 'cause I'm sure I look horrible, especially by adult standards. She looks up at the sky behind me. "Clay's not here, sweetie. He just left a couple minutes ago. I'm surprised you didn't see him driving down the hill."

I turn around to see what she's looking at. The sky looks ominous. It's multicolored blue, white, and black, like a haunted watercolor painting—the perfect backdrop for me, a wreck of a person. "But...his truck's here." I have to make this convincing.

"Oh, Tammy drove."

Tears fill my eyes before I can stop them.

"Come in, sweetie." She opens the screen door. "Are you okay?"

I nod and follow her through the house to the screened-in porch out back. I throw my muddy backpack on the floor. The dampness on my skin starts to evaporate. I sit on a chair facing the backyard.

Susan looks outside, her head tilted upward to the sky, with a totally relaxed expression on her face. "The wind is soothing, don't you think?"

"I hope it rains. There's nothing like rain." I wipe my nose with my arm. And I hope Tammy dies a painful death tonight—maybe bad fish poisoning.

"I couldn't agree more." She sits on the sofa, next to a table that's holding a half-read novel and a bottle of red wine. "Clay loves rain too."

I burst out crying.

"What's wrong, Sam?"

I wipe my eyes with my T-shirt sleeve and try to stop crying by holding my breath. I have to tell her how I'm feeling. If I keep this inside, I'll explode, burst into bloody pieces. "There's this person I really like and I'm not sure if they like me back." My face rushes with red, hot blood. That was hard to say.

"What do you feel in your heart?"

"I think they like me but won't admit it to themselves because they're scared."

Sharky runs in and lies down by my feet. He feels soft and warm.

Susan looks at him. "I think he likes you."

He likes me.

No, she's talking about the dog.

We look at each other. An embarrassing connection forms.

Moms know everything. She has to know Clay likes me, if he does.

I want to ask her, but I'm way too ashamed. My tears have

dried, forming salty paths down both cheeks. I lick what I can reach with my tongue. The salt tastes good. I put my hand under my chin and watch it rain outside. Now my hand's been there too long. It looks posed. I look out the window. Now it looks like I'm trying to avoid being intimate, avoiding eye contact whenever the situation gets tense, like I don't understand how to get close because my parents were cold when I was growing up. I'll just be what she expects me to be—if I only knew what that is. I wish I could go jack off. I should have just done it on Clay's bed after they left. I'd probably feel normal right now if I had. That's what I need to do. Now I just feel trapped.

"Would you like some dinner? I made some pasta."

Clay and Tammy just left her, and I saw how that made her feel. "Yeah, I know…uh…I mean, yeah. Sure."

She walks into the kitchen.

"Thank you." I listen to the music. It's great. My stoned daze is wearing off. My eyes feel droopy.

She walks in, carrying a bowl of pasta and a big glass of red wine. She hands me the bowl formally, like I'm an official guest.

"Thanks."

She doesn't look me in the eye. Maybe she knows I'm sad about something that isn't the easiest thing in the world to talk about. If she knew it was about Clay, I bet she'd freak out. Not that she'd be freaked out about him being queer or whatever, but she wouldn't like the thought of her blood, her son, making me feel so sad. She looks out into the backyard. "I'm worried about that Japanese maple. It looks so fragile in this wind."

I see what she's talking about, a newly planted tree tied up with two stakes, and I tell her, "I'm sure it will be okay. It's a tree. They're used to that sort of thing."

She laughs and touches me on the shoulder, cautiously, like I'd jump if she did anything more—but I love it. I love being touched by her. I take a bite of the pasta, which is excellent.

She drinks wine and watches the wind sweep the lawn and clear away dead leaves and branches.

My knife slips in between the tongs of the fork. It looks sexual. When Clay's on my mind, anything can be taken sexually.

She looks down at my silverware, then quickly looks away.

The screens billow in, then get sucked out by the wind. The screen door at the front of the house opens, then slams shut.

"Who is it that you like?" Susan looks at me with a sense of adventure on her face.

I can feel Clay's name forming on my tongue. What if she gets angry? All these people around trying to steal her son from her. "No one you know. Why didn't Clay and Tammy eat here with you?" I take a huge gulp of wine.

"It's complicated. Tammy wants me to think it's because she wants to be alone with him, but I think she's a little jealous of me. She's possessive. I don't think Clay will put up with that forever. He's a free spirit."

Is she saying this because she knows? Why else would she tell me about Tammy? This is so fucking great. She doesn't like Tammy any-more. She's ready for me. "Clay told me something about not being around when she's here." I can't believe I just said that.

"I'm sure. She thinks you'll steal him away."

"But…that's stupid."

She fills my glass. Her teeth and tongue are stained red. "Is it?"
Oh, fuck. She knows.

I look out into the backyard. The ferns are look white because they are being blown to one side and the wooden fence is rattling hard. "Something big's going down."

"Last time I saw winds like this, I heard roofs flying off of houses. It really makes you appreciate life, doesn't it?"

"Without it, we'd be dead." I smile. Lightning lights my face so bright, I'm sure she can see it needs to be washed.

She takes the empty wine bottle into the kitchen.

I'm pretty sure this is fun. I wish Clay was here with us. I think he would be jealous if he knew I was here with his mom in this storm having a great time. I hope he's having a horrible time.

Susan walks back in with a joint and another bottle of wine.

"Oh, my God, that's so cool."

"It's only a joint. Don't be a square. It's a special occasion. And don't ever come around and ask me for pot. We'll say this one's for Kahuna Kilokilo, the Hawaiian god who watches the skies for omens, and Kahuna Kilo Hoku, the expert of weather. Pray for him to spare the roof and the trees." She takes a hit and coughs.

I take a big hit and hand it back to her.

The music picks up, a happy song. The Japanese maple is holding up all right—as I suspected.

Joni Mitchell does a song about what we're doing: laughing and drinking.

We sing along together, smiling the entire time. I feel sorta stupid, letting myself dork out so much, but I know the record well from hanging out with Jared's sister, Kendra, and it's the perfect song for the occasion.

A huge gust of wind blows. Aluminum lawn furniture gets tossed across the backyard, barely making it over the fence into the next house's yard.

The emergency hurricane siren blows. It sounds out-of-date, but utterly serious and desperate.

A big branch falls from an old mango tree near the back of the yard where it meets the neighbor's yard. It's a violent, cracking, spiked sound. It crashes onto this lightweight aluminum lawn shed Clay uses for a workshop. The sky is deep blue with a black tint. Far away, I hear what sounds like a house being ripped apart, board by board. Big, full, loud, amplified crunches and squeaky strains. I tell Susan, "Hope we're gonna be okay here."

The lights go out. It takes us a second to realize. The hurricane siren blares again, growing louder when the wind shifts in our direction. "Where's Clay?" I sort of whisper. A horrible image flashes in my mind of Clay thrown in some water-swollen ditch, bewildered and terrified, trying to get up before he drowns, but not being able to because his leg is shattered.

A power transformer explodes on the next street over, shooting up white sparks. Artificial snow-white flashes make the house behind us backlit for milliseconds. Shutters fly off the back of the house next door. They fly across the yard and ram into the fence. The potted hanging spider plants knock against each other in the wind. Soil flies up and sticks on the wet screen. The lights on the next street over go off with a flash.

Clay's dog cowers under the chair I'm sitting in, which makes me scared. Animals have an excellent sense of oncoming tragedy, when to be scared and what to ignore. He starts barking fiercely, like he's defending himself.

Susan gets up quickly, runs out the flapping screen door into the rain and wind. She kicks dirt and mud around the base of the young tree. Her big, flowing, hibiscus-flowered muumuu whips around like a flag on a windy day. As she gets soaked, I can see the shape of her body underneath her dress. She's skinny and her kneecaps stick out like mine. Her breasts are like a high school girl's. Her hair is soaked. She's possessed. She'll do anything for that tree. Suddenly, she stops and looks up into the sky. Wind and rain pelt her. "You have to feel this, Sam. Come out here."

Several metal sheets whip through the sky above the backyard.

I walk outside. The raindrops feel like icicles. The wind feels like it could carry me away. I hear the sound of a big tree branch breaking. It crackles through the air like electricity. It feels like nothing I've ever felt, and makes all my problems seem small. I'm speechless for a while, at one with the sky, then tell her, "This is incredible."

She nods crazily. "Would you look at that moon? It's absolutely stunning. Well, it's gone now. Watch for it, Sam. It's worth the wait."

The moon pokes through thick, black clouds. I'm amazed it's still up there in its calm, cold vacuum, untouched by all this.

I see two Hawaiian guys in the carport beyond the yard.

They look like brothers. They walk to the back of the carport and grab surfboards. They peel away in a pickup truck, tires spinning on the wet pavement.

We walk inside, soaked and exhilarated. I'm happy nature can be as angry, angsty, and crazy as me.

Susan picks up the wine bottle, searching for something. "Where's your glass, Sam?"

"Uhh…" I'm too stoned to remember. I spot it, lying on the floor, shattered, reflecting light in a hundred directions, like a star. "Oh, shit. Sorry."

"Storms have a way of disguising the reality of our plane of existence." She sounds like such a stoner.

"Yeah." I start laughing. The wind picks up even stronger. I hear a horrible, loud metal bang.

"That sounded like a car accident." Susan looks toward the house, with a terrified look on her face.

"Yeah, and totally close." I get up and follow her to the front door. She swings it open. The warm rain stings our faces. "Oh, my God!"

"Oh, fuck."

Her car, a blue Toyota, is dwarfed by a thick tree branch lying on its totally smashed-in hood. It looks like a car dressed up as a tree for Halloween.

She looks up at the sky, and the rain beats down on her face.

"You don't know how many times I've wanted to do this myself!" she shouts, laughing.

Quickly, the sky turns a deep midnight blue. The winds stop. The trees regain their composure. A couple more leaves fall, then all is still—too still.

We walk out to the street, where newspapers touch down and get glued to wet pavement. The air haunts slowly around and fills our lungs with oxygen picked up from hundreds, maybe thousands of miles away.

"I think we're in the eye, Sam." She looks straight up to the sky, where some stars shine through.

I see a bit of Clay in her profile. "How long will it last?"

"Maybe twenty minutes, maybe less."

I feel the circle of energy surrounding us.

"The hurricane plays games with us, just like people play games with each other."

I feel like I should say something like she said, something deep-sounding. "Yeah," I say. "It's cool."

I'm such a loser.

The eye feels less centered now. My head wants to tilt to one side.

She slips on wet leaves, spasms, and raises her arms to catch her balance. "It's coming, Sam. The big part of the storm is coming."

"I hope so." I'm starting to spin. I'm forgetting the words that leave my mouth as soon as I say them, and I don't want to say anything stupid or give myself away. She'll think I'm using her to get to Clay, and I'm not, even though I wouldn't put that past me. I'd do anything for him to love me. I think I'd kill.

The winds pick up quickly.

I see headlights coming up the hill.

Clay drives up the street in Tammy's car. The windshield is shiny and clean, except for a few lime-green leaves. My peripheral vision vanishes like I'm in a tunnel. I start to sweat. My eyes never stray from Clay's face. They're red and watery, but I don't care if he knows I've been crying.

I'm an emotional haiku poet.

I have a right to cry about the boy I love.

11

Angry typhoon, friend,
over sea, your brisk winds blow;
discontented eyes.

Tammy sits in her car like a queen, with no reaction to the fucked-up Toyota.

Clay parks her stupid car, jumps out, and runs over to where his mom's hood is totally smashed in. He starts laughing. "Gnarly! What the fuck happened here?"

"Kahuna Kilo Hoku granted my wish and finally destroyed this rusting hunk of metal." Susan smiles at him. "We were worried about you."

Clay looks at me and doesn't look away. We could be on wild horses jumping over valleys, and we could keep this eye contact.

Tammy gets out of the car.

The folk music stops. Weird, instrumental stuff that sounds like the musical equivalent of having a bad trip starts playing inside on the stereo.

I feel my eyes crossing. My vision blurs. I look at Clay's fuzzy face. I can't hear anything but flutes in a sound tunnel, echoing indistinct drones. I'm dizzy. My stomach's feels like it's going to float away. I'm defying gravity. I'm falling. Everything's fading.

I'm underwater. It's my worst nightmare. Sharks are circling me, their big fangs piercing through depths of cold, dark water. Scavenger fish are organizing efforts. The cold penetrates me to my bones. Swirling trees in circles, with color rings flaring off their surfaces. Strange light barely makes it to my brain. I smell cut grass. I lose my breath. Cold water soaks through the back of my shirt. I try to focus my eyes. A shape, a body, is holding me.

"Sam? Sam?"

I'm thinking *What?* but my mouth can't make the "W" sound. I see Clay's dragon tattoo on his arm, and it looks like it's floating above his skin.

He slides his hands underneath me.

I see him through hazy clouds.

He's holding me.

I feel his heartbeat.

Susan walks over to me. "Sam? Are you with us?"

Tammy makes a grunting sound, like she's about to throw up.

Clay looks at her, then loosens his grip on me and sits up straight, like he's just helping out one of his surf brahs who wiped out on a massive wave.

Tammy peers at us. She doesn't move from the driveway. She just stares—scared, sad, cold, still.

Susan leans down and rubs my leg. "You okay?"

"I don't know."

She rubs Clay's head affectionately, then looks at Tammy.

Clay looks at her too. I can see him struggling—halfway between anger and feeling sorry for her.

She's alone on the driveway.

Susan gestures to her. "Come on in, dear. It's going to start pouring again any second. I've got some nice wine. Come in and have a glass."

But Tammy won't move from her place on the driveway. She won't let her feet touch the grass and dirt. She can't help the look on her face, like she's seeing something paranormal, and it scares her.

Big raindrops start plopping on the cement, the beginning of a huge tropical soak.

Susan takes a step toward her. "I've got some comfy clothes for you in my bedroom. Come dry off."

She stumbles forward, almost falling off the driveway.

Clay looks down at me, still sitting in the wet grass in the rain. "Do you feel all right, dude?"

"Uhh...yeah."

Tammy stops on the front porch and just stands there, looking at us.

Clay looks at her.

Susan holds the screen door open.

Tammy just stares, like she's going to throw up, and mindlessly wanders to the door. Her high heel gets caught in a crack and breaks off. She falls over. Her butt smacks down in a puddle in the grass. She says "fuck," then stands up quickly. The back of her skirt is muddy. It sticks to her butt. Her hair's a stringy mess. Streams of hair spray–laden rain run down her face. She squints her eyes and looks at us for a split second. Then her expression totally changes and—presto chango!—she looks graceful and honest, and I'm almost impressed. She looks away, and Susan ushers her into the house and wipes the back of her skirt to avoid getting mud on the carpet.

I can see her underwear for a second—silky and leopard-printed with mud stains. I burst out laughing, then feel horrible for her. I tell Clay, "Shouldn't you go inside or something?"

He falls back into the wet grass shouting, "I don't know what to do."

We both stand up and a curtain of rain showers us, making smacking sounds on the pavement and aluminum roofs and cars. A raindrop catches his eyelash and sticks. Another drop streams down his face and caresses his lip. "Come on, man." He walks to the front door.

I follow him inside, watching sexy-looking raindrops evaporate from his neck. Being in the house makes what happened outside seem even more outrageous. Situations like that can only take place outside, with all the forces of chaos around. I don't know where Tammy is.

She's probably making herself over in the bathroom.

Clay sits down at the dining room table and lights up a cigarette, like he hasn't done anything wrong.

I watch him, waiting for the moment when, in his own dumb-ass way, he'll smack his forehead and realize that he just fucked Tammy over for me. It doesn't happen. Instead, he just keeps taking hits off his cigarette and looking vaguely out the window.

"Girls are weird, right?" He shrugs his shoulders. That's supposed to be enough.

"I came over to see if you wanted to go watch the storm from the park."

"That sounds nice," he says in a sort of jokey way that makes me feel like the joke.

The radio music goes off and the local report starts. "Waves are building to eight and ten feet on Oahu's eastern shores from Makapu to Sunset. Damage reports have been filed from the Big island to Molokai. Stay tuned for further developments."

Clay puts out his cigarette in a plant and says, "Fuck, I wanna surf."

"You're crazy."

He looks like a dog on a chain, ready to bite through it. "You wanna go down there with me?"

"Where?"

"The beach, stupid."

"Uh...no. You can't surf in a storm. You'll kill yourself."

He gets up and scratches his head.

I see the waistband of his underwear and the thin line of hair going down to his dick when his shirt rises.

He raises his arms and takes his shirt off in one solid motion. "Well, I'm going. You can come if you want."

"OK, let's just hang out, though. Watch the wind."

Clay goes out the back door and brings in a long board and a short board.

"Who's that for?"

"Tammy."

My heart drops.

"Just kidding." He smiles at me in a very direct, confident way.

"Ha. Ha. Fuck you."

I get my backpack from the screened-in porch and follow him into the kitchen. He hands me the short board and grabs a towel from the laundry room, flinging it over his shoulder in the kitchen doorway.

I cower behind him, trying to be invisible. "Laterz, Momason. We're outz to surf."

"What do you mean 'out to surf'? You're *not* leaving Tammy here. You deal with this. Go in there and take a shower with her."

She doesn't want to hang out with Tammy, either.

Clay smells his armpits. "I'm clean. Why's she so upset, anyway?"

Fuck. I feel like I'm gonna lose it. I want to kill him.

He knows why she's upset. He knows everything.

Susan turns red. She's gonna start screaming any second.

Clay steps closer to her. "Mom, seriously, she's fine. You're gonna be here, aren't you?" He rubs her shoulders, lowers his voice and whispers with a babyish tone, "You can take care of her."

"I'm too tired for this bullshit, Clay. I mean it! Don't leave this house! This isn't my responsibility!"

Tammy appears at the end of the hall, and stares at me, still wearing her muddy dress. She looks like Carrie from that horror movie.

I get a chill in my spine that makes me squirm. I want out of here. I can't take the guilt of being the person who caused Clay to lose interest in her.

"I'm outz. We'll talk later about your hippie rules." Clay storms down the hall.

I glance at Tammy, then look at Susan, who's furious.

I feel responsible for all of it. They're all going to end up hating me. I walk out to the front yard. Clay straps both boards into the back of his truck, and we get in the cab. It's quiet. I zip my pack open and closed over and over. "Tammy's gonna be pissed off."

"What? Oh, no, she's cool."

"I saw what you just did. You know that, right? The whole surfing thing's bullshit."

"Uhh, yeah, I know," he says sarcastically.

"Well, that fucking sucks. Why don't you just tell her we wanna hang without her around?"

He just ignores me and almost smiles.

I grab a beer from a six-pack on the seat between us and open the cap with my teeth. I fill my mouth with beer, nearly downing the whole bottle. "Fuck!" I throw the bottle out the window and it smashes on the driveway.

"Dude, you look sexy when you're pissed off."

"Fuck, Clay, be serious."

"I was."

I ask him if he knows how fucked-up he is.

He says, "Yup. I was born fucked-up."

A big palm frond hits the hood of the truck.

He starts the truck and backs out of the driveway. He drives off fast over debris-covered streets like it's a sunny day.

I grip the dashboard and reach around to put my seat belt on.
"You don't need that. Relax, man."

"Like I trust you."

We pull into the beach parking lot and he jumps out, grabs his
surfboard from the back of the truck, and runs to the ocean. He
looks back at me. "Laterz."

I get out of the truck and stand in the wind. It's so strong, I can
lean into it with all my weight.

He paddles out through wide areas of storm-strewn, bubbly
white water. He looks like a seal, getting smaller and smaller. The
winds start up strong and gusty again. A strong salt mist and
foamy bubbles coat the beach. The cold rain picks up to a full-on
pour. I get back inside the truck. Fuck him. He's a fraud and a liar.
I feel like shit about the way he treated Tammy. Why should I be
the only one?

I start up the truck, peel out on the slick fallen leaves, and take
off down the road.

The second band of the hurricane is here. It's hard to keep the
truck straight as I barrel down the road.

I feel like I'm going crazy. Is Clay thinking about me, or about
Tammy at home with his mom? I wonder if he's thinking at all, or
if he's relying only on survival instincts now, out in the water that
looks like an old oil painting that's shoved in the back corner of my
garage where the world is flat and the big wooden ship is almost
falling off the edge. I pull over and down a beer for confidence. I
light a cigarette that's wet halfway up. The noise of the storm is
deafening. There's a sharp crash every couple seconds. I'm soaked
and my teeth are chattering. The beer tastes good. I'm one with the
chaos. I'm as careless as the storm. I peel off from the side of the road
and turn up a dirt sugarcane road. The dirt is bright orange. It
splashes up on the windshield as I bounce along the road. I slam on
the brakes, and the truck starts to slide off the road toward a ditch.

"Fuck!"

Everything stops. The rain picks up. I don't remember getting here. The truck sits diagonal in a three-foot ditch. I rev it up and slam on the accelerator. It sprays bright-orange mud behind. I'm stuck. I guess this is where I'm meant to be.

I can distinguish every scent inside Clay's truck: cigarettes, spilled beer, dirty clothes, some oil, gasoline, Clay's skin, come on my dirty T-shirt.

I practice looking tough, doing Ninja jabs, slicing through the air. I make mean looks at the mirror, trying to look like a samurai or black belt.

"Hi-yah!" I break a plastic fast-food drink holder. "Man, Clay. Why won't you just tell her to fuck off? Why are you so fucked-up?"

The future just isn't what it used to be.

I put in a tape. It says PUNK ROCK '93 on the front in Clay's chicken-scrawl handwriting, with some hieroglyphic-looking drawings of skateboarders doing tricks on the back of the scratched-up plastic case.

A song by DI plays. Fast drums, high treble guitars with a low, half-intelligible, young, scratchy voice screaming. "Down with the government! Down with the cops. Down with the government!"

Clay's like this music.

I open another bottle of beer with my teeth. I feel like pouring it all over myself.

I look in the mirror. Dark circles under my eyes, sweaty face. I hit myself right below my eye. I do it three more times. My eye becomes hot and numb. I do it twenty more times, harder each time. My brain feels like it's being jarred, woken up. It starts to feel like a need.

I take a huge gulp of beer, keep it in my mouth, swallow as much as I can, then spit the rest on the dashboard and windshield in front of me. My eye is swelling.

I grab the mirror off the dash and lie back on the seat. I look up to myself in the mirror. I have an incredible-looking black eye. It's blue and purple already. It looks Japanese, swollen into a slit. I reach down and find Clay's old skate shoes, with soles barely left, and throw them as hard as I can at the roof. They ricochet and hit me in the chest.

"Fuck!"

I throw the shoes over and over as fast as I can. One cracks the interior dome light. I'm falling. There's no bottom, and I don't give a shit. A vision of Clay floats above me, like a pink candy heart on Valentine's Day with fucking "Won't you be mine?" on it. I take out my haiku notebook and try to write, but I'm seeing double, triple. The notebook slides off my chest and onto the floor. The deafening punk rock music disappears. It slips into my unconscious as a monotone of shallow guitar noise. I'm slipping. I reach over, but miss the door handle. My hand slams the door panel. I reach up and pull the handle. The door flings open.

I fall out of the truck upside down and backward. My body slides out and lands in a mud puddle. I roll over, then give up.

It's pouring warm large tropical drops. I taste the water in the puddle. It's orange. I'm orange.

Four inches of rain fall over my body.

I'm filthy and drunk, almost passed out.

I picture myself from above.

A muddy, fucked-up pickup truck shoved in a ditch across the road pointing at a tree, a boy beaten up, lying pathetically outside the truck's open door in a big orange puddle with an empty beer bottle in his hand. The truck's radio blaring punk rock across miles and miles of sugar cane fields. Storm clouds and the biggest storm to hit all season looming overhead, appearing steady and predictable in contrast. As my mind flies farther up, I see the ocean on all sides. Farther up, the shape of Oahu, then the chain of islands, then, the pure isolation of where I am.

How small must I be, and how far away, until I disappear completely?

12

Mad typhoon left cracked
trees, littered leaves and sacred
broken dreams for me.

I'm wet and coated with red dirt. My eye is swollen and my mouth is dry. My head pounds. The light looks like morning light, white and fresh and diffused by fog—but I'm not sure.

"Fuck, I feel like shit! Ahh!"

No one can hear me. The trees and mud suck up all sound.

I feel like an animal that lost its ability to survive in the wild. I look on the outside how I feel inside—like someone not capable of being in public.

"I hate you, world! I hate you, Clay! I hate you, Sam! I fucking hate you!"

I get up and slam the truck door shut, then I spit on it. I run into the forest on the other side of the road, over rocks and streams, with twigs and branches scraping me and tearing cuts into my face. Part of me thinks the cuts will look cool when I finally emerge from the forest and confront Clay. I jump into a stream and small fish scatter. They probably know what I'm feeling better than I do from analyzing my sweat dripping into the stream. I jump up and do as many pull-ups as I can on a low-hanging branch till I'm sweaty and hot. I compose a haiku in my head and scream it out. "Shit fuck asshole fuck, liar fuckface shithead boy, asshole dumb-ass fuck!"

The humidity is high, and the forest is the same temperature as my body, which makes it all the easier to go crazy. I jump out of the stream and duck through a banyan tree's complex root system. A rock turns my ankle the wrong way. I fall hard and fast, onto a dirt path covered with vibrant pink petals from a mountain apple tree. I'm out of breath and my heart is beating fast, making my chest rise and fall dramatically. I fall back and look up to the blooming mountain apple tree.

Clay enters my mind like a flash of lightning enters the atmosphere.

I start crying as a pink blossom falls on my chest. It's such a shame to ignore true beauty. The great haiku poets would look down on me for wasting this moment.

I haven't been living. I've been acting, for myself and the forest— which probably thinks I look pretty stupid. I grab a stick and draw Clay's dragon tattoo in the mud. I get my dick out, thinking of Clay's tattoos, inked on his thin muscular arms. I stand up and arch backward. My dick is the center of my existence. I come on the drawing of Clay's dragon, proud of myself for having such an inspired orgasm.

An unnatural-looking point of light shines through the trees. I follow it with my eyes till I make out a spiked punk rock bracelet.

It's Clay.

I pull up my pants as fast as I can, panicking that he'll see this whole weird scene and judge me as psycho or a weirdo or someone he doesn't want to be involved with.

He looks tired, with gray circles under his eyes. He's still wearing his surf shorts. He stops in front of me. The tiny hairs on his leg are glued to his skin with salt crystals. He looks at the dragon in the mud. He sort of glances at his arm, then looks down again. "Man," he says, "I can't handle this."

I feel helpless and busted. "Can't handle what?"

He ignores me and takes a deep breath. He closes his eyes.

Why won't he comment on my black eye, my cuts, my mud-covered body? I think I'm short-circuiting his brain. I want to hear his master plan. I'm sure he has one, hidden in his expressions and silence and contemplative looks. I'm sure that maybe someday soon he'll face himself and admit he likes me, then leave Tammy and start being real. Isn't that why he left with me last night? Why isn't he telling me the time line, in charts and graphs, like stock performances on the news? Maybe he's not capable of loving. Maybe I'm too young to be in this sort of position, and this kind of shit shouldn't happen to me. It might fuck up my ability to trust or love or be loved.

Maybe he knows this and he's downright evil. Maybe he wants to toughen me up like he's done to himself, and he wants me to lose faith in him—so I don't expect too much.

I feel desperate in his silence.

He gets up and takes a good look at my face, showing no emotion.

I want to look him in the eye, but I'm too scared, so I stare at his shark's-tooth necklace. Why can't it just be like it used to be? We aren't supposed to be angry with each other. We are each other's happiness, each other's escape.

He starts walking back to his truck.

I get up and I follow him.

He gets in. "Throw some wood or some shit underneath the back tires so I can get out of here."

I find some big stones and wedge them under the back tires, and Clay peels out backward. Orange mud flies up and cakes the wheel well.

He puts a tape in the deck, turns it up really loud.

I think he wants to leave me here. I run to the passenger door and jump in, shoving my notebook into my pack and zipping it up so he doesn't see.

We fly over bumps and muddy puddles. He doesn't seem to care if I get knocked around.

I'm confused, because I can't remember why I came here last night. I just remember the feeling I had. Disillusioned, abandoned, exploited, and guilty for him leaving Tammy, even though that should make me feel good.

We turn onto the main beach road that leads to our houses. A view of the ocean rises over the horizon as he drive over the last hill.

He stares out at the water. "Why'd you leave last night? Trying to get attention or something?"

"I don't know. I don't want to talk about it. You never want to talk about anything, anyway. You must do all that with Tammy."

"No, I don't."

"You never say shit."

"Why does everybody always expect me to talk about shit? Fuck, brah, I just wanna go to Japan and become a samurai."

"Whatever, Clay. You're full of shit."

"You are, man."

"How'd you find me?"

"I was hiking. I wasn't looking for you." He turns a corner way too fast.

"Like I believe that."

"You're just freaking out. Just chill. You're fucking crazy."

"Look in the mirror, dude." I grab the mirror from the seat and shove it in his face.

He smacks my hand and the mirror away from him.

It hits the windshield, cracks, and lands on my lap. It hurts my leg.

"I should fucking hit you, man. Swear to God, I don't know what's wrong with you. I fucking looked all night long for your sorry ass." He freezes. He realizes what he admitted. This pisses him off even more. He speeds up faster and runs a stop sign. Veins throb in his temples and arms under tattoos that already look pissed off and tough. He's becoming a pit bull.

I want to hit him. "You're acting like an idiot. Slow down." I hold on to the dashboard.

"Sam, I'm warning you, man, you better shut the fuck up."

"No, face up to me. Fucking baby." *Tell me you love me. That's all I want to hear. Tell me you were sad when I left last night.* I see his fist tighten and his arm pull back.

His teeth are clenched hard, making his jaw muscles shake.

Sweat drips down the sides of my torso.

He punches the seat inches away from where I'm sitting and rocks back and forth, like a caged animal, too wild for this small space.

I try to put the mirror back on, but the bracket is broken now too.

He turns the radio way up and pushes my hand away from the window. His anger smells like a rancid variation of how he smells during sex. "Fuck the mirror!" We nearly hit a car going by in the other lane. He lays on the horn. "Fuck you, bitch. Fucking idiot!"

I'm sick of this. I want to make him hurt. I want him to cry and feel a loss of control. I don't care what the repercussions are. I don't care what he thinks. I want to kill him. I can't help it. I cock my fist back and punch him in the shoulder as hard as I can.

He slams on the breaks. The tires squeal to a stop in the middle of the lane.

"Get the fuck out!"

He reaches across me with his muscled arm.

I hunch down, afraid he's going to hit me.

He pulls the door handle and shoves the door open on my side.

I look down and see the road. It's rough and hard.

"Leave me the fuck alone!" Every word is punctuated. He pushes me out.

I fall onto the side of the road, my elbows and butt taking most of it.

He throws the rear view mirror at me. It hits me in the forehead with a sharp sting. Then my backpack comes flying into the ditch. He peels out, the back of the truck fishtailing and black smoke flying up.

I lie back on the gravel, bleeding, out of breath, full of adrenaline, and confused. I feel guilty.

The sun becomes a white, blinding haze, blurred by my tears. The salt in my tears burns the scrapes on my face. The sting feels appropriate. My bruises feel deserved. I set chaos into motion. I feel like I should be pissed off, or turned on, or arrogant and brooding, but all I am is hopeless and sad. I thought falling in love was supposed to feel good.

I can only imagine what the people driving by in cars this Friday morning think of me. I'm dirty, cut up, bruised, with dried blood on my face. I look so obviously discarded, lying on the side of the road. I feel like I'll never stop crying. There's only one thing I can do. I have to get up and go on. I stand up and climb up the ditch to the side of the road. I'm dizzy. I lose my balance and fall on my knees over the white line.

A teal convertible rental car screeches toward me.

"Oh, fuck."

It squeals to a stop only feet in front of me.

I'm being paid back by the universe for screwing with Clay. He hates tourists more than he hates anything. It was him, that asshole. He sent this car.

A tourist lady in a big straw hat jumps out and runs over to me with a terrified look on her face.

"Are you all right?"

"What's it look like?" I stand up and brush the dirt off my shorts.

"You should really be more careful." She walks back to her stupid car.

"Fuck off, bitch."

She jumps in and drives off.

13

Gusty winds
ferns quivering, panicked
oncoming storm.

I walk home, thinking of a haiku about what happened, but I can't come up with one, so I go through the ones I've memorized about Clay and about how I felt when I thought he'd just drop everything, including his stupid surfer-boy ego, and fall in love with me. I've got a million haiku in my backpack. I walk into Coconut Grove, a neighborhood of old beach shacks, a shortcut to my house. My fucking knee hurts, and a thick trickle of blood is dripping down my leg right over the Band-Aid that Clay's mom gave me. God, I'm pathetic. Cuts on top of cuts. I'm not meant to be uninjured, I guess. My blood is meant to spill out of me and clump in the hairs on my chins. I walk down the street looking at houses, wishing I could have one of my own. A lot of dudes in their twenties live here when they move out of their parents' houses because this neighborhood's cheap and fun and there are usually some good parties on Friday nights, not that I've been to any, except the one Clay took me to, and that's probably the last time that's going to happen.

I hear a girl's voice yell. "Hey, Sammy-boy! What you doin' in my hood?"

I stop and turn around, but no one's there. I start walking again.

"Sam! It's Kendra!"

I stop and turn around, and there she is in a purple bikini by a tall wooden fence—and smiling, holding a green garden hose in the front yard of her new house.

She looks happy and carefree and all that, so my misery stands out even more. I wonder if she sees my confusion.

"Hey." I slowly walk over to her front yard, which is basically just sandy dirt with some dead yellow grass and weeds in big clumps and two cartoonish-looking pot plants growing side-by-side near the front door. "Nice pot plants."

"Yeah. They're growing like crazy, but I think I have two females, or two males, or something, because they won't make THC. If you smoke it, nothing happens." She throws the hose down, still running. "Come see my new abode, Sammy." She runs up to me and hugs me, then notices that my knee is bleeding over another Band-Aid. "What happened?"

"Skating. I'm perfecting my kick-flip." *Yeah, right—as if I could possibly perfect a kick-flip.*

"Well, come inside. I've got some alcohol or something. You think rum would work?"

"Maybe in my mouth. I don't know about the scrapes. I bailed pretty hard." I follow her up the three steps into her house, which is basically empty except for a flowered rattan couch and chair that obviously came from the Salvation Army down the street, and a couple surfing posters and old dried leis on the wall. "Nice place."

I would want my own house to be cooler than this, but I'm still jealous that she has one to herself. I follow her into the kitchen and over to her table, a card table with a tiki-patterned tablecloth. I scan a photo collage on the kitchen wall. There it is: the photo that Kendra took of me, Clay, and Steve passed out in Steve's room at the party. It's in a collage with tons of other party photos. I check it out as much as I can without letting Kendra know I care about it. I'm lying just inches from Clay, just inches from his chest. I think about lying there and how in love I felt, and I wish time would reverse. I set my backpack on a chair and sit down in another one.

Kendra gets a bottle of cheap rum from the cabinet and pours out two shot glasses. She hands one to me, picks up hers, and we both throw them back.

The rum burns my throat, but almost instantly I feel a little better. I guess I'm already on the road to becoming an alcoholic, drinking to numb my problems.

"Here." She pours another shot and dumps it out on my knee. It burns like crazy. The rest runs down my leg. She soaks up the runoff with a paper towel that has pictures of little loafs of bread on it. "That should do it." She gently wipes the blood from my shin.

I take the paper towel from her. "I'll do it. My blood might be poisonous." I'm afraid she can smell me. I smell like balls and sweat and anger and confusion, and I don't want her to think I never take baths. The paper dyes red when it touches my cut.

Kendra pours another two shots. "Here…"

We down them and then another two. She doesn't want to leave just a little bit in the bottom of the bottle. I'm pretty drunk now, which happened really fast. Kendra's drunk too, but not as drunk as I am.

She's been partying for a lot longer than me, but she's turned red because she's Asian. Most Asians turn red when they drink. I like it. I associate my friends being red with having fun because it usually means that Jared and I came up with some little-boy scheme to get some brews or a fifth of some crap.

Clay doesn't turn red—he just gets more aggressive, more confident, more sexy.

"I'm glad you came over, Sammy, but where's your board? You said you were skating."

"I broke it."

"Ahh...I see," she says like a mystic would say, all-knowing and sort of evil. "You seen Clay lately?"

"Here and there." I look down at my hands and feel really, really sad all at once, and I can't control it at all, which is scary and sort of feels good at the same time. I feel tears forming in my eyes. *Damn you, fucking salty tears! Don't ruin this for me. Don't tell her things I'm too afraid to say myself.* My body is betraying me. The tears come rushing out.

Kendra looks like she's going to cry too, and she does. But she's also smiling. "What? What is it?"

"Nothing. Aloha all around. Nothing at all." I start crying even harder, like almost sobbing, and it's so pathetic that I can't stop it.

"Sammy, you know I know you're gay or whatever, right?"

"What?" Any little second to compose myself is why I just said that. I heard her perfectly clear.

"That I know you're gay. I've known you were since you were like ten or something." She gets up and goes to the fridge for a couple cans of guava juice. "Are you and Clay like...?" She sits down and pops open her can of guava. "I've always suspected he was, but he couldn't admit it, which torments him and makes him act so...you know, the tough surfer-boy act."

"I'm not sure."

"About Clay or about you?"

"Both. I mean me—no, I mean him." I bury my head in my arms on the table and talk into the tablecloth, which smells like fake pineapple for some reason. "I'm totally in love with him." My ears start ringing and my heart goes nuts. This is fucking gnarly, major, ripping, shredding shit that I've never told anyone before ever and probably never will again.

"Does he like you back?"

I lift my head up from the table. Kendra's so cool. "I think so, but he's so…closed, fucked-up—you know how Clay is. He's a lizard." I reach for my backpack to get my haikus. I would never do this if I wasn't drunk, but right now, Kendra seems like the perfect audience. I've never read them to anyone but Jared and he doesn't take me seriously, and I have such a strong urge to share with her it's killing me. "You want to hear a poem I wrote?"

"You write poetry? That's so cute."

"Shut up."

"I do too, Sammy. I've been trying to get published since I was like seventeen." So Kendra is doing something. I always thought she was just happy working for her dad at his psychiatry office. "Read me one of yours, and I'll read you one of mine." She goes and gets a folder from her bedroom and comes back and sits down. "OK, you first."

I get really nervous suddenly. It's a weird feeling but I sort of like it. I unzip my backpack and find one about Clay that I write probably soon after we first did it in his room. "I write haikus. They're not true haikus like five-seven-five, but they're like haikus. They say in English, haikus don' t have to stick to the formula because the words are so different from Japanese words. Anyway…" I hold up a paper with about six poems on it and pick one to read. "'His tattoo looks at me and smiles. I'm hard—in love.'" Fuck, I'm embarrassed, but Kendra looks slightly impressed. "I'll read another one. That one's not very good. Okay… 'Chameleon surfer-boy, riding waves by day, imagination by cool evening.'"

"Sam, I think you're on to something. Okay, here's mine—God, this is so great you write poetry! Okay, here's mine." She holds up a piece of notebook paper. "'Hawaiian sunsets from white sand to white sand, won't you take my caramel Asian female hand,

and caress it with care, then breathe some fresh air, and tell me thy love that you're there.'"

OK, Kendra's a poetry dork, but I am too, I guess, so I guess I can live with it. "That's cool." I shove my haikus back in their dark backpack and ask for another shot of something.

"Yeah, Sammy, for a fellow poet, anything." She stands up and opens the cabinet above the stove. "Vodka, dark rum, amaretto—I don't even know what that is..." She searches through the bottles.

"Vodka's cool."

She takes the bottle down, pours me a shot, and hands it to me.

I gulp it back, almost gagging on its fucking lighter-fluid taste. "Ah!" I lean back and almost fall back in my chair.

"Easy, boy." She laughs and eats some mochi crunch seaweed crackers out of the plastic bag with Japanese writing on it.

"Eh!"

Kendra and I both jump. We turn to look at the front door, which is wide open on the far side of her almost-empty living room, and there stands Clay looking sweaty and ripped and angry and scary and sad and sort of needy.

"What's up?" he calls out.

I look at Kendra. "Nothing. What's up with you?"

"Hey, Clay-boy. Amazing. You haven't stopped over here since I got my new couch."

"That thing's fucking new?" I guess living with your parents has some small advantages.

Kendra stands up. "Come in, dude."

He walks in, obviously freaked out that I'm here. What, is Kendra like the therapist of every gay boy on the island? He sits down on the chair across from me, acting like he hardly knows me.

I give him a dirty look, as mean as I can, even though he looks kinda sweaty and vulnerable and hot.

"You wanna shot, Clay? Me and Sammy here were just boozin' up the afternoon."

He glances at me, then at Kendra. "Sure, sistah. Pour it."

Kendra pours him a shot of vodka, then she pours herself and me another one each. She sets Clay's and mine on the table, then sits down with us. We all sort of look at one another, but it's like we're all embarrassed about something. Clay won't look at me. I won't look at him. We're both just staring at Kendra, and she's looking back and forth between us, like she's waiting for us to jump up on the table and make out or start punching each other. We all take our shot.

"What've you been up to today? Any waves out at Sandy's?" Kendra shuffles papers on the table—her poems.

"No, just chilling." He shifts his weight and leans back in his chair with his arms behind his head, probably a combination of trying to look casual and unconsciously wanting to smell his own armpits. "I'm thinking about going camping. The Big Island or Maui or Na Pali Coast would rip." He sort of looks at me, like the least he can without not looking at me. "You wanna come, little brah?"

I look at Kendra.

She looks at Clay.

Clay looks like he's going to cry right here on the spot, though I don't think he knows it.

Kendra stands up. "I have to move my clothes to the dryer. Be right back." She walks out the back door to her detached roach-filled garage.

Clay's face changes immediately. "You wanna come?"

"I don't know," I say, as bratty as I can manage. "Maybe…"

He leans forward, then he rubs my leg under the table, up into my cutoffs, just inches from my balls. "Come on, dude. It'll be rad—all nature, good *mana,* and no people…"

"Yeah." I can't even think with Clay's hand near my dick, and anyway I'm starting to spin from the alcohol, and my head feels like it's going to shoot off.

Kendra opens her back door.

Clay pulls his hand away in a flash and leans back in his chair.

Kendra holds up a tiny tank top, like only big enough for Barbie. "I hate dryers. When I was little, we hung things out on a clothesline. You strong boys think you could build one for me?"

Clay almost falls backward, and I almost laugh. "Sure."

Kendra throws me the tank top and I hold it up to my chest.

Clay says, "So you wanna come or not, Sam?"

I look back and forth between Clay and Kendra for a second. She's so warm, so normal, so nice to me. Clay's so fucked-up, so arrogant, so insane. I can't not go with him. I'll regret it forever. "Yeah. Sounds cool."

"OK, excellent. I'll give you a ride. Let's prepare the gear." Clay heads to the door.

"Bye." I look at Kendra, and she looks kind of worried, but what the fuck? I grab my pack and follow Clay outside and get in his truck, which is still muddy as shit from the cane road last night. I look at him now that we're alone.

"What?"

"How'd you find me here?"

"Coincidence."

"Yeah, right. You totally looked for me."

He looks cagey, paranoid. "I gotta get out of here."

"Why?"

"I need to get the fuck out of here."

"Why?"

"I just do, man. Is that all right with you?"

This is so fucking rad.

14

Fragile spring blossoms
feel the same fear I do:
terrified of wind.

I watch out the window as Clay drives like a maniac.

Samoans drive around, looking tough. Boys with new girl-friends hang out in the park and smoke cigarettes. Skateboarders ride wide-open, newly paved streets. Everyone is normal but us.

We pull into his driveway.

Susan stands up from planting flowers. "Clay, my ray of sunshine," she says.

I get out of the truck and jump down to the pavement. "More like an eclipse."

She laughs.

Clay makes an exaggerated sad face, like "poor me."

"What's up?" Susan asks.

"I can't lose this nag." Clay points to me and walks up to the house.

She notices my black eye and the scrapes on my cheek. "Oh, my God. What happened?" She gives Clay a suspicious look.

"Don't look at me! I didn't do it." He walks inside, slamming the screen door behind him.

She looks at me.

"These Marine guys jumped me."

Susan nods, like she knows everything, and she understands. "Those stupid grunts."

I walk into the house, down the hall, passing blocks of light on the woven mats. Clay's door is mostly closed, like his personality.

The room is dim. Sun shines through the bamboo shade and illuminates torn-out pages from surfing magazines taped on the wall in a collage. Cobwebby streaks of smoke hang low in the air.

Clay's smoking a roach. He looks relaxed and exquisite, leaning back on his bed with his joint delicately pressed between two fingers, smoking pot in his own accomplished-looking way.

I know he doesn't want me to be here. To him, I'm the source of his problems.

He needs time alone to revamp his idea of himself, to fool himself into thinking that he's the person he wants so desperately to be—that faraway surfer-boy with the forever-pleasing personality. He looks around his room, while his cheeks are puffed out from his hit of pot, reassessing himself. "We'll go to Kalalau beach. Hike in," he says, like he's an army logistics commander and he just figured out the warpath. He starts shoving things in a bag. He stuffs clean clothes, dirty clothes, a pair of socks that don't match, a big bag of fluorescent-green pot, a few lighters, and matches into his black *Thrasher* backpack. He looks insane, jumping around the room like a frog. He's too busy scavenging things off the floor to notice my questioning, doubting eyes.

"What about clothes? I'm not going home."

"You can wear my shit. Here." He throws shorts and T-shirts with surfing logos at me.

I let the shirts hit me in the face. One drapes over my head. I can see him through a worn-thin yellow T-shirt with a shark on the back.

He looks at me, but he can't see my eyes through the T-shirt and he doesn't know I can see him. He looks scared.

I grab the shirt off my head and shove everything into my pack.

"Go get my pup tent. It's in the carport."

I get up quickly and open the door to the hall, causing a vacuum effect that sucks the blinds to the screen. What an unstable atmosphere in Clay's room. I wonder if it's him or me.

Outside, Susan pulls weeds from the flower bed and stacks fallen dead branches from the hurricane. She's already cut up and moved the huge mango-tree branch that smashed her car.

I admire the order she creates. It's so different from my screwed-up life.

She looks up at me as I try to sneak by through the screen door in the enclosed patio. "Sam, where are you off to?"

"Clay told me to get the tent from the carport. We're going to hike Kalalau."

"Oh, my God. That'll be amazing." Her eyes fill with some hippie-love fascination—that's the only way I can describe it. She doesn't know it's Clay's militia hideout plan to escape from the peering eyes of the world. She stands up and pulls down her muumuu, wiping loose dirt and leaves off. "I'll show you where it is."

I follow her to the carport.

She looks to an upper shelf and grabs the tent. "You all right?"

"Yeah, you know, he's weird." I can't believe I'm talking about Clay to his mom, like he's my boyfriend. This is great and scary.

"He cares for you, Sam. I can tell. You keep him honest."

"Yeah, I guess."

"You two have a real connection. I can feel it."

Clay walks outside with a pouty expression.

"I'm still angry at you, *young man*. You better call Tammy before you leave. I'm not going to smooth things over for you."

We all look at one another. She's outrageous to say this in front of me.

"OK, Mom." He responds in a droning tone. He puts his arm around her and looks at me arrogantly because he's the center of attention. "We're going camping."

"I heard." She winks at me. "I'm jealous."

The sun comes out from behind a cloud and shines on their faces. It makes them a beautiful soft yellow and illuminates their matching intense dark-brown eyes.

I look into her eyes, then his.

"I love you, Mom." He's such a conniving little boy. He knows how to play people for his advantage. It scares me, and at the same time I think it's super cool.

"I can't believe you can still do this to me." Her tone changes, like she's talking to a friend. "What do you want me to tell her if she calls?"

"Tell her she's ugly."

A barefoot, short Hawaiian-Portuguese guy with no shirt on and long, flowered surf shorts walks up the driveway. He's amazing-looking—pure and strong.

"Eh, brah," he says to Clay, "is Eddy ready to go?"

Clay nods, apprehensively, like he dreads what he has to do.

Susan hugs the guy. "Hi, Manny. Howzit?"

"Is Clay boy ignorin' his responsibilities again?" He says "responsibilities" like he's never said it before, like it's a really complicated word.

"Clay, listen to your friend."

Clay gets a mean look. "I'll call her when we get back!"

"Okay, okay..." Susan puts her arm around him to make up.

He shoves her hand off of his shoulder and steps away, like he's embarrassed by her affection.

"Where you going?" Manny asks.

"Me and Sam gonna hike Na Pali."

Manny looks at me. "I'm Manny." He holds out his hand to shake.

"Manny, Sam-boy, my little brah."

I feel important being introduced to Manny as "brah." I reach for Manny's hand, but he starts doing all this secret-handshake surfer-boy shit.

Our hands just bump a couple times, and I feel really stupid. "Who's Eddy?"

Clay practically explodes. "My Jackson chameleon, stupid."

"Why's it named Eddy?"

Clay and Manny look at each other like they can't believe what they're hearing.

"Where'd you get this guy?" Manny asks.

Clay practically attacks me with enthusiasm. "Eddy Akua. Only the best big-wave surfer of all times."

I feel stupid. How could I forget? Every surfer on Oahu has an "Eddy Would Go" sticker on the back of his pickup truck. They all like him 'cause he's got the biggest balls and does things they're too scared to do, but he died doing it, so now he's got immortal status in all their dumb-ass surfer brains.

I follow them into Clay's room. I feel like a little brother or some dumb kid following around the older cool guys. I should have just stayed there with Kendra, taking shots till I passed out so I could forget about all this psycho bullshit.

Clay picks up Eddy and gives him a kiss on the mouth. "I'll come visit you." He looks towards Manny. "You better take good care of him."

It's so like Clay to only express true emotions to a reptile.

Manny takes the lizard.

"You're holding him wrong." Clay pulls Eddy's tail over Manny's thumb. "I'm serious. Take care of him." He looks at Eddy lovingly.

"I *will,* brah. Quit saying that." Manny hands him a couple twenties for the chameleon. "Blame Tammy, not me. She's da one who tinks Eddy stinks."

Clay just stands there.

"OK, I'm out. Teach this one some tings." Manny looks at me and smiles. He walks out the door and screams, "Bye, Mrs. A. You're lookin' good."

She laughs, and Manny squeals off in his souped-up truck.

Clay sits on his bed.

I sit next to him, and he stands up quickly, like he just thought of something he has to do. It's just an act. He looks around at the floor, then throws our packs out in the hall. "Let's go, man."

15

In search of pure wilds
primitive urges force me
to get a boner.

We take off in a little propeller plane over Pearl Harbor. Clay orders us little bottles of vodka.

The flight attendant gives them to us for free.

I think it's her attempt to flirt with him. What a bitch.

"Welcome aboard and aloha. We're expecting a smooth thirty-five minute flight to Kauai. Please relax and enjoy the view. Mahalo."

The island looks green, lush, and tiny from the plane. I can't believe my whole world's contained in such a small place. I'm glad we're leaving, even though it's just to another tiny island.

We land in Lihue on an old airstrip. We get the backpacks and the tent and jump in a shuttle bus. It winds down a curvy road surrounded by jungle.

I watch Clay.

The veins in his neck stick out and a layer of sweat makes his skin shiny. He watches the passing forest closely, like a wolf searching for prey. His muscles look puffed up and strong, and his eyes are clear and intense.

He's turning wild.

The old local van driver drops us off at the head of the Kalalau Trail. "Good luck, brahs. Careful. Watch for da spirits." He smiles and drives away, leaving us alone with our fucked-up selves.

The wet dirt path looks inviting and ominous at the same time. Green-leafed plants would eagerly take the path over if given a week or two without shoes stomping around killing saplings and moss. The path weaves into a forest that tourists call "rainforest." "Rainforest" sounds too distant and foreign to mean here. We're only hours from our mowed lawns, food-filled kitchens, and come-stained sheets.

I follow Clay into the forest, watching imperfect shapes of sun and shade caress his shoulders and neck. I look back. A glare from a reflector on the road blinds me for a second.

I want to disappear with him into the coolness of the wild. We'll become animals, free from civilization. Clay's skin will let in the humid forest and the wild energy of the untamed side of him will prevail. He'll be even sexier than he is now.

We'll be unrestrained with each other. Our relationship will find its natural essence.

We walk for a couple miles into the forest.

I follow him 'cause he acts like he knows where he's going. We walk for miles, occasionally talking about a bright-colored bird or a cool-looking tree.

When it's almost getting dark, he throws his backpack and the tent down on the ground in an opening in the forest. Trees grow in a circle around him. A cool stream with moss-covered rocks runs by. He surveys the site and picks a spot for the tent.

I take my shoes off and shake out rocks that slipped in while we were hiking.

Clay gathers shiny, round dark stones for a fire pit, and makes a perfect circle that looks ancient. He assembles the tent, an old Army pup tent with an anarchy sign drawn on the side in black

permanent marker, and lays out two brown sleeping bags to pad
our backs from roots and rocks.

I'm impressed with the setup. It's neatly organized and very
normal-looking for a couple of psychopaths to spend the night in.
I can tell he's proud of the campsite. I want to embarrass him.

"Clay, this is really romantic."

He ignores me and starts fidgeting. He rearranges the fire-pit
stones, then opens his bag and refolds his clothes.

I feel a sense of power, being able to admit what's really going
on here—a lovers' camping trip, like a honeymoon. He deserves it.

"Why'd you sell Eddy?"

"Too much work."

"It's because Tammy doesn't like him, isn't it?"

"Shut up, man!"

He jumps up, steps out of his shorts, and runs naked to the
deep part of the stream. He puts his cigarette down and jumps in,
holding his balls. The splashing water makes rainbows in the
sunlight.

I find flat stones and throw them so they skip along the water,
dangerously close to him. I want him to know I'm capable of
anything.

He flashes me a mean look and sits down in the streambed. His
arm sticks out of the water at an acute angle, piercing the surface
like a dead branch. He leans back on the edge casually and arrogantly, to show me that he knows I won't hit him. He reaches for
his smokes and lights up.

In the sunlight he makes slightly blue smoke weave like a
cobra. It scoots along the surface of the rippling water, coating it
with hazy film.

I throw another rock. The splash sizzles on his cigarette.
"Sorry." I didn't want to say that, but I couldn't help it. It just came
out. Saying sorry ruins my effect.

Clay throws his wet cigarette at me and slides underwater. He comes up with his head back and streams of water following the gently curving lines of his shoulders, chest, and arms. Beads of water form, clinging to his dragon-tattooed arm, making it all slippery and reptilian.

Chemicals rush through my body. "Let's make a fire." I say.

He jumps out of the stream naked. "No fire, brah, kine explosion." He grabs a lighter and flicks it over and over in his left hand. He piles some wood into a pyramid, reaches for his backpack, and grabs a bottle of lighter fluid. He sprays it on the woodpile, like he's peeing, then lights a match and throws it on. It explodes.

I feel a blast of heat on my chin. "Jesus."

He squirts more on. "Watch this, brah." He lights the stream of fluid coming out of the bottle, then holds the bottle in front of his crotch. It looks like he's shooting fire from his dick.

"You're gonna burn your dick off, stupid." I get up to brush the ashes off. "God, you look like a fucking demon."

He jumps around squirting fire and howling, catching a branch above him and hanging, throwing his feet in all directions, mumbling gibberish, really scratchy-sounding masculine punk rock riffs. "You'll never escape! Your soul is mine."

A chill runs up my spine. The sky has lost its color. I think of stories I've heard of night marchers. They come up from the sea in long rows, in the form of ancient Hawaiians, all holding torches, marching to the tops of mountains and dormant volcanoes. If they see a haole, they kill him. I guess they figure you're trying to impede their progress. They want the islands to be sovereign.

"Quit. Seriously. You're freaking me out."

"Oh, am I?" His voice is taunting and haunted.

"Just act normal. Sit down and talk or something. Put your shorts on." I sound like a parent. Sometimes, I'm more full of bullshit than he is.

"You're no fun." He stands up and looks down to his dick and then up to me, all proud.

I feel like I should be thankful that he's looking at me, like his attention is a gift. This is fucked-up. He's brainwashed me. I forget what real people act like. And I feel like a lame-o suburbanite who can't handle being in nature.

A branch falls from a tree.

I jump, scared by the loud crackling noise.

"No worries, brah. I know this island and these waves better than anyone." He holds his head up high and sort of flexes his chest. "I'm Clay. From red-colored earth. I was born with crazy eyes, crazy thoughts, cold blood." He stops on "blood" for dramatic effect and looks around like he's a predator looking for a kill. His lighter fluid supply runs out. He jumps down and crouches by the fire.

"Are you expecting me to take you seriously?"

"You better." He drools accidentally and catches it with his hand.

"You're not Hawaiian. You don't give a shit. You just want me to think you have some sort of power so I'll *need* you or whatever." I see reflections of the fire on his sweaty skin and in his "crazy" eyes. "You're full of shit."

"You tink so?"

"Yup."

"Maybe you're right." He leans back and lies on the ground, and spits. It flies up and lands on his neck. "*E ho mai 'ike, mai luna mai e.*" He chants in a deep voice and stares at me intensely. "*I na mea huna no'eau a na olele e.*"

I stare back, pretending he's not scaring me. "What are you doing?"

"*E ho mai, e ho mai, e ho mai.*" He chants the same words over and over and searches the sky, like he knows what he's looking for. "When the fire goes out, you'll believe me. You'll need me.

Only I know the chants." He jumps up and runs off.

I feel the vibrations in the ground from him running. The sound reminds me of rabbits thumping their back feet to signal *danger* to other rabbits. When he gets far enough away, I can't hear him anymore. The forest has triggered the most instinctual corners of his brain, the parts that make him want to fight for dominance, inflate his ego, and strengthen his arms.

Trees rustle. My pulse rate goes up, and my reflexes act as fast as lightning, whipping my head to find the noise. There's a little movement down by the stream, but I can't see it. The firelight is blinding me, like there's a flashlight pointed at my face.

A piece of wood pops loudly. I jump. My hair stands on end. It feels weird, like gravity has stopped functioning.

The air pressure changes quickly and my ears pop. The fire sputters, as if it's been sprinkled with water.

Clay was right.

I need him. I'm terrified. I throw sticks on the fire, but they won't light. My eyes adjust to the dark shadows and I hear a stream of water dripping. I think I hear breathing. I look toward the tent. No movement there, except a slightly blowing door flap.

Something's coming at me!

I lunge to my knees, and squeeze my head between my legs, like the crash position on an airplane. "Clay! Come here!" Sweat drips down my torso.

Clay comes running with his dick pointing at me. "*Mai ha ho oku'i a ka halawai!*"

I've lost feeling in my body. "Fuck! You stupid fucker." I feel like I got my breath knocked out of me.

"I had to pee." He ducks into the tent. "Night." He's evil. He knows he's making me lose trust in humankind and he doesn't care.

The wind blows tiny sparks into the trees.

I climb into the tent. "Asshole." I imagine a huge forest fire caused by me and Clay. It would be a perfect expression of how I feel. I take off my clothes, damp from humidity and sweat, and climb into the tent. I try to relax with some stupid yoga breathing technique my dad does when his stocks plummet. I count my breaths. Five seconds in, five seconds hold, five seconds out. I watch the dwindling fire through the nylon wall of the tent. It dies out, then comes back to life, as if a spirit is tending it and supplying it with new wood.

Clay springs up and flops on top of me. His weight pushes me into the ground.

My elbows sink into the soft, damp dirt, making indentations under the tent's flimsy floor. I can't take a breath because my chest is constricted.

He bites my bare chest, leaving warm wet spots on my skin.

I look at him. "Why are you doing this?"

He then licks my chest and down my stomach. "Because I want to, little brah."

"Why couldn't it be like this the whole night?"

He jumps up and stands on his feet. "It was." He raises his arms over his head. He looks heroic with his chest stretched out and his armpits exposed. The tips of his fingers scrape the tent ceiling and nearly catch the support that's holding it together. He throws down his underwear with one hand and flings them to the side with his leg. His dick is pointing up and hard. His teeth are easy to see even in this dim light.

A white caution tag on the tent wall reads: WARNING: IF APPROACHED BY WILDLIFE, THIS TENT DOES NOT OFFER ADE-QUATE PROTECTION. What if the wildlife is in the tent?

Strong rushes of doubt rise up in me. Something's wrong. I feel taken. "Clay?"

He sighs, like I'm annoying him.

"Can we just talk? I wanna ask you something."

He shakes his head "no" and rolls me over with his head like a bear rolling over his prey. He pulls my underwear down to my ankles and starts licking me.

I thrust into his mouth. We will have happiness and a lifelong bond. I grasp his thigh with one hand. It feels strong and hot.

He puts his hand on top of mine on his thigh and applies pressure and squeezes it while he sucks me off.

I move my hand and jerk his off. He thrusts into my hand in the darkness.

The idea of Clay and me having sex without weirdness makes me so happy. There's no parent on the other side of the door, no friend of his lurking dangerously close to catching us, no macho punk rock attitude while driving down the road jerking off. I want this to last as long as possible. "Clay?"

He thrusts into my hand. "Yeah?"

"This is so great, I mean…we're having so much fun with each other, and, like, there's nothing weird about it. This is so cool."

"Shut up."

"But, I just wanted you to know how much this means to me. You know what I mean?"

He covers my mouth with his hand. His hand smells like his dick.

"But, wait. Are you loving this?"

He stops touching me and lies down beside me. The energy between us goes from manic craziness to dull in half a second. He sits up. His dick slips away from my hand. He lies still for a second and then starts jerking himself off. He comes on the floor of the tent. "Cool, brah. Night." He lies down with his back to me.

I want to hit him as hard as I can. I want to make his face bloody and his legs unable to move so he can't escape me. Maybe then he'll know how strong my love is.

16

Warm summer morning
no light thing being a boy
wind blowing steady.

Clay is pissing out the door flap when I wake up. His butt is squeezed tightly as he shoots his piss as far as he can. He walks outside naked and picks a mountain apple off a tree.

I watch him secretly.

He crunches a big bite and looks up at the sky with a moaning yawn. He looks like primitive man.

I wish I felt as comfortable naked as he does. I slide on my underwear and Clay's faded black T-shirt, and walk out to see him.

He leans over the stream and takes a messy gulp of water. He notices me behind him and cups his dick and balls with his hands. He ducks into the tent, shaking water off his face, and comes back out in boxer shorts with Hawaiian tiki drawings on them.

I'm confused why he's acting so modest after last night. I roll my eyes at him.

"What's that look for?" He looks away and busies himself by packing up our shit in the backpacks.

"Your underwear are hilarious."

"It's a traditional tapa pattern," he says rudely.

"Sorry. God. I wish you were naked, that's all." My heart beats fast from having said something so honest to him.

He looks off, with his head tilted, like he doesn't understand why I would say that. "Not now." He begins pacing the perimeter of our site, like a guard dog.

I feel my face turn red. I was dumb to think I could be affectionate without Clay regulating my feelings.

Daytime is back, and he wants us to be serious, communicate in code, and hide our emotions. He has to start worrying about what people think of him and how to pick the right part of himself to make each situation smooth.

My defenses rise immediately to match his. I stand up straighter and resist any mannerisms that could be considered unmasculine. I have to stop laughing casually about things I think are funny. That's too girlish. Now's the time to speak to him with lots of "dude" and "brah" and "man" added in.

He distances himself from what he's saying with those words, by sounding like every other stupid surfer in Hawaii.

"What do you wanna do today?" I finally ask.

"Surf," he snaps. "Think. Be alone. Motor out of here."

My heart drops. I clench my teeth to stop from getting angry or sad. "I guess I'll just walk back to town then."

"Fine, go. I don't care." He sits down and hides his face in his hands.

"OK, I will."

He screams with his jaws clenched and jerks himself up. He runs up to a tree and hits the rough bark as hard as he can. His hand starts bleeding. He clutches his fist, like he's trying to restrain the head of a poisonous snake. "Fuck! Look what you made me do!"

"I didn't do shit."

He wipes his head with his fist and smears blood across his forehead. He looks me in the eye. An obvious ploy for sympathy.

I stare at him. "I'm not stupid, you know. I see what you're doing."

He looks at me suspiciously and turns away and starts throwing rocks into the stream as hard as he can. Small drops of blood fly off his injured hand.

I go to stand in front of him, blocking the stream.

He leans down, picks up a rock, and throws it. It whizzes by my head and a string of blood splatters my face. He walks away.

I follow him and stand up to him, inches from his face. "You're not some tough guy. Why would you even want to be? Most of your friends are fucking *dumb,* and you let them tell you how to act."

"That's bullshit."

"No, it isn't. You're never yourself. You think people will make fun of you if you like me. You can't bear the thought of life without everyone accepting you."

His chest is puffed out, and his eyes look as furious as they can get. "What do you want from me?" His voice cracks; I can feel his breath on my face like fire.

"You, that's all, nothing else!"

His eyes get watery, but he wipes them immediately, acting like a swarm of gnats flew in them and irritated them. He wants to say something mean, but doesn't.

"Just act like you. Don't try to be tough and all that shit."

He stops throwing rocks and looks down at his feet. His head hangs low and his face contorts, like he's going to cry. "Quit fucking with me."

"You're fucking with yourself. I'm just telling you the truth."

He jumps up and hangs on a branch and does pull-ups, tapping his chin on the top of the swaying branch, over and over, with a determined look on his face. The veins in his neck pop out. He looks possessed by his confusion.

"Clay? Stop it."

"Leave me alone, dude." He jumps down and wipes the sweat off his forehead with his arm. He looks like he's going to turn into a werewolf.

"Fine. Fuck it. Be miserable." I start to take down the tent.

He puts his hand down the front of his shorts and rubs his balls, then smells his hand and walks away to the stream.

I can see his reflection on the water's surface, quivering in the currents.

He dives into the water and stays under, holding his breath.

"Fuck you." I flip him off.

If he's too embarrassed to be real with me, fine. I hope he feels threatened. He doesn't give a shit, anyway.

I walk away, carrying more than my share of the stuff, so he knows I don't need his help. I take one last look back.

He's floating like a corpse facedown in the water. Some bubbles burst at the surface by his head.

I hope he drowns. I stomp around a corner of a switchback trail and up a steep hill. I stop to take a breath. My eyes are drawn down the hill, following a bird's plummet, where I have a perfect view of Clay.

He rises up out of the water, gasping for air.

I sit down, light a cigarette, and watch him. I taste his blood on my lips. I make a gun with my hand and blow his brains out a couple times.

He lies on the ground, dripping wet, shiny in the sunlight. He leans up on his arms and his head is back, probably seeing everything upside down. He scratches his balls through his shorts and looks around in quick intervals, like he's keeping watch. He starts maniacally doing sit-ups, stopping every twenty or so to look at his flexed stomach muscles.

Three bright-yellow birds watch him from their perches on the branch that he used for pull-ups.

The smoke from my cigarette drifts down the hillside, illuminated by beams of sunlight. I lie on my stomach as low as I can get.

His head falls back and thumps on the hollow-sounding earth. He bursts out crying. He kicks his legs around in frustration.

I lose my breath. I've never made anyone react this strongly before, except making my parents utterly frustrated, and that's normal. I watch him so intensely that he goes out of focus.

Maybe he does care. Maybe he really is confused. He rolls over, burying his face in his arms and screaming as loud as he can. His low-pitched moans echo off the valley walls. Scared birds take flight quickly, their wings slapping together.

I feel like I shouldn't be watching, but I'm fascinated because I caused this—and horrified that we have come to this. I can't resist.

He stops crying and stands up, then his face clenches up, and he falls over sobbing again.

I gotta take off. Think. Breathe.

I reach the top of the hill perched over the ocean and white crescent beach of Kalalau. It's outstanding. The smell of salt and campfires mixes with the flowers of the forests. This beach has a legendary reputation, and seeing it makes my heart beat faster. I think of a haiku, but a lame one: White sandy beach, aren't you scared of, all these complicated humans?

Once, a whole group of hippies lived here, naked and free, till hepatitis and typhoid infected their water supply and everyone got STDs.

The ancient Hawaiians who lived near here were known for their love of celebration and ritual dances. They chewed hallucinogenic roots to find their inner selves. They also performed human sacrifices.

I see a fire burning and some people cooking over it. I imagine the rancid smell of a human body burning and melting, killed for

Pele, the goddess of fire, the goddess who supposedly created these islands. I descend the steep trail into the valley, the tent on my back. A chill slithers up my spine.

Waterfalls plunge from the cliffs and smack into pools. The ocean churns with big waves that go from pastel blue to midnight blue the farther out you look. The cliffs are covered with moss and all shades of greens and browns and are eroded into sharp pyramids and cartoon-like cones and jags and caves.

Clay told me on the plane that one of his goals since he was a little kid was to come here and experience this place. He said he wanted to feel the *mana,* the Hawaiian word for the kind of power a place holds. He'd be with me now if he weren't such an asshole.

I'd love to see his face looking out at this perfect beach. I'd see inside his head.

He'd be real.

Campsites are set up along the back of the beach. Tents flutter in the sea breeze like grounded parachutes. People sit around in groups. They look drunk from the natural beauty and seclusion. A few surfboards rest against a weathered pine tree.

Two naked blond girls lie in the gentle surf, browned and caressed by the delicate sun. Their pubic hair's shaved off, and the skin where the hair used to be is untanned. The pale white skin looks obscene.

I step on the sand at the bottom of the trail, and the beauty of this place overtakes me. I get nervous. I feel like I'm losing control, being changed by the environment.

A guy notices me walking onto the beach. I feel like he's gonna scream, "Get outta here. This is my territory," but he turns around to watch a girl walk past.

What if Clay doesn't come?

I'll end up hiding in the tent till I can get out of here.

These hippie beach people intimidate me. They all look so relaxed and confident.

I find an open place, isolated yet close enough to the other tents not to feel alone. I plop down on the warm sand and take my shoes off and run my feet through the fine white powder. The sun is hot and pure. I feel my skin darkening.

A guy about my age, with a lanky, sinewy body, a shaved head, bright green eyes, and an air of intelligence about him, intensely writes in a journal. He looks like a younger Clay, with a similar tattoo and the same shaped head and bony hands, but he's skinnier and not nearly as tough-looking. He's the hippie Clay.

I set up Clay's tent, which is a lot more confusing than taking it down was. I keep glancing at the guy and thinking he's Clay and almost talking to him. It's a weird feeling, like people aren't so hard to replace. I should know exactly what Clay looks like—he's all I think about—but my eyes catch the boy for half a second, and I think he's Clay. I whisper to myself, "That's not Clay. You don't know that guy."

The boy notices me staring at him.

I look away as quickly as I can and try to seem involved in putting up the tent. I try to act all tough, handling things like I don't give a shit about them.

The boy's stare is calm and relaxed. His eyes penetrate me and make me feel vulnerable. He doesn't look away when I look at him.

I guess he's less self-conscious than I am.

His stillness makes me feel inadequate. His calm, confident demeanor makes me more flighty and jumpy than ever. He's working a spell on me. He's evil.

I'm getting sweaty. I'm standing all wrong. I don't know what to do with my hands. Before, they were just *there,* and now they're a hassle, another decision to make and inevitably get wrong. I look like a skittish dog. I'd like to move the tent, pick a different site, but I don't want to be rude—or admit defeat.

He glances up at me again from his pretentious journal. The sun makes his eyes look glimmering and clever.

I almost turn inside out, feeling judged.

He's trying to figure me out. I'm sure he's getting me all wrong. I bet he thinks I think I write lame, gushy, emotional poetry and that my hair color and clothes are an expression of my personality. What bullshit. My haikus are real and my hair colors are just because I happen to like them.

His stupid pen gliding across his wheat-grain recycled paper makes me want to be an asshole.

I could look all poetic and take out my notebook, but I'm not that much of a poseur. "Man, what are you staring at?" I say in a fake deep, jockish, dumb-ass voice. I feel really absurd right after the sounds leave my lips. I sounded like Clay.

The kid looks over at me and points to himself and casually mouths, "Me?" with no sound coming out.

Oh, fuck. I can't keep this tough guy thing up for long.

I play dumb, with a low voice, and act like I'm the spaced-out surfer type. "What? Uh, no, I was...forget it." I turn bright red and my face gets really hot. I fool around with the tent, acting like the stakes aren't secured properly yet, like I'm the type of guy who does things right or not at all. That'll throw him. I get up to go swimming, but there are four big muscle guys throwing girls off their shoulders into the water. I'm embarrassed to take off my shirt and let them see my skinny chest.

They're all wearing Hawaiian flower-print long shorts and have dark tans and slight goatees that make them look like devils. The girls are laughing and flirting. Their beer is floating in the surf, keeping cool.

I sit back down awkwardly. I feel trapped.

A naked older couple walks past me, blocking the sun for a

second. They have no tan lines and look like they feel really comfortable naked in front of people.

I stare right at their crotches to see if they care, but they don't. It's gross. They're too old to be naked. But they look free and natural, or whatever nudists feel about being naked.

A hippie family—a mom, dad, and their three naked kids—make some sort of stew in a big pot over a fire. I'm hungry.

The kid who was writing in the journal is doing tai chi by his tent, almost right next to me. He takes his shirt off. He's wearing loose drawstring pants that hang low on his waist. His arms are thin, but I can see the different muscles under his skin, all separate from one another. He looks stupidly serious as his arms rise slowly to feel his inner light or whatever. He looks at me again, breaking the concentration of one of his poses, just to make me feel shallow and meaningless for not devoting myself to concentration and for finding pleasure in making fun of others.

Fuck him. I'm not going to let him make me feel worthless. When Clay comes, we'll beat the shit out of him. I hope he's intimidated by Clay.

He'll hate all Clay's macho hang-ups and surfer-boy expressions.

I'd love to watch his calm, meditative state melt into insecurity. I go into the tent and lie with my head near the open flap door. I watch the kid do poses. I'm fascinated at how long he can keep this act up and not laugh at himself. As I watch him move, I can see the shape of his dick through his pants. I get a boner and I'm mad at myself for it. Why can't my dick listen to my mind? I hate him, but I'd jerk off to him. This feels irreconcilable, and it pisses me off. I give him a dirty look.

Balancing on one leg with his arms raised high, he smiles at me in a really bratty way, like he knows why I hate him and he likes it.

I'm probably imagining all of this. My mind goes crazy when I'm alone.

He sort of laughs and then looks away and closes his eyes, concentrating on this stupid pose, standing on one leg with his arms out like scissors.

I want to go over to him and push him over and jump on him, kick his face with his smart-aleck smile and clever eyes. After that, I want to strip him naked and rub my face all over his body, smelling from his knees to his dick to his head. I watch him, to make sure he doesn't realize what I'm thinking. I examine him to see if he knows. If he did, I would leave, pack up the tent, and run away from him.

He doesn't. If he did, he wouldn't keep doing these poses. He's not as clever as he thinks he is.

Two girls stare at me like I'm amusing.

I stand up and imagine Clay walking. I copy what I can remember—his long gait, arms not moving, head up, almost tilted back a little, shoulders back, chest out, like a less exaggerated version of a soldier.

Why are they looking at me and whispering? Maybe they like me. No, they're way too old to like a skinny sixteen-year-old psychotic.

I walk farther away, looking back at them, trying to be scary and intimidating.

They run over, tits bouncing, to the dumb tai chi kid and surround him with attention. The kid looks bored, so they walk away, sit down in the sun, take their tops off, and try to look sexy for guys walking past. Their poses are obvious and their skin is shiny from oil. They look like the kind of girls who would fall in love with Clay in seconds and help keep his ego burning high.

I hate them. I walk away, down toward the end of the beach. Everyone's fucked-up and I don't want to see anyone. I sit down on the white sand and look out to the ocean. *There has to be someone in the world who understands me.*

A Frisbee bangs into the back of my head. I turn around and four naked hippies are standing in a large square all staring at me.

A tall, skinny guy with a beard waves at me. "Sorry, brother. Could you throw that back?"

I grab the Frisbee, stand up, and throw it as far as I can out into the ocean. A big wave crashes on top of it. They won't see it till it washes up and that could be days from now with the riptides. I walk past the hippies and smile.

They're shocked but too free-loving to get pissed off. "Man…"

"Go get it yourself, love children." I head for the tent. For a remote beach that we had to hike nine hours to get to, there sure isn't much peace here.

In the distance, I see the tai chi kid is hanging with some guy outside his tent.

The new guy is holding tai chi kid's arm and directing his leg with his hands. They're close enough for me to have to say hi or something, but the sun's in my eyes, so I can act like I don't see them.

The new guy looks like Clay. Same color hair, same olive skin, same tattoo. Oh, fuck, it's the real Clay. He's hanging out with that dumb-ass hippie.

It can't be.

I walk closer to the guys. I don't want to walk past them to go to the tent. I hold my head down and walk up to them.

"Hey," an unfamiliar voice says.

Clay's hand is on the kid's thigh, directing the movement of his leg.

A surge of bad chemicals rushes through me. Pure dread. This is the worst possible scenario. I glare at the point of contact. I feel a mean look take over my face.

Clay's such a fake, acting like he wasn't just crying hysterically an hour before. He has no right to talk to him. He's supposed to hate him, and the kid's supposed to think Clay's shallow. What the fuck's going on?

I thought the hippie kid would be *my* friend, even though I hated him. I'm furious. I try to make my expression look reckless and driven, so they think I don't care that they're hanging out. I stand up straight and force my shoulders back, trying to look tough.

They don't notice. They keep doing karate moves.

I can feel Clay's distanced posture immediately. He avoids eye contact with me and looks away just before I catch his eye.

The kid acts the same, but even more arrogant now that he's stolen my only friend.

I hate how easily Clay can befriend people. He just walks up like a hero and does what he wants. I give the kid a mean look for Clay to see.

He ignores me, obviously and rudely, making me feel like the bad guy.

"You wanna roll a joint?"

The kid ignores me.

Clay looks at him. "You wanna smoke, Anar?" He knows his name: Anar. What kind of a name is that? He probably made it up, that dumb hippie.

I'm really pissed off now. "We don't have that much."

"Don't be stingy, Sam."

I feel like an unfriendly asshole, the worst quality in front of a hippie boy.

Anar looks at me and almost laughs. I feel stupid. I can't say anything right.

Clay rolls a joint, and Anar watches his expert rolling abilities over his shoulder. Abilities that used to be reserved for me and him. Anar's leg touches Clay's back.

I monitor the spot where contact is made, watching for slight movements, like Anar's leg applying more pressure to Clay's back or Clay leaning back into Anar's leg.

Clay hands Anar the joint.

Anar takes a big hit off the joint and hands it to me.

I want to slap his hand away, then knock him to the ground. I don't look him in the eyes as I grab the joint from his hand. I suck in the THC, hoping for super powers.

The light is slowly leaving the sky. Soon, the darkness will bring out the essence of things as they truly exist. People's facades will fade away and their animal selves will come out. I'm ready for the kill.

"I gotta take a shower." Clay walks over to a waterfall coming off the cliff and starts undressing. He points at the waterfall, plunging fifty feet from the cliff. "Look at this! Man, this is so rad," he says to Anar.

Anar nods at Clay, but then stares a little too long. He looks back at me.

I hope he feels stupid for staring at Clay naked. I give him a look of disapproval, and ask, "Who are *you* here with?"

"My sister and her friend." He points to them, asleep and topless on beach towels. "I think they smoked too much today."

"Looks like it." Campfires pop up all along the beach. Pools of red-orange light illuminate groups of people, tired from a day in the sun and horny from being naked in nature all day.

The air is warm, and molecules are moving quickly. In the isolation of this beach, we are all a bigger part of one another than we would normally be. Being so far away from society gives everyone a particular buzz, an edge of craziness. It's exhilarating for some people and scary for others. The air is full of adventure and possibility.

I can't hate Anar anymore. I need him. Sitting close to him, in the fading light, not talking, I get turned on in this strange hippie way that I've never really felt before. I like it. He smells like cedar wood and puppies. He's sexy. We're both really stoned and weird connections are flying between us. When we look at each other, it's embarrassing, but the embarrassment feels adventurous.

Clay seems old and experienced compared to Anar. I'm happy to stare at someone who doesn't know what the hell he's doing and doesn't try to act like he does. He's just a cool-looking, smart-ass dork, in a really unique, scrappy way.

"Hey, bring me a towel, will you?" Clay yells from the waterfall.

"Get it yourself."

Anar grabs a green towel. He's about to stand up. This can't happen.

I jump up quickly and grab the towel from his hand, feeling stupid for looking so obedient, especially when that's not my motive. I slow down and walk leisurely over to Clay. "I don't wanna have to hang out with that hippie wanna-be all night." I look back at Anar, who turns when he sees me staring.

I know how he feels, when you start to hang out with new people and you feel like they have to get together and approve you or something. I keep staring at him, like we're talking a lot of shit about him, not that I'm not.

"He's cool."

I don't want him to know that I approve of Anar, not even in the slightest. "Oh, I see. You're all normal now, like nothing ever happened." I stare at Clay waiting for his reaction.

"Lighten up, brah." He towels himself off in his obsessed-with-his-own-body kind of way, looking at his muscles flex as he raises his arm. He punches me in the shoulder, like that's supposed to be enough to say sorry.

I roll my eyes at his vanity and walk away with my mind set on winning Anar's admiration away from him. I'll read him my poetry if I have to.

17

Pine falls from fire,
smoke turns clear blue sky dark gray
seeds cultivated.

We build a fire that lights up our faces with the same warm glow as a rising sun. Clay pretends he's a young but wise Hawaiian prince and tells scary stories about Hawaiian legends, with a spooked-out look on his face for effect.

"*Ka huakai o ka po,*" he sings in a guttural whisper. "The marchers of the night. My mom's friend saw them here before. Picture this. A strong wind blows, like tonight, to clear the path for dead chiefs, retracing their ceremonial marches from the outrigger canoes to the mountains. Burning torches, red and intense. I think tonight is *Po Kane,* the twenty-seventh phase of the moon. That's when they march. Between sunset and two." He jerks his head up and looks to the cliffs. "I saw something!" He points to the ridge.

Anar looks up quickly.

"It's some dumb-ass hippie with a lantern." I act like the stories don't scare me—I've heard them a million times before—but they feel really possible here on this isolated beach. I could scream as loud as I possibly could and still miss the ears of civilization by miles. I feel both trapped and protected here, by the churning sea on one side and the steep cliffs and sharp volcanic mountains on the other.

Clay holds his hand up, palm facing out, as if he's about to enlighten us.

A dog stops playing and looks at him.

"Remember, if you see them, don't look them in the eye. Take off all your clothes and lie flat on the ground. If you're lucky, they'll ignore you." He sticks the end of a big piece of gnarled driftwood into the fire till the tip glows bright orange, then he stands and traces hieroglyphs in the air. The hot ember makes trails in the darkness of turtles and birds. "We should be safe. I think." He talks with a Hawaiian pidgin accent, so we're more likely to believe his made-up ritual.

I look at Anar and roll my eyes.

Anar dismisses me and looks at Clay attentively, like he knows more than everyone else who lives here.

He doesn't, and fuck hippie-ass Anar for acting like he does.

"Where'd you learn about all that?" Anar's really into this.

Clay loves his loyalty and rewards him with attention, snapping out of his scary mode. "Friends, personal experience, surfing."

I want to laugh.

"Where you from, brah?" Clay asks, like he's equally fascinated by Anar.

"My parents live on Maui. We've lived there since I was twelve."

Oh, he's one of *those*. He's rich, smokes a lot of pot, and has ultraliberal hippie parents. He's kind of confused, his parents give him no guidance at all, and he spends all his energy trying really hard to be cool, even though he lives in the middle of nowhere and has no idea how normal people live.

"Cool, man. I love Maui." Clay says that about every island. "The Garden Isle."

What a dork. All the islands have these nicknames that are

supposedly what the ancient Hawaiians called them, but I think the tourist board thought them up. Whenever someone says one of the names, I get cold chills of embarrassment.

"It's cool. Really beautiful. You guys from Oahu?"

"Yeah, Kailua. It sucks." I have to put an end to this every-place-is-lovely bullshit. All I can think of is my prison-like school, macho Samoans driving around picking on kids, blond muscle surfer-boys in pickup trucks with KAILUA BOYS stickers on the back, a stupid gang whose members beat their girlfriends and talk like Hawaiians even though they're white.

"It doesn't suck. Cool brahs, hot chicks, good waves. Windward breezes keep your mind clear."

If he says "the Gathering Place," Oahu's nickname, I swear I'll throw up.

He shows Anar his arm, halfway flexed, the tattoo of Oahu with a big plumeria flower where Kailua is. He flexes more as Anar takes it into his hands. He glances up at me for a second to see if I notice his flexed arm.

I flash him a mean look, trying to make him feel stupid. "You don't really like it, Clay. You just don't know any other way."

He ignores me. He grabs a stick and throws it for this hyper dog to fetch, then he gets down on all fours and encourages a tug-of-war.

The dog growls.

"Watch this, Anar. I have a connection with dogs." He speaks in a really friendly voice, kind of how Anar talks, like everything is equally interesting and sharing your thoughts is healthy because then you get more back from others, and all that stupid hippie shit. He's being totally fake, as he molds himself into a version that makes Anar feel important. He grabs the dog's face. "You remind me of Sharky, boy."

Anar watches him. He looks amused and entertained, like it's really fun to watch some guy play with a dirty mutt in the sand.

This is really sick. I've seen how different Clay is around his friends, but that's pretty normal for a surfer in Hawaii who listens to punk rock music, parties a lot, and smokes weed. I had no idea he had the capability of being this peaceful, sensitive hippie boy. I don't want to know this. Is nothing sacred? Why's he have to be so brilliant at such a fucked-up skill? A genius of deception. That sounds like the name of a movie or something, or a book about a man with three separate families, all in different states.

I feel betrayed. Why can't he be a genius at expressing himself, making me feel loved and cared about?

"If you look straight into their eyes, you can see their souls," Clay says to Anar, trying to hold the unwilling dog's face to his.

I was the idiot who believed him when he said I was cool and cool-looking and interesting to him and smart and funny and that he liked me for me. I was seeing an act. Seeing him convert to hippiedom puts an entirely new slant on the rest of his personality. What came off before as spaced-out surfer-boy now seems like overly open-minded and downright desperate, which I really hate in people.

"You into drumming—you know, bongos and all that shit? I went with my best brah to Maui last year and everyone was drumming. It's really cool, under the stars—the ancient tribal rhythm."

"Yeah, I know a couple guys that are into it."

"I'd like to get into that shit." Clay nods a couple times.

What a lie. He hates hippies. Well, he did yesterday and every other day before that. He's making me lose trust in people, like a dog that's been beaten too many times. The dog just walks around like the victim with its tail between its legs. That's going to be me.

"It's really cool meeting you, dude. I like to meet all different types of people."

"You guys been friends a long time?" Anar innocently asks me.

I make my way out of the haze of thought. "Yeah, well, we knew each other when I was like twelve, then we didn't see each other till last year."

"I'm glad you guys showed up. I was going crazy with my sister and her friend. All they wanna do is meet guys. They're so boring." With a dumb smile, Anar watches Clay play with the dog. He looks at Clay with an admiration that even I find incredibly naive. Maybe Clay should go out with him. He could just do what he wants without having to feel judged and dissected. Love should be simple like that, I guess. I forget how to feel love as a simple emotion. For me, love's a jumbled mass of hidden feelings, indirect motivation, and uncontrollable lust.

"How old's your sister?"

"Twenty-one. She's a nursing student."

"I hate nurses," I say quietly.

"Oh?" He doesn't know the full impact of my declaration. "You have any brothers or sisters?"

"No. Thank God. The house is already too small for just me and my parents. I need a lot of space, you know, to have a clear mind." I sound like Clay.

"Yeah, it's hard living in one big room with my parents."

Clay looks up all the sudden. "How do you jack off?" Of course he had to bring up Anar's dick, that asshole. I bet he wants to see it. I hate him for it. He runs after the dog toward the ocean.

Now I can't stop picturing Anar naked and coming up with dumb see-through schemes to get him into the tent alone. I get a boner as I picture Clay and Anar sucking each other off. What's happening to me?

Clay looks up at me and Anar talking, but he's too far away to hear us.

I smile and laugh, trying to make him think I'm having a great time with him and that Anar's mine, not his.

Clay jogs away, throwing the stick for the dog to fetch down the beach. "Do you believe that stuff about night marchers?" Anar asks.

Here's my chance to have some control around here. "There are people who swear they have seen them. I don't know. Weirder shit happens in Hawaii."

"Yeah, I guess so."

"Got a girlfriend?" I ask strongly, like Clay would.

"Nope. Never have."

"What do you mean, never?"

"Never liked anyone." He looks uncomfortable and shy.

"So what's the deal? How could you never like anyone? There must be some hot girls on Maui." I can't believe I'm doing this. I'll rot in hell.

Anar looks away from me and glances down at his hands. "I don't know."

"I've heard stories about Maui girls." I smile at him and wink.

"Whatever story you heard about *Maui girls*"—he exaggerates the words, making me feel stupid for trying to be so cool—"has to be total bullshit."

We hang out in silence. Finally, I say, "So, how long are you gonna camp here?"

"A couple more days. We've already been here for three."

Tiny crystals of salt make his eyebrows sparkle in the firelight. I want to lick them off.

"How long are you guys staying?"

"I don't know. Till whenever I get sick of it."

Clay comes running up and throws me a bottle of beer, which almost slams into my face. Then he presents another one to Anar like he's a waiter trying to get a good tip. "There's some cool Australian guys over there. I taught them how to say *vagina* in Hawaiian." He does a couple karate chops, then sits down on the sand and lies back, looking up to the almost-full moon.

Anar asks, "How?"

"Duh: *pu nani*. Who doesn't know that?" I can see the shape of Clay's dick through his shorts and the thickening of his torso near his chest, lit by the fire.

Anar watches him, waiting for his next words.

"Anar's sister is a nursing student," I say to Clay.

Clay raises his head, like a dog hearing an intruder. "So?"

I look at Anar. "Clay's girlfriend's a nurse."

Anar nods.

Here's my chance to win this pathetic competition. "Have you heard the story about that nurse at Honolulu Hospital? She was going in at night when the hospital was almost empty and performing frontal lobotomies on male patients, then she'd make them fall in love with her. The guys didn't even know what hit them. She made them into who she wanted them to be, and they didn't even remember who they were before they met her."

"What happened to her?" Anar's politely riveted.

"She gave her last lobotomy to this surfer, and he felt obligated to sleep with her and put up with her, like all the others, but—"

"Shut up, man." Clay sits up.

"What's your problem?"

"You think I'm stupid?"

I look at Anar, who looks confused. "So, anyway, the surfer tried to enjoy himself every time he fucked her, but she was really horrible. She didn't even know how to give a good hand job."

"Shut the fuck up!" Clay rubs his bicep.

"Make me."

Anar looks back and forth between us, trying to figure out which one of us is the bad guy.

Clay stands up. His intense glare is made stronger by the flames reflecting in his eyes. He walks over to me and stops so close that all I can see is the front of his shorts with a couple black hairs sticking out the top.

"Move," I say. "You're blocking my view, dumb-ass."

He leans over in my face, stares at me with a look somewhere between hurt and anger, and shoves me backward.

I fall back into the sand and stare up at the black sky. Through the corner of my eye, I see Clay grab his beer out of the sand. He kicks sand in my face as he runs off.

I don't want to sit up and look away from the solace of the dark sky, but I have no choice. I have to face Anar. There's no one else.

He's in shock. He's looking at me like he wants to rescue me, but he's not sure if I'm cool. All he knows of Clay is a sweet, cute surfer-boy who's patient, strong, and wants to get into playing bongos. All he knows of me is a bitter, conniving little prick who has huge inconsistencies in his personality and tries to act bigger than he is. "What was that about?" He sort of sounds like he's taking my side.

"His girlfriend, Tammy. She doesn't like me, and I don't like her. I used to go out with her, and he's always been jealous." If I tell the truth, he'll think I'm psychotic.

Anar helps me up and sits down next to me.

I can smell him. I get a boner that looks obvious poking out the thin fabric of my shorts, but I don't mind. I hope he'll notice, but I don't know what I'll do if he does.

He leans back on his arms, his leg touching mine.

I concentrate on the point of contact and press my thigh into him as hard as I can without being totally blatant about it. I don't know if he's queer or whatever, and if he's not I'm gonna feel really stupid. Our faces are close.

He moves his leg a little.

All my instincts tell me to touch Anar as much as I possibly can. Of course my brain says *no!*—because I love Clay and want to be with him forever, but I'm worried that loving Clay is turning into a habit, rather than a desire. I'm ready to never see him again, as painful as I think that will be. I turn my head toward Anar. The distance between us becomes more meaningful than just close. It becomes intimate and visceral. I feel heat radiating off him. I hear his shallow breathing.

"You all right?" he whispers.

A smile comes across my face that I have no control over. I press my leg more obviously into his. If he's not into this, I've made a really big fool of myself now. I'm pressing just hard enough to make my intentions pretty obvious, enough to feel stupid if he's not into me or doesn't like boys at all.

He leaves his leg in the same place. Good sign.

I can hardly breathe, and my hands are shaking.

He slides his hand onto my arm. It's softer than Clay's hand.

A torrent of dizzy happiness rings through my entire body. I want to look at his hand to see if it looks cool on my arm, but I can't escape from his calming gaze. If I do, I'll panic and start thinking about Clay's face crying in the woods earlier today.

He was crying over me.

I look out into the black sea.

The waves are building. Sets of eight-footers are increasing. Another hurricane is out at sea, waiting till we least expect it to wreck our tidy lives and houses and erode away the mountains slightly more, making them lose some of their familiarity. The mountains elude us by seeming so permanent. They can change as fast as we do.

I need to change. I want to feel every part of Anar. I roll over on top of him and pull him close to me, my arms around him with my hands clasped together against his back. I rub down to his butt, inside his shorts, then I slide my hands around to the front.

His dick feels hot on my skin. He's going to fall in love with me, I know it.

I'll end up hurting him. I want to be in his arms forever, but I know deep inside myself that the possibility isn't here. What will I do with myself, forever full of this new ability to fall in love and act on it all in minutes? I'll never sleep as soundly.

I kiss Anar, and his lips taste like salt and his tongue is wet and strong. He kisses me back like he can't get enough. I grind my dick into his stomach, delving into his body and his soul, not clear on what I'll find. I smell his skin, tangy and moist. I'm afraid to speak, afraid it will ruin the spell, but my senses tell me that we can't do this on the beach, in front of the world. "Let's go in your tent," I whisper.

We duck into the mildewy scent of his tent. A lantern is burning. I find his sleeping bag because it smells like him. One of his pubic hairs lies on the plaid interior lining, which makes him real, and I almost back out.

He dims the light, which makes him seem experienced at this and makes me feel dumb, like I'm being taken by some hippie slut. We pull our shorts down and wrap ourselves in each other's bodies, our skinny legs poking each other by accident.

I squirm down his body till I reach his dick. It's just like mine. I hold it in my palm and he thrusts a little into my hand, which is pretty courageous of him, since we hardy know each other. I jack him off and he comes in my hand and I shoot at the same time. It's weird.

It smells like how magnolia bushes smell when they're blooming.

Dread comes over me. There's evidence of Anar on my skin, my largest organ, as Mrs. Daly said in health class. Sperm is swimming around my hand, sperm that I hardly know. It's like inviting some door-to-door salesman in for dinner, wine and all, and letting him use your bed and toothbrush. I've turned into a hippie slut.

I almost jump up, scared at what I've become. My head hits the top of the tent and the plastic support rods slip apart and the tent comes collapsing down on us.

He laughs, even though I tried to escape and failed, and rolls over beside me holding up the material around us.

He's going to tell his rich ultraliberal parents that my dad's a conservative working against the Hawaii Natives Fund, and they'll force me to move in to escape the repression of my evil dad's morals, which are based on greed and capitalism.

I'll sleep in his room, and we'll cuddle and come together every night under the safe roof of his parents' house till we're hippies no longer, till we're normal and old and boring. I love and hate the idea at the same time. Mostly, I love it; I can't help it. I want to tell him all this, but I'm afraid. What if he doesn't like me? The surf shorts I borrowed from Clay are staring at me from the tent floor, looking useless and dirty. I throw a blanket over them and notice stubble on Anar's chin.

He looks wise.

I think he has some Japanese in him from generations ago. I think I trust him. I hold the plastic rod up and build a makeshift tepee out of the tent.

A fire outside the tent is burning brightly. I can see guys and girls standing around it, casting shadows in shapes like Indonesian shadow puppets on the orange tent wall. Their heads are exaggerated because they stretch upwards on the pointy roof of the tepee.

A shadowy figure approaches closely. It looks like a huge monster. It walks by the partly open door flap.

I see legs walk by. I think it's Clay. I scramble to put on my shorts under the plastic-feeling material.

"Where are you doing?" Anar raises his head, looking concerned.

"I'll be right back." I duck out of the mess of tent, accidentally making the center rod fall again.

Anar struggles to get it up, but then rolls over, letting the tent fall on him, letting the chaos win.

Clay spots me right away. "What's up, Sam?"

I look back at the fallen tent with Anar inside squirming like a larvae in a cocoon. "Uh…nothing. Hanging out with that kid. Where'd you go?"

Clay looks like he's sleepwalking. "Hung out with these dudes, drank a beer, smoked a J." He looks over at the fallen tent.

"I think he's sleeping," I tell Clay. "Don't bother him."

He leans down and pulls up the floppy material to see in his tent. He drops the nylon and throws his beer down hard. Beer foam splashes onto my chest.

"What's wrong?" I try to grab his upper arm, to harness the dragon.

"Don't touch me."

"Clay." I put my hand on his shoulder. My body resonates with a dull hum that feels like someone's slipped me too many downers. It's humiliation. If I were a samurai, I'd get out my sword and kill myself without a moment's delay. Rid the world of my disgrace, dishonor, repulsion.

I have to resist an urge to run into Anar's tent and hug him and listen to him say he loves me.

Clay runs down the beach, not looking back.

"Wait!" I have to tell him the truth. I have to make him understand that I know I fucked up. I thought he hated me.

Clay disappears into the dark, crooked shadows of cliffs.

Anar puts the tent back together, from the inside, and turns up his kerosene lantern to high, providing a moon for himself.

The waves build in size and consistency, and a breeze makes the lazy air expressive and vocal.

Anar sticks his head out of his tent. "Sam?"

I don't know what to do or say. I wish he'd just fall asleep.

"Yeah?"

"What are you doing? Come back in. It looks like a storm's coming."

I duck inside. "Yeah, it does."

This is hurricane season, but never since I can remember have storms come as often as this year. Nature is figuring me out, and it's spooky. I'm dealing with a force that makes me as small as a particle of antimatter in a universe that is so big it scares me to think about it.

Anar looks confused.

"It's out to get me," I explain.

"For what?"

"I can't tell you."

He looks down to his sandy feet and then back up to me. "I'm not worthy of conversation, only a...forget it..."

Oh, fuck. He's vocalizing his thoughts. I hate when people do that, which means I'll be doing it soon.

"Where'd Clay go?" he asks.

"Down the beach. I'm sick of his bullshit."

Just as I say this, a thin band of lightning strikes the sea, not very far out. Lightning is rare in Hawaii—very rare. I've only seen it like five times maybe. An empty, vague, painful sensation pervades my body. It hurts really bad and it's hard to breathe. I feel sick. I have to throw up. I crouch at the door. Acidy liquid burns my throat and tongue and pours out of my mouth.

Anar looks too confused to help.

I stand up, a bitter taste in my mouth. I spit out a bunch of little pieces of gross matter that tastes like my stomach lining. I feel my chest. I'm coated in a sticky layer of sweat. I think this is what malaria must feel like. This lying is killing me. "I have to go."

I run away before he gets a chance to respond. I don't want to piss him off because I need him to be here as a base camp. I'm scared to see Clay. I might need a hug when I come back. I imagine I'm a spaceship forging space no one's ever been to before. I keep Anar in my mind, sitting with headphones on in the heated, dry control room in Houston or whatever.

He guides me through layers of static radio waves.

This is Anar in Ground Control. Sam, do you copy? You're entering a thin, unstable outer layer of universe. Come in, Sam. This is Control. I'm losing you. Come in, Sam.

18

Humid summer night
moon judges as mosquitoes
search for deep rich blood.

When I find Clay, he's wearing a black hooded sweatshirt that covers his face. He looks like the grim reaper, sitting on the edge of a tide pool in the pounding surf, ignoring waves that smack him in the face and almost knock him over. His sweatshirt sucks up water and hangs heavy.

I'm scared of him. I'm ashamed and proud and confused.

He's lit by bluish moonlight. He throws his hood back, and the tint of the full moon's glow shines on his skin.

I think of Anar's hazel eyes. I wish I could stare into them and feel their easy acceptance

"I know you're there, stupid."

"I wanna talk."

"Leave me alone," he says quietly.

"I want to tell you the truth."

"I know the truth."

"I'm dying. I'm sorry I haven't told you before now. It's leukemia. I have six months, maybe seven."

"I don't care. Go hang out with that kid. He'll talk to you. I don't want to. 'I'm not capable of dealing with things,' remember?"

He imitates my voice, making me sound like a whiny brat.

"I love you, Clay." This is the first time I've ever been able to say this, even though I've thought it hundreds of times. Saying it makes me feel amazing, like it's my reason for living, the source of all happiness.

He just sits there with water splashing him in the face, looking out to the dark sea.

I look up at the sharply eroded cliffs, and all of nature has new meaning. The waterfalls emanate tears. The waves are rolls of sad emotions that I can't overcome. Dead branches are reminders of what was once flourishing. The beauty of it all feels eternally untouchable.

I look at Clay. His head is down, and he's completely soaked.

I've never seen him so still, even during sleep. I want the resilient, escapist Clay back, the one who wants to forget about it all and just fool around. I look at him till my eyes go blurry. I hear the conversations of groups scattered around the beach, growing louder and more abrasive as they drink more.

A whole group erupts into evil-sounding laughter.

Clay looks over his shoulder to the laughing group of three guys and four bikini girls down the beach about fifty yards. He probably wishes he could just hang out with them and turn into that cool-boy surfer and forget about my psycho head-trip—and me—altogether. He stands up and scratches. It's the most normal movement he's made in a long time.

My heart beats faster.

He takes his sweatshirt off and throws it down on the sand.

A light shower begins that mists my face with warm drops of water. They taste like salt. A dark monstrous-looking cloud bank looms out to sea, lit by the bluish full moon. The front looks hundreds of miles long and as thick as oil.

I imagine Clay's dragon tattoo protecting us from the powerful forces of the tropical storm, but I know it won't.

He walks farther into the churning water with the elegance of jazz, jumping over crashing surf.

I stand up on a huge rock and watch him.

He walks deeper into the sea. The shifting water reaches his nipples and embraces his chest. He dives into a rounded swell and comes up in the face of increasingly brutal sets. They smack into him with their full power.

I run to the water's edge. The waves are loud and furious. I want to dive in and help him, but I'm too scared. I'd be a useless handicap anyway. I feel helpless. I have to find help. I look around frantically.

The Australian surfers' boards are leaning against a coconut tree in the sand.

I run over to them, a hundred yards away.

They sit around like wise soothsayers and sip their beers casually, as if nothing horrible's happening. Their plump bellies and worked-out bodies disgust me. They're gluttonous and arrogant and lazy.

I sneak back to the coconut tree, steal a short surfboard, and run off with it. I run to Anar, awkwardly dragging the heavy board under my arm. The tail fins make grooves in the sand. I drop it and duck down to look in his tent.

He's lying down. His long, sinewy back is curved in a gentle crescent.

For a split second, I want to cuddle with him and let Clay walk into the sea as far as he wants to go. "Anar!" Feelings of lust and guilt and fear rush through my veins. "You have to help me!"

He sits up and I see his flat chest muscles straining. "Fuck off. Are you insane?"

"Clay's in trouble. He's in the ocean. He's getting so far I can barely see him. I'm afraid he's not gonna come back." Tears spill out of my eyes and make my vision blurry.

He gets up, ducks out the door, and looks to the ocean. He grabs the board under his arm, runs into the water, and paddles out through the violent waves.

I stand on the shore, scared as shit, relying on someone I just exploited to rescue someone I just fucked over. I was following my heart, I thought, and now I've sent two people I love into violent water to save each other. I stand there, useless. I feel like I'm watching television. I can see the problem, but I can't do anything about it. Saline mist burns my eyes and makes the tears come out even faster. I lose sight of them. There's only black, rushing water.

Clay is killing himself.

I am dry and still. My brain forms figures and shapes out of the patterns of rushing water. The clouds part from the moon, and I see millions of subtly different colors from azure blue reflective surfaces to white fizzy bubbles to deep green waves. I wonder if my brain is fooling me into seeing these colors—like some gland designed to handle death and heavy stress is making me trip.

I imagine Clay sucking water into his lungs.

He must be devastated if he's willing to have spent his whole life surfing, staying on top of the waves, and he now wants to die underneath them.

I twist around. There are a couple lingering campfires slowly being extinguished by the tropical shower.

Everyone on the beach is having too much fun hanging out and talking to notice what's going on. To them, I must look like some worried kid watching the ocean, hoping for something to happen.

"Sam!" Anar's voice barely resonates over the waves. "Sam!"

I run into the water, up to my balls. The waves crash over my head. The water burns the inside of my nose. I get knocked over and twisted around underwater. I'm gonna drown too. I gasp for air and inhale tons of water, then come up coughing. Another wave comes towering over me. I aim for the beach. I crash on the sand, out of breath, sand coating my back and scalp. I feel its gritty texture in my mouth. I cough up water that's warm from my lungs and stomach. I see Anar hanging on the back of the surfboard.

He pushes the board over a monster wave. He bobs way up in the crest of the wave and the board almost flips in the surf. The riptide sucks out and Anar kicks hard and shoves the board onto the beach. The fin snaps off. The surface of the board is coated with wax so the water beads up.

Clay's lying on top like a corpse, not moving.

"Clay?" Anar leans down to feel if he's breathing. "Fuck!"

He looks up at me, cowering above the wreckage of Clay's limp body, like, *Look what you've done.* He looks pissed off and scared for me at the same time.

"Clay?" I lean down.

He doesn't respond.

My ears pop and a shrill high-pitched buzz infiltrates my head. Big, warm raindrops increase. I see them, but I can't feel them because my mind is shut down. There's loud vague noise, like the sky is screaming.

Clay looks dead.

Anar and I stare at him, paralyzed.

"Oh, my God." Anar leans down and cocks Clay's head back and pushes on his chest. "Luna! Come here!" he screams toward his sister's tent.

I don't like the look of his hands on Clay, but I don't know where else to look. I'm scared to see a sign of death on Clay's skin. I'm afraid I'll see it turn gray and dead. I can't touch him because he might be cold.

"Luna! Hurry!" Anar rubs Clay's chest in quick, bird-like strokes.

His sister runs up with a serious, almost professional look on her face. She's wearing her bikini bottom and no top. Her breasts have probably never seen this side of her. "What's going on?"

"He drowned. He was…" I point to the ocean, which crashes dangerously close.

She crouches next to him and puts her ear to his chest and places her finger on his throat. One breast rubs his ribs. Her skills look desperate and deliberate. The economy and precision of her movements scare me. She's touching him like a patient. "He's not breathing," she bluntly announces, as if talking to a doctor. Panic takes over her expression. "Okay," she says, as if willing herself to remember the CPR class she passed because she slept with the T.A.

"Oh, fuck," I say without thinking. "Do something!"

She pushes his chest with severe movements that look too hard and violent. "Come on! Come on, breathe! One and two and three…"

She pushes her lips into his and blows a big breath in his mouth that makes his cheeks puff out. She pushes his chest and counts off again, fifteen times in a row. Her movements are quick and exaggerated. Her breasts joggle wildly. It looks like they're fucking in some weird porno, but with all my emotions caught up inside of it. She counts and pushes and blows and checks.

"Get the fuck off of him!" I scream.

Anar looks at me, shocked. A flash of realization runs through his face.

I can't look at him. All I feel is guilt.

He holds me in his arms and pulls my head close to him, like a wrestling move. He squeezes me pretty hard, almost too hard, like he's devastated he had to see me defend Clay.

I feel passion and comfort and anger in his arms. I can hear his shallow breathing in my ear. The pressure feels good on my shoulders. I want him to squeeze even harder. I deserve to be squeezed to death. I can't hear. All I see are blurry snapshots: Clay's ribs. Anar's sister's hair covering Clay's face, her mouth announcing numbers. Anar's hands rubbing together. The hairs on Clay's calf. The sand coating the edge of the black leash attached to the waxy, cream-colored surfboard. Flames painted on the board sticking out from under Clay's armpit. The reflection of fire in Anar's eyes.

19

Bamboo shoots
moving in—shooting up,
through the floor.

Clay wrenches up, his knees forcing up to his chest. His stomach muscles flex and he takes a huge gulp of air and coughs and gags. Water shoots out of his mouth at Anar's sister's face. He opens his eyes.

I jerk away from Anar before Clay can look at me.

Luna wipes her eyes and resumes her professional act. "How do you feel? " She wipes his forehead with the side of her hand.

"Dizzy…" Clay keeps coughing.

"Cough it up. That's right. Come on."

This girl is starting to annoy me. What is it with nurses? She should leave us alone so we can have our big tear-filled moment of survival. So I can say, "Thank God you're okay. I love you forever. Let's ditch these weirdos and do it." We should be able to stare longingly into each other's eyes till we get boners. I want to talk to him. I want to tell him that I'm going crazy and that I love him more than I thought possible—that the thought of him dying is unbearable to me—that I never want to leave his side again, but Anar is monitoring me like a doctor studying an X-ray for a cracked bone.

"You need to rest," Luna says to Clay. She stands up, her boobs bouncing, and looks at Anar and me. "Take him to his tent. Use the surfboard as a stretcher."

I take the end with his feet, because I don't want to look into his eyes till we're alone together. Luna walks beside us, watching Clay like she's his lover or something sick like that. She holds her hand over his heart while we carry him over the sand.

I jerk my end of the surfboard stretcher away from her, pretending I lost my balance for a second. Her hand scrapes along Clay's chest and falls off to her side. "Careful!" she scolds.

Clay lies back with his eyes closed, taking deep breaths that make his chest expand. He's being dramatic. He likes being argued over and feeling the attention from the girl, and he likes being carried over the sand like a young prince on his royal surfboard. "I feel like I'm floating. There's so many stars."

What's he talking about? I grab his foot softly, so he'll feel like I'm taking care of him, that I'm making it possible for him to feel important and cared for.

Anar glares at me disapprovingly, then stares at Clay's lower stomach, just above the waistband of his shorts, which hang low on his hips, to show he is trying to piss me off.

"Stop it!"

"I saved him."

Luna gives me a mean look. "You guys, shut up!"

We set the surfboard down on the sand, and I drag Clay by his armpits into the tent.

Luna rushes around and supports his neck with her hands, as if he just broke his spine or something.

A heavier shower starts up, and rain pours down in thick sheets.

Anar follow us into the tent and we all sit like Indians around Clay, who's lying spread out and shirtless on his brown plaid sleeping bag.

Luna fusses with him. She rolls up my sleeping bag to make a pillow and dries him with a T-shirt.

Clay sits up and takes a deep breath. "I'm fine. Don't worry about it."

I can see a smirk behind his innocent expression.

I won't be surprised if he falls back, unconscious, with his hand over his forehead, like an old-time movie star.

"Lie down. I need to check you out. I'm Luna, by the way. It's nice to meet you, even though the circumstances are pretty trippy." She sounds flirty. *What a slut, taking advantage of the sick and needy. It must run in their stupid Maui hippie family.*

He lies back, always receptive and willing to be flirted with. "I'm Clay." He smiles.

She puts her hand on his neck and watches her dumb waterproof watch, counting. I don't like her making Clay into numbers and charts. "You seem okay. I'm gonna stay and watch you for a while. I've seen a stable patient go into a coma with barely any notice." She laughs. "I guess I shouldn't have said that. Anar, can you get Clay some water?" She looks at me. "For some reason, near-drowning victims are usually dehydrated when they're revived." Her tone is emotionless when she talks to me, compared to her tone with Clay, which is embellished with all the girliness she can muster.

Anar comes in with a fresh bottle of spring water and presents it to Clay like a waiter. "Here you go, man. Drink some of this." He rests the bottle on Clay's chest. What a kiss-ass.

"Thanks."

I grab the bottle out of Anar's hand and give it to Clay.

He leans his head up and takes a big masculine drink. His throat pumps and throbs as the water goes down his esophagus.

Anar watches Clay drink. He makes sure Clay notices him by leaning over him with an earnest look on his face. He's trying to steal Clay's attention away from me. This is a fucking conspiracy. He shoots me a deceitful look.

Clay's still mine, even if I did cause his near-death and Anar and Luna rescued him.

He probably doesn't trust me at all.

I didn't save him.

That might have been the test he set up. He might have thought to himself, *If Sam doesn't save me, it's over.* I can't take anymore of this bullshit.

"You did a good job, Anar. I'm impressed." Luna talks like a proud teacher or parent of a ten-year-old who got an A on his stupid spelling test.

Anar smiles and glows at her approval. "Clay's been up at the drum circle in Haleakala. He knows Maui."

"I bet we've seen each other there before." Her eyes wander over Clay's torso and dwell around his belly button to his crotch. "How long have you been surfing? You must have some pretty strong lungs." She rubs his stomach and up to his chest and looks at her watch, like she's making medical calculations, but she's faking it. She just wants to touch him.

"Ten years, about. Yeah, I think they're pretty strong. Big wave surfing takes pretty good lung capacity." He squirms, yawns, and smiles, like he's getting off on her fussing over him. "You'd know from those Maui rips. Jaws takes some lung power."

What the fuck? I can't watch this. It's got to stop.

"Hey, nurse. Could you take a look at my arm? I think I fucked it up in the surf. My elbow's killing me."

"I think Clay's situation is a bit worse right now. I'll look at it tomorrow, but that's not my field of study." She answers me in a bitchy tone, like she can't believe I had the balls to complain about one of my tiny problems around Clay, who was unconscious for minutes, basically dead.

I hate myself. I lean over Clay's face. "How are you feeling?" I whisper.

"Tired, a little dizzy. I feel pretty good, considering—"

She cuts him off, to keep his attention away from me. "That's normal. Keep drinking. And breathe deeply." She pushes a little on his diaphragm. "Does that hurt?"

Anar gives me a mean look. "He could be better."

"You could shut the fuck up. You don't have anything to do with this...hippie boy."

"Oh, yeah. I only saved him." He looks at Clay for a reaction.

Clay arches up, with a look of disbelief. "You brought me in? Fuck, man. I don't know what to say. Come here."

Anar crawls over to him, and Clay embraces him, unabashedly and fully.

"Thank you so much, man. I really can't say enough, brother."

"No worries, bro. You're worth risking my life for any day."

"Get the fuck off of him." I crawl over and try to pull Anar's hands off Clay's back.

"What's your problem?" Luna looks at me like I'm crazy.

"Sam, what's up?" Clay lets go of Anar.

"Don't you see what's going on here?" I say, and Anar fakes a dramatic look of outrage.

Luna takes charge. "He needs to be relaxed, not stressed. He almost died. I hate to take control here, but I am the only trained medical practitioner." She sounds strong and professional, like she has to say this sort of thing all the time to freaked-out patients' friends and family.

"But, it's my tent."

Clay looks at me. "No it isn't. It's my tent." He's turning against me. "Let them stay. They're taking care of me." Clay turns on his side and covers his head with the sleeping bag. "I'm tired... dreamy."

Dreamy? I lean close to Anar. "Come on, man. Please?"

Anar leans over and presses his lips to my ear. "He's *mine*."

This kid's a sadistic motherfucker. I did it with a psychopath. He has evil plans in the works. He stands up and holds the door flap open. "Come on, Luna. We should let Clay sleep."

She longingly looks at Clay and follows Anar out, with hesitation. "I'll be right over there in the rose-colored tent. Call for me if you need to." How can this stoned, naked girl act professional with any degree of seriousness? Her tits look like torpedoes.

Clay smiles, then rolls over and closes his eyes.

The heat from Clay's wet body is making the tent hot and stuffy, and it smells like the ocean. I examine his skin for damage. "Clay?" I whisper in his ear.

He moans, asleep.

I touch the smooth skin on his upper arm. It's cold and damp. Little blond hairs on his chest, barely visible, stick up, like he has chills. The air in the tent has an electric buzz. I roll him over. His arm flops above his head, exposing his armpit. I'm terrified to really look at him, but I have to. I'm picturing a big gash or wide bloody cut on the back of his head, with his cranium exposed, his brains leaking out. There has to be something wrong with him.

He acted too normal after trying to kill himself.

I lean down and smell his armpit as deeply as I can. There's just a tiny remnant of his musky scent mixed with saltwater and surf-board wax. Maybe it's a little different. I try to remember him lying in his bed, surrounded by his dirty clothes. He smells sharper or something. I rub his arm, over his tattoo. The ink of his dragon looks darker in the flickering glow of the burning kerosene wick. The dragon's arched back perfectly follows the intersection of his bicep and shoulder muscle, like he was born with it on his arm.

He's not tough and untouchable-looking, like he usually is. It's obvious in the soft curve of his lips. His cheeks are flushed. Salt crystals make his eyelashes sparkle.

I lift his head. I trace his eyebrows and down his sunburned nose, with my finger. I touch my lips to his and suck in his exhalation, which tastes like sweet pepper. I look down his torso, from the perspective he sees.

His dick swells in his blue surf shorts. I guess his body's all right. His dick's working perfectly and mysteriously, like always.

I scoot under him and rest his head on my lap. Big drops of rain fall on the roof of the tent in random patterns. I stare at his sleeping face and imagine the sky above. I hold my hands together, like people do when they pray. I stare at the tent ceiling.

Please, clouds, raindrops, winds, try to help Clay forgive me. Please give him the strength to recover and learn to love me the way I love him.

Lightning strikes, followed by ground-shaking, deep, roaring thunder.

It's nature's way of saying go fuck yourself.

His head thrashes around in my lap and squishes my balls into my leg.

"Yeah! Oh! Yeah."

Is he dreaming of a dark-skinned stoic Hawaiian with a lei around his neck, or a blond bikini girl with a suntan? His arms flex, causing the veins to stick out. His legs make a paddling movement.

I almost want to call the nurse over, but I know she'll take control and Anar will follow her in. He'll sabotage my good intentions by making me look evil.

I can fix this. I slide my hands down his torso, into his shorts.

He stops convulsing. His dick is hard and damp, pointing toward his stomach. I cup his balls, pull his shorts down below them, and start beating him off. I don't know if he's really asleep and he feels like he's having a wet dream, or if he's awake and likes it. Touching him feels different than I remember. I'm not used to seeing him respond to my touch so openly. I hope he wakes up and tells me he loves me and asks me if I want to move into his room with him. I have to test him, say something that he couldn't sleep through. "Clay? All your friends know about you and me and what we do with each other."

He does nothing. He's asleep.

I jerk him off faster.

His dick rises up in a strong pulse, and he shoots onto his stomach, like ink thrown on rice paper to make Japanese characters.

He came for me. No one can take him away.

I pull my shorts down and get out my dick and hold it in my hand. *This boner is from him,* I think. *He gave it to me.*

I rub his chest. His heart flutters. Three quick beats in a row. *Oh, my God. I fucked him up by jerking him off. I overexcited his heart.*

I use my left hand to beat off, which is difficult, because I'm right-handed. I like it because it feels more like someone is doing it to me. I rub Clay's thigh and down his leg, and I'm done in seconds.

He twitches, rolls over, opens his eyes, and sits up.

I pull my shorts up as fast as I can and push them into my crotch to wipe up the mess.

"Could you get me a beer?" he asks.

I feel, for a second, like I was dreaming this whole thing and I just woke up. "Uhh…sure, I guess. Hold on." I get up and duck outside and walk past the other tents. They're lit from within by flickering lanterns.

I try to get a good look inside Anar's tent. I see his sister reading tarot cards for her friend, whose legs are sunburned and plump, like turkey that's been roasting for hours.

I stand outside the Australians' tent, perfecting a look that isn't scared or nervous or weird or like the psycho-queer poetry-boy I really am. I relax my mouth and let the tension out of my shoulders. "Hey. What's up?" I practice. I peek in. It's warm, inviting, and cozy compared to the dark, gray, and confusing environment of our dreary tent.

They're sitting Indian-style in a circle, smoking a joint under the yellow glow of a kerosene lantern. Their thick, tanned thighs are splayed out with half-full beers resting on their crotches. One guy looks up at me. "Eh, mate."

I can't compete with his gracious nature. "Hey," I almost say, but the sound hardly leaves my mouth. I feel damaged and tired. I have too many problems with people I already know to meet new people and exert any sort of social effort.

"You think I get a couple brews from you?"

"Cooler's outside."

The raindrops feel like bullets hitting my face. I stick my hand into the icy, slushy water and grab two beers. My hands sting and feel numb from the ice. I should go back in and say thanks, but I know I'll do it wrong, so I run back. This beer could be the last opportunity I ever get to do a favor for him, before he rejects me and tells me to go fuck myself.

Someone is running after me. The rain beans me in the eyes too hard to see clearly. I get a chill up my spine, scared of the spooky figure behind me.

"Sam!"

I ignore it.

"Sam!"

It's Anar. I stop and let him catch up with me.

"You didn't see me in there." He's smiling.

"See you in *where*?"

"Those Aussie guys' tent. I was sitting right there, and you didn't even notice me."

A couple hours ago I couldn't notice anyone but him. Weird.

"Oh…uh…what were you doing hanging out with *them*?"

"I went over to give 'em their board back, and then I just ended up hanging out. They're really cool. I told them the whole story. How I rescued Clay. They were pretty impressed."

He's using my boyfriend's near-death, triggered by our jerking off together, to get cool points with some dumb jocks. What an asshole. "Why should they know?" I snap.

"You stole the guy's board. *You're* obviously not a surfer. It's an old limited-edition handmade board that he's had since he was sixteen in Perth. One of the first short boards ever made, and you broke the fin off. What was I supposed to do, just tell him he should live with it?"

I look away. A couple is fucking in the surf, right out in the open, in the rain. "They're assholes. Who cares?"

"I do, and they're not assholes. A couple of those guys have been around the world."

"Yeah, and I bet they told you all about it while you sat there like an admiring little brother."

"Sounds like you with Clay," he says.

"Fuck off, dude. He almost died! Hippie…" I walk away. A girl with flowers and peace signs painted on her cheeks with glow-in-the-dark green paint runs past me, topless in the pouring rain.

"I saved him," Anar calls out. "You owe me."

I keep on walking and leave him standing there. Outside our tent, I pause to readjust my face. I can't look pissed off from my argument with Anar, and I can't still seem cool-acting from having to deal with the surfers. All I can manage is a bland sadness.

I duck into the tent, wet and pathetic.

He's sitting up like he just went to a movie and dinner, completely normal.

"Clay?"

"Yeah."

I begin to cry. I didn't feel it coming. The tears just flowed out. "I'm scared. I'm so sorry. I love you. I can't stand the thought of being without you."

"Do you know what just happened to me?" He acts like he didn't hear me. His face shines like he's in a cult. "I died and came back. It was so amazing. There was *real* peace. It was calm. No one around." His voice is full of wonder and naïveté, like he's amazed how words sound coming off his tongue. "There were fish, and glowing rays. The current was stronger than I've ever felt. Can you imagine the way true peace feels? Tranquility amid violence?"

What the fuck? Hippie-boy speak?

"Do you feel all right?" I wrap his flannel sleeping bag around him, and he pulls it up to his neck and tucks it under his chin like a little boy.

"I'm sorry, Clay. I fucked up. I hate Anar."

"You look so cute," he says dreamily. "I can't believe how cool you look. You're like a mystic sea-boy." He looks at me like I'm a swirling psychedelic poster and he's tripping. Something's not connecting in his head.

"Where's that guy?" he says.

"I don't know," I say. "Asleep, I guess."

"I feel good. Really good. I don't know…yeah, like…really awesome-good." He turns over and takes a sip of beer. "You can't just ignore him, you know. He's full of light. It would be cruel to blind yourself of his aura. He's a powerful being."

"OK…"

"You learned all your bad qualities from me. Take solace."

I can't keep my hands still. I feel cornered, weirded-out, guilty, embarrassed, and worried. This is really confusing. *Yell at me. Punch me in the eye. Be the macho surfer-boy I knew before.*

Guys out on the beach chant in Hawaiian. "*E ulu I ka lani, e ulu I ka honua, e ulu I ka pae aina o Hawai'i.*" It's louder than the wind and rain.

"I bet you wanna escape right now. Don't deny your feelings. Run away if it feels right."

Fuck. He's the anti-Clay. I want to scream: *Leave me alone, you demonic alter ego!*

He closes his eyes, like he's thinking about something that makes him happy. I'm not sure if I'm imagining his expression or if it's really there. There's only this flickering kerosene lantern to see by.

I ask him: "Why'd you go into the ocean?"

"You know." He rests his head back on his arms.

A sharp chill runs up my spine. The lantern is blown out by a strangely cold gust of wind that felt like it came straight from the Arctic.

"Something was in the water, Sam. This feeling. It's like I *understand.*"

"Understand what?" I try to light my lighter. I keep flicking it, but it just hurts my thumb.

"I know why you did that with Anar. I know how the world works..."

My lighter lights like magic. It burns really bright for a few seconds. "Oh." I'm too stunned and scared to say anything else.

"You thought it would make everything better," he says. "I don't blame you."

"You should. I was acting just like I accused Tammy of being."

Clay looks at me. "It's different. You have good intentions. Tammy's just insecure about me. She caught me jerking off to a picture of you." He looks amused. His eyes follow my hands and my every movement, while I shift my legs and adjust my T-shirt to get more comfortable.

I sit helpless in the face of my own creation.

He's everything I wanted him to be.

I hate him. I ruined him. My thoughts changed reality. I feel like we're in a different dimension. I should have kept my thoughts to myself. I want his arrogance back, his tough-boy charm. I should have left him alone. A roar coming from the ocean builds. I'm scared. The earth is coming to get me.

Down the beach, people yell and howl like animals. The rain pours down even harder.

I look out the tent door and see silhouettes in the rain.

The ghosts from the '60s have come alive to antagonize us.

I let my eyes focus and adjust to the darkness.

Girls throw off their bikini tops and drop their bottoms on the sand. The suits look like jellyfish washed up on shore. Boys fling their shirts off and jump out of their shorts. The color of skin replaces the colors of flower-printed fabrics.

A guy flexes his thick white thighs, like in a tribal dance. Two girls run by, naked. One carries a dead fish in her hand.

A man with a fire torch, burning bright despite the rain, dances, then throws it as far as he can, leaving a fiery trail in the sky. Another thin blond guy jumps around. His dick is halfway to a boner as he watches naked girls run past him.

A tall girl with long black hair like Pele's masturbates in the surf with her back arched dramatically.

A couple has sex in the surf. They're painted with warrior body paint. The girl rides him on top, with her arms flexed, like a body-builder's. The guy moans and pushes into her as hard as he can.

Clay and I are doomed. Someone or something out there sees our inevitable demise. I zip up the tent door, leaving only a small-screened window to look through.

A strong wind picks up. The tent would fly away if we weren't inside. This storm could cut us off from the world by covering the tall mountains in orange, slippery, impassable mud.

Clay won't be able to fend for himself in his new weakened state. He'll starve.

"Let's go outside!" he says like a little boy, as he sits up with a hopeful expression.

I look out the window flap, half-expecting some guy to be out there casting a spell on our tent, an explanation for Clay's burst of energy.

He moves up beside me and looks intently out the window. "Come on."

"No. You have to rest. You don't know what you're saying. Something happened to you…"

He looks at me, confused.

Chanting echoes off the cliff walls. Primal pond scum is organizing and forming multicellular creatures right before my eyes. The world is rebeginning. I don't believe in God, but this is an awful lot like what those Christian freaks said would happen in the year 2000.

I need to calm down. I light the lantern with my HANG LOOSE HAWAII lighter and look into Clay's eyes.

He looks back at me romantically. His eyes reflect the lantern's glow.

"Stay here," I say forcefully, then I run over to Anar's tent.

A tan muscular guy runs past me, calling out Hawaiian words, like a tribal chief. Tea leaves tied around his biceps and red lines painted on his body accentuate his muscles. He looks like a warrior.

A naked girl runs toward me. She turns quickly, to avoid a collision. Her long, black hair slaps me in the face, stinging my eyes. Then she runs away like a maniac.

Primitive-looking fire torches burn fiercely in a grass hut that's probably been here since the '60s. Hawaiian guys with green leafy leis lying on their shoulders stand around in a semicircle, flexing their chests, calling out chants in scratchy, guttural Hawaiian, like they're preparing for a sacrifice.

I feel like when I was a kid running down a dark hallway, imagining a murderer running up behind me. I lean down and peek inside Anar's tent. Dark-red candles are burning. I don't know where the hell they came from.

They look up at me. Anar lies on his stomach, in his shorts, and his sister and her blonde friend sit Indian-style, playing hangman on a piece of crinkled notebook paper.

Anar smiles. "Hi, Sam." He sits up and reaches to his feet, doing some tai chi stretch.

I sit down next to him. "Clay's acting really strange. I think something might be wrong with him."

"How's he acting?" Luna asks with a professional tone in her voice.

"I'm not sure how to put it," I say. "He's just not himself."

"Is he mumbling, having trouble breathing?" prods Luna.

"No, he's talking normal. It's what he's talking *about*."

She thinks for a moment. "I've dealt with a lot of near-drowning victims…tourists trying to swim at Jaws, getting caught by riptides. Sometimes they're in a degree of shock for days. It's not unusual to be out of it, lethargic, tired. He may seem dull or even dumb. The brain needs time to recover."

I don't want to tell them this, but I have to get Clay back. "He says he *understands*."

"Understands what?" Anar interrupts.

"*Understands*. Like, everything…people, life…"

Luna's friend sits up and acts interested, even though she was in a pot-induced nap during the tragedy. "Maybe, he, like, saw the other side."

I get a chill. I hope not.

Clay bursts into the tent. His bare chest drips with big, clear drops of water. He looks shiny and clean and magically vibrant. His skin glows with health. He looks at Luna, then her friend, then Anar, then his eyes stop on me.

I can't have eye contact with him in front of these freaks. I look at Anar, then at his sister. I close my eyes. I can't find a place to look that doesn't have some sort of meaning. I look at the tent door, through Clay's legs.

He tilts his head sideways. "What's up?" he asks like he wants to party.

I want out of here. I get up and duck out the door. "Come on, Clay."

He follows me out, runs behind me, and tackles me onto the sand.

I fall sideways with him on top of me into the wet sand. The tiny grains stick to my skin. My arms look like a sand monster's, covered with tiny, round jewel-like pebbles. It's like the whole universe is sticking to me. Each grain of sand is different. Infinite possibilities of color and size and shape.

He lies on top of me and breathes into my ear. The drawn-out pulses of air feel like they're penetrating me, calming my tense muscles and spine, making me go limp. It feels like good drugs.

My body makes an indentation in the sand.

Clay rolls off me and I roll over next to him.

Seawater rushes in and fills the mold of me. I'm water—salty, buoyant, cleansing, with the ability to disguise and dilute small amounts of pollution. I could harbor animals that glow in the dark and have more tentacles than octopuses, and fish the color of fire. I could flow according to moon phases and tidal rhythms, and I could build up into waves for dolphins and surfers to catch.

Clay opens his eyes and looks up into the rain. He looks at my face, like he's looking into a mirror. "Wanna go?" he asks.

"Yeah, I wanna go, but I'm not sure we should. We have to stay here till this is figured out. Don't we?"

"Oh, Sam," he says. "I love you."

I can't even fathom that he said that. I want to hurl, but I haven't eaten anything all day. "You're acting really weird. I can't handle this."

He giggles. "I know. I love you."

I sit up and look at him to see if he's being sarcastic. His skin looks baby blue. He asks me, "Think you'll be okay getting back by yourself?"

I look up to the sky to find the North Star. "Why? Where are *you* going?"

A light sprinkle starts.

"I have to find out where I went when I was underwater."

"I *know* where you went. Underwater. It's not that complicated."

"I think I was an animal, like a seal or maybe a whale."

Just the mention of a whale makes me think of the lame '70s when everyone was painting those creepy murals on every building. Huge paintings of whales and dolphins diving through perfect waves with planets and moons and unicorns and rainbows above them. "A whale? Dude, you almost drowned. If you were a whale, you could have used your blowhole."

He just looks at me, wondering why I would say such a stupid thing. "I'm going on a vision quest," he proudly announces.

"What's that—a Nintendo game?"

"Don't be so sarcastic."

"I'm not."

"Yes, you are. You're all defensive."

I hate this trap. "OK, what's a vision quest?"

He sits up, as if he'll think clearer looking out to sea. "It's a Native American journey that every boy takes once before being accepted into his pueblo as a man. He takes peyote, then walks alone into the wilderness to learn about himself and his place in the order of things. Also, you learn to identify with an animal that rules your spirit. You find out where you came from, and maybe where you're headed. But I'll just get high."

I hide my smirk with my hand. My fingers smell like Clay's dick. "How do you know about this?" If he says, "There's a lot you don't know about me," I'll freak out.

"I read about it when I was taking classes at Pacific."

"Oh, I see. Community college wisdom." I burst out laughing at the thought of him with eye paint and feathers on his head.

"If you're gonna be judgmental, then I shouldn't have even told you."

"You're fucking crazy. Do you even know what you're saying? What's your name? Do you even know your name?"

"Don't doubt me now. I'm Clay. The one with fire in his eyes."

I can't deal with this. I want to run away into the woods, but I don't know where to go and I'd get scared. It's only one more night. That's all I have to handle.

He'll be back to normal when he comes back. He has to be.

I don't know what I'll do if he isn't. *I can do this. Breathe.* "When are you going?"

"Morning, I guess."

"You don't sound very sure."

"I'm sure." He squeezes my shoulder firmly and smiles like a brainwashed lunatic.

Maybe it's Clay that caused the craziness on the beach. Then he walks slowly to the tent.

I follow. There's nowhere else to go.

The lantern burns dimly in the tent. Our shapes are indented in the sleeping bags, like ghosts of him and me had just been lying there, through all that went on, molding to each other, sharing warmth and love.

Part Three

20

*Don't understand
this summer, plumeria
won't share his colors.*

I wake up. I feel like total shit. My head is pounding. This is a
bad sign, but it's stupid to try to read anything into a hangover.

Clay leans against his backpack looking out to sea, his golden
brown back absorbing the warmth of the sun. His dragon tattoo
watches me and tells him I'm awake. He turns his head. "How do
you feel, little Sammy?"

"Like shit. You?"

"Promising."

I want to groan. "You still going?"

"Yup. But there's something I want to do first. A ritual with
you." He ducks into the tent and comes out holding a Swiss Army
knife. He balances the blade gently on his leg.

I stare at the sharp metal, gleaming in the sunlight, but my
view gets drawn up the legs of his surf shorts, where his skin is
whiter and more naked-looking.

He twists his arm around awkwardly to look at his shoulder
and tattoo, a slender dragon clutching an empty ball in its men-
acing claws. He points to the circle and traces it sensually.
"Here's where your name is going. I've been saving this spot
since I was fifteen." He spits on the blade and rubs it on his

shorts till it shines. "Hand me a lighter?"

I hand him my green lighter. On its side, there's a white outline of a hand signing "Hang loose."

He holds the flame on the blade for a minute and then he grabs an expensive-looking pen, with CLAY ANDERSON—PIPELINE JUNIOR SURFING CHAMPION engraved on it, and unscrews the cap and pours some drops of black ink over his tattoo. He dabs it off with a balled-up sock and picks up the knife and places the tip of the blade on his skin. His movements are ritualistic and steady, like he's a shaman about to exorcise an evil spirit or cure me of a century-long hex. He bites his bottom lip and slices a letter "S" in the left side of the ball.

My stomach clenches up. I imagine the sharp burning and freezing sensations on his skin.

He shouldn't be doing this. When his brain resumes its normal arrogant rhythms, he'll regret this. He'll blame me for this scratched in, amateurish cutout in the middle of his beautifully blank tattoo. His face turns red and the veins in his temple stick out. His arm muscles tense up, making his forearm look like the arms of old sculptures of the great warrior Kamehameha. He moves to the "A" quickly, without breathing, and then slices three out of four lines of the "M". Blood drips down his arm. He looks like an injured soldier. "Here. Finish it." He presents the knife to me like it's a royal staff.

I don't want to be blamed for this.

If he ever comes back, my name will be proof that he was out of his mind, and if he stays the hippie he is now, I don't want my name on his arm anyway. I still have a chance to make it say something besides Sam. I can change the three lines of the "M" to an "N" and add an "E" and make it say SANE; although that's definitely not the case, it sounds tough.

Guys he knows would get tattoos that say SANE on the back of their necks in Old English script or Polynesian tiki letters.

I couldn't squeeze in SANCTIFY, but that sounds pretty gnarly too. I wipe the blade on my shorts and it makes a thin red line of blood on the fabric. I hold his shoulder, slippery from his sweat, and take a deep breath. I push the blade on his skin till it pierces through with a slight pop and carefully slice that last line of the "M".

He looks down at it and mouths, "Sam."

It looks sort of cool, with thin blood trails on the letters. It's about as punk rock as anything I've ever seen. I'd really love it if he told a dick joke or I saw some of his obsessive self-conscious bull-shit right now, or a fake-tough look, or a moment where I wasn't sure if he wanted to hit me or kiss me. This straight-out "I love you" crap is unsatisfying—and it's all I ever wanted from him.

"OK, man. It's official."

I don't know what's official, but I smile at him. I dab his cuts, and my name imprints smeared blood letters on the white sock. The black ink settles in the cuts, becoming permanent as I wipe the excess blood away. I secretly lick a little off my finger. It tastes strong, like iron.

He grabs me and kisses me, forcing his lips into mine. The taste of the iron-filled blood penetrates my mouth. His stubble scrapes my chin.

I get a boner immediately and feel a rush of confusion. I don't want the new Clay to turn me on.

"I love you." I had to say it.

"I love you too, my mystic sea-boy. Here's my truck keys. I'll see you when my animal spirit asks to come back. Maybe in a couple days, maybe more." He abruptly stands up, grabs his bag, and walks away, like a superhero who's just saved lives, with a slight limp and heavy, thoughtful breaths.

I stand up. "Aren't you going to take anything?"

"Gonna live off the land." He salutes and disappears into the forest.

I'll remember him like this forever. It's one of those moments that I can already be sentimental about, like seeing a son grow to be a man or sending a boy off to war, knowing he might not come back. I hope he doesn't get an infection from my name. My stomach growls—which comforts me in a weird way, as if it's saying "Life goes on."

I take the bendable plastic rods out of the tent and the green nylon falls.

A tiny bright-green gecko runs out from under it.

I guess he saw the whole thing between us. I wish I could ask him for advice from his perspective. Clay's "I love you" meant nothing, since he's not himself. It had no more importance than hearing a prerecorded message on an answering machine.

Anar steps out of his tent, rubbing sleep from his eyes. He couldn't have worse timing.

I sit by myself on the sand, feeling empty, next to a collapsed tent and mess of strewn wet clothes, sleeping bags, and camping equipment. I look like the model for the "fallen from grace" catalog.

He must love seeing me so pathetic.

I'm giving him something by sitting here. In the folds of the tattered-looking, discarded-halfway-through-the-job tent are expressions of my desperation and anxiety. My foot taps relentlessly and sweat runs down my sides. My head pounds and my mouth is dry. I secretly watch Anar's delicate-looking feet dig into the sand as he stretches. The sunlight on his skin gives him an angelic quality. His calf muscles flex, then release. The lines sewn on the shorts accentuate his hipbones and the thickening of his upper legs. They make him look more masculine.

Don't talk to me. Don't talk to me. Don't talk to me.

"Hey, Sam. Beautiful morning, huh?"

"Yeah, I guess. If you're into sun."

"How's Clay?"

"He's fine."

"He seemed pretty out of it last night when he burst into the tent—something in his eyes."

"What do you care?" I say.

"Where'd he go? I saw him take off about a half-hour ago."

I look at Clay's footprints. "I'm catching up with him later."

"Yeah, sure."

"Listen, stupid. That's not going to work. You're just jealous."

A big, puffy cloud shades me, but Anar remains in the sun. I can see the dividing line between us.

"Hey"—he holds his hands up in front of him—"just reporting what I saw, man. He seemed pretty messed up to me. My sister said she was worried about him. She said she thinks he could have a brain malfunction."

"You're lying. Shut up. He's the same. He's better!" I'm lying. He's changed. He's horrible.

"You'll see." He runs out to the ocean and dives into a wave.

21

Lost boy soul
deep green jungle without
sympathy for him.

The shady green of the forest soothes my eyes and the cool, wet clay-mud trail feels good on my bare feet. I feel like I'm out on a safari or bird-watching expedition, except I'm looking for Clay, a rare species that can blend into natural environments as easily as a ghost. Maybe he's changed into his spirit animal already. A chameleon darts in front of me and up onto a big volcanic rock. That could be him.

I run up the trail, barely hanging on to the two backpacks that make my shoulders red and raw. I walk up a steep hill. I recognize a huge boulder on the top. It's the place where I stopped to watch Clay cry. I throw down the bags, take my shirt off, lie back, and watch the trees.

This is the place that I felt I won him over in a way, as if you can ever break a wild horse.

The tree branches stir loudly in the wind. I sit up and face the breeze so it dries me. I see where our campsite was. I scan the area and look for signs of us having been there. One of Clay's shirts hangs on a branch. He forgot it. A half-burnt log is still in the fire pit. There's no sign of the confusion I felt, the frustration and lust.

Amazingly, the site looks like anyone could have used it, from serial murderers on the lam to a happy couple who smoke lots of pot. This disappoints me. When we were there, it was important.

I start my walk back to the road to wait for the shuttle to the airport. I walk for hours and finally see the edge of the forest. It's bright and glaring after three days of no concrete.

The van pulls up almost magically.

I get in. "Hey."

The guy looks back. "Aloha, brah. Howzit?"

"Pretty weird, man." I stare out the window, the trees becoming blurs of green.

The plane ride makes me feel like I'm being pulled into another dimension. We land, and I run ahead of everyone down the aisle. I crave the familiar smells of Clay's truck. I stand up straight, breathe in the air, run to the parking lot, and find the car. I grab the key out of my pocket. There's another key on the ring—his house key, I guess—and there's a small locker-type key that probably unlocks the carport storage where he keeps his surfboards and BMX bike. I unlock the door and hop in. The interior smells like a mixture of the ocean, Clay's sweat, and dirt. I look through the grimy windshield and push his *Punk Rock '93* tape into the player. I pull out onto the road as the music starts.

It's a song called "You Don't Understand" that Clay sings to himself whenever he's pissed off or he thinks something is lame. I guess he wouldn't identify with it anymore. I take the long way home, out to the country and along the north shore, the Kamehameha Highway to Kaneohe.

Hawaiian kids wait at the bus stops, and boys holding surfboards under their arms skateboard by on the shoulder. Driving this pickup, I feel like I belong to this pack of wolves that roam these parts, the beaches where the best-shaped waves in the world arch over and fall into themselves at the last possible moment. Half-naked guys, with deep tans and bleached hair, wax their surfboards on the side of the road, on the open tailgates of their pickups. Some of them nod to me, like I'm one of them.

I didn't know it was so easy to be Clay—from a distance, anyway. I'm wearing his shorts. My skin's been tanned the same color as his. I've got his truck with his Etnies skateboard-shoe keychain hanging out of the ignition. I smell like him too. I feel free, cruising down the road, looking at people who think I'm like them.

The ocean looks as sparkly as diamonds and delicately blue, and the wind coming in the window is soft and moist. I pull into the Waimea Bay Beach parking lot, a place I would never have gone alone before, scared of being confronted by assholes. But now I'm comfortable, and the people look nice. It's my beach as much as it is theirs.

The occasional drift of stringy pot smoke rises into the air from the groups of people gathered in the picnic areas. I park the truck in an open space on the grass beside the full parking lot.

Two girls sit on the back tailgate of an old El Camino and three Hawaiian guys sit below them on the ground with their legs crossed. One is plump, jolly, and stoic at the same time, and the other two are slim, with their whole upper arms pattered with triangular Polynesian tattoo bands. One has long windblown hair covering half his face, making him look important and deep. They're playing small polished ukuleles. The most modern looking of the three, a skinny guy with a flower behind his ear, sings in Hawaiian. The staccato rhythm and exaggerated vowels sound cool and foreign. The sun lights them with a warm yellow glow. It's incredible to see such tough-looking guys, macho assholes, sit around and sing gentle and beautiful music, as soft as the ocean breeze.

I get out of the truck. Clay's surf shorts are long and blue with lighter blue waves, shaped like fire, down the sides. The sun makes the material shiny and accentuates the tanned color of my skin. I think my calves are a little more muscular from the hike, if it's possible that quickly, and my arms look more defined, with some veins sticking out like on Clay's arms. I walk down the row of cars and trucks, dangling and twirling the keychain, passing all kinds of people—pink tourists in teal sedans, local families with packed lunches and young kids, and groups of kids from my age to out of high school.

Guys with tight, flat chests come out of the bathroom changing area in flower-printed shorts and white puka shell necklaces. Mocha-colored girls come out of the other side of the shelter wearing bright bikinis.

I walk across the grassy picnic area onto the hot white sand.

Marines with dumb tattoos throw footballs around, happy to be in the hot sun, far away from their Midwestern homes.

The beach is wide and shaped like an open clamshell, sloping and rounded at the front of a half-oval shaped bay. Cliffs at the back are covered with trees that hide steep trails up to the road where people park when the lot's full.

At the far end of the beach is "the rock." That's what everybody who lives here calls it. It's a black peninsula, a sudden outcrop of jagged lava with a flat top. It rises fifty feet above the waves.

I walk down the beach past Japanese tourists. The combination of shadows and sunlit areas on my body make me look like Clay— with muscles and substance to my torso. I feel salty mist off the ocean, and it makes tiny transparent hairs on my chest stick together with minuscule white grains of salt. My eyes follow the almost invisible mist into the water below the looming rock. Lots of boogie-boarders are all squashed into what looks like water swirling in a cauldron.

I run into the water. It's as warm as piss and feels good on my skin, rinsing away the smelly sweat of two days of worrying and Clay almost dying and total complete panic and sex and work and hiking. I swim over to the rock, grab on to the sharp outcropping.

A big Hawaiian-Samoan kid I'd normally be terrified of boosts me up and I scramble up the rock.

A Vietnamese kid with a buzz-cut flies over me, holding his knees to his chest. He looks like a ball.

I reach the top and pull myself up.

It's packed from ledge to ledge with teenagers and big tattooed Hawaiian and Portuguese guys and pretty local tomboys with long black hair. All the colors of tan skin blend into one another, making a painting of golden browns and yellows. There's a NO JUMPING sign ignored by all and pools of saltwater in the cracks and crevasses of the sun-baked and foot-worn rock.

I feel like I've stepped into a stranger's living room. Everyone hangs out here, on the top of the rock, for hours at a time, talking, gossiping, screaming, kissing, and always, finally, jumping, but I never have.

"Try jump, brah," an older Hawaiian boy says to me, but he's distracted by his friend showing off with a triple flip into the water. "So, trow party?" The local guys always say that when they think someone's showing off.

I sit down on the rock and lie back to let the sun, mist, and drips of water rolling off the arms and chests and shaking heads of the wet jumpers clean and refresh me. I feel almost ecstatic watching my comrades. We're all trapped on this island together away from the world, and I actually feel all right about that now. I stare into the sky till I fall asleep.

Silence wakes me. The comforting sounds of chaos are gone. Me and the low sun are all that's left on top of the rock. I'm lying on a green palm-leaf-pattern beach towel that's not mine or Clay's.

I don't know where it came from. It smells like someone else's laundry. I guess someone left it for me, or didn't want to wake me to get it.

The sky has turned an electric blue with burnt-looking edges. The light has a buzz, like electric particles or spirits are flying around, getting ready to dash and hide for the night.

I get up and stretch.

Just a few people remain on the beach, flapping their towels, rinsing off sand in the showers. Three girls smoke a joint and watch the sunset.

I jump down off the rock and walk down the beach with the towel over my shoulder.

Surfers are gathered around the lifeguard stand, drinking beer, watching the light fade, and talking about girls or cars or waves. The lifeguard's the center of attention in the crowd—the pack leader whom they all look up to in some little boy sort of way.

I scale down the rock and walk past them and recognize a few from Steve's party.

"Hey, bro," a tough-looking black-haired guy says to me.

"Aloha." I nod and walk by him.

Clay's truck is the only car left in the lot. It stands out like a mohawked punk rocker alone in a mall, not concerned about much else other than himself.

I get inside and breathe in deeply.

The guys all look over at me and nod their heads. Maybe they recognize Clay's truck.

I'm sure they know him. I turn the parking lights on—the orange ones without the headlights—like all the cool Hawaii guys do at dusk, and the instrument panel lights up video game–orange. It makes the truck more fun to drive. I pull out onto the road and drive away.

I pass by fields of cartoon-looking banana trees, horse pastures, small towns with hard-to-say Hawaiian names like Kaaawa, with half closed-down shopping centers and poi factories. More beaches along the road—Shark's Cove, Pipeline, Sunset, an island shaped like a cone with a brim called "Chinaman's Hat." Houses light up as I drive past.

With Clay gone, I feel more complete. I don't want to go home. I already feel like I'm home in Clay's truck, and going to my real house will feel false and empty, and I'll get depressed. Maybe it's his life I've been in love with and not him.

22

An era is over
dead leaves drop; hard to find that
familiar maple.

I pull into Clay's driveway and hear Sharky barking from the backyard. I didn't even have to think to drive here. I catch a view of myself in the truck's side mirror and see a bit of uncertainty in my face. I squint my eyes, suck in my cheeks, and puff out my lips like a tough punk rocker. I hold my breath and turn off the engine. It rattles and makes some quirky metal clicks and adjustments while it cools.

The neighborhood is lit by odd dark-blue light. It's hard not to be seduced by it, but I have something I need to do.

I stare at the house. Low eaves shield it from the light. I jump out and slam the truck door.

I imagine Clay's spirit is watching me, possessing me, guiding me. I hold my stomach in, my shoulders back, and puff my chest out. I widen my stance and lower my center of gravity, like I'm standing on a surfboard riding a monster wave. I imitate Clay's conniving, smirky smile. "Hey, brah. How's da waves? Big rights out at Sunsets. Killer, brah." I reach out to the glass and touch my lips in the reflection. I do the complicated surfer handshake. I'm him. I nail it. "Eh, dude, howzit?" I watch my lips form the words.

I consider sneaking through his window, but he wouldn't do that. Sneaking around's more my style. I feel Clay begging me to use all the freedom and confidence he has.

I walk to the front door and hear movement somewhere in the house. I clear my throat and think of Clay. "Hey. I'm home." I hear my fake, deep voice bounce off the walls inside the house. Sharky runs up to me with his ears back, not barking. "Hey, boy." I lean down and pet him down his back.

Susan walks out from the hall with a smile on her face. "I thought I heard you two drive up."

I open the screen door and walk in. The house is all lit up and it smells clean and fresh. The dog-like scents of Clay have vanished. I replace them with my own dirty camping nature musk. I have to bring balance to the house. It needs it.

She needs it.

I give her a kiss on her lips, like Clay does. It makes the same smacking sound that Clay's kisses make.

Her eyes pop open wide. She's surprised I'm so forward. She thinks of me as shy. "Where's Hammerhead?" She looks out the door at his truck. She sees no movement. She checks a moment longer, then looks at me. Her brow lowers. She strokes her long hair with her hand and holds it back.

I stand and smile at her, trying to be cute in all the ways I can think of. I hold my head down and stare up at her with sad-looking eyes. I scratch my stomach, raise my T-shirt up, and stroke my chest gently with my hand, like I'm too sexy, even for myself, to be around without touching.

She looks at me strangely. "You two didn't get into a fight, did you?"

I cock my head sideways. "No, I just couldn't wait to get back to see the hottest woman in Kaneohe, that's all." I smile nervously and sort of salute her, in a really jerky, overly masculine way.

She laughs, a little charmed, then gets serious. "Where's Clay?"

"In the woods. He'll be home in a couple days. Don't ask. Spiritual quest."

"Clay? Are you *sure* everything's all right?

I flex my bicep and look down to see how it looks, reinforcing the tough look on my face by gritting my teeth so my jaw muscles swell. I stretch, drop my backpack on the floor, and examine the veins in my forearm.

She watches my whole muscle act, which I immediately feel stupid for doing.

I nod a couple times. "It's just, you know, I'm kinda pissed off. This fascist world…it gets inside my brain."

"I know what you mean." She lets me off the hook. A motocross motorcycle rally comes on the TV. I imitate the noise of the engine and hold my arms out like I'm riding one over a big dirt ramp.

She watches me and examines me as I move around her, like my head might pop open at any time and a big-toothed blue monster might spring out of my skinny neck.

I feel scrutinized, picked apart. I scratch my leg and dick.

"Does he have enough food?"

"Yeah, he's *fine*."

She comes alive, like she'd forgotten her lines and just remembered them. Her expression completely changes from worry and concern to all-knowing and clever. Her posture changes. "So, how was it?" she asks pleasantly, rocking back and forth from one foot to another, like she's excited to hear about the trip.

I look down the hallway. I'm drawn to Clay's room. I walk toward it in steady, measured, and assured long strides. His scuffed-up wooden door with stickers on it looks like the entrance to nirvana. Every instinct I have tells me to go in. I shove open the door and slam it behind me.

I hear Susan close the washing machine lid and start it going.

My body relaxes. I was holding my breath the whole time I was talking to her. My neck and shoulders are tense and pained after flexing for so long. I lock the door and fall back on his bed. I got away with it. My identity is pliable. I can just choose a new me and stick with it.

Clay's rubber slippers lie carelessly on the floor. Letters and photos and shit are sprawled out all over the floor.

I crawl over to the photos. I try not to see Tammy's face and expression in them. I'm afraid if I look into her eyes, she'll beam Clay out of me, take him away, like only a scorned girlfriend could do. I throw the photos into the trash can.

Susan knocks at the door.

I quickly shove all the letters under the bed and resume Clay's surfer-boy posture. It feels familiar already. I squeeze my throat with my hand to make my voice sound rough. "Yeah? What's up?"

"Are you hungry? I'm making dinner. I'd love your company."

What the hell is she doing? Is she insane?

"Uhh, I don't know." I picture her standing outside the door, waiting for the other shoe to drop, waiting for me to say, "Yes, please, that would be great," in the stupid kiss-ass way that polite pretty boy Sam would.

I hear her outside the door, breathing, waiting, creaking the floorboards. "Are you spying on me?" She shifts her weight.

"Every move." She sneaks away, leaving me with the horrific implications of what she just said.

I go over and sit down on Clay's bed and envision him in here before we left and what he'd be thinking: *My lizard's gone. That sucks. Fuck, it's a mess in here. I need some money. Where's my pot? Oh, yeah, it's in that drawer.*

I go over and get the bag and roll a joint. I kick back on the bed, fling my shoes and shirt off, and light up. I stare at the *Apocalypse Now* poster and try to think like Clay some more: *I wanna make a movie like that. I'm hungry. I wanna go out. I need some cash.*

I leave Clay's room to look for Susan. I walk slowly, arrogantly, and confidently. I spot her through the doorway to her bedroom. A talk-radio show is blaring from the living room. I clear my throat, clench my fists, and walk in.

She's setting up her easel and sorting tubes of acrylic paints, the kind Jared uses to paint Japanese action heroes and bloody shark-bite victims.

I've never been in her room. The door has always been closed. I can smell her flowery perfumes and essential oils. This room's like Clay's womb. It has perfect soft light and big ferns, and the bed's covered with a tapa-pattern bedspread. It's the same fabric as the pair of boxer shorts Clay wore at the campsite. Maybe she made them for him. In that case, I should have made fun of them even more. That's probably why he's sensitive about them. I wonder if the new "hippie-boy Clay" would care or think it's cool that his mom made his boxers. "Hi."

She backs out of the closet and straightens, like I scared her. She's different in her room, like maybe I am in mine. She's more complete, more expressed by the things around her.

"Hi. What's up?" She always says that to Clay.

I sit on her bed and rub the soft comforter. This is the place where he was made, maybe even the bed she and Clay's dad fucked in to make that one sperm join her one egg to make such a peculiar creature. Maybe a little of Sonny's sperm remains, resistant to washing off, and I could harvest it, make a new Clay in a test tube so he can have a fresh start, a new body and mind. It would give me a second chance too. I scoot up and lie back on the pillows.

"Take your shoes off on the bed."

Oh, my God. That felt real. She's my mom. I kick my shoes off and rest my head back. I flex my arm muscles. "Can I have some money? I'm really craving a plate lunch." I wait patiently and

attentively for her response with the right amount of pressure and
guilt-provoking neediness in my eyes.

She grabs her macramé purse off the floor.

I want to tell her to stop, not to give me a cent. I don't deserve
it. I'm not her kid. I'm a freak-imitation psycho boy who should
go the fuck home.

She pulls out her brown leather wallet.

No! I can't believe it.

"Forty would be dope." I take a deep breath. "I haven't seen my
bros in a long time. I thought I'd take a few out." That was stupid.
I only have one friend, and Jared would be pretty weirded out if I
wanted to take him out to dinner. He always pays. Do I mean
Clay's friends? I wouldn't be able to talk if it was them; I'd be so
uncomfortable.

"How about this? Mow the grass tomorrow morning, and you
get forty."

"So, it's a bribe? Okay, sure." I'm getting the hang of this.

She rolls her eyes and hands me two twenties.

I bow my head to her, samurai-style.

She bows back, like a bashful geisha girl. "Be careful. Don't be
out late. You know how mothers worry," she says, like it's script-
ed. She spins around and walks down the hallway to listen to her
hippie news program on the radio.

"Bye." I grab the keys from my pocket, adjust my dick in my
shorts, and head to the front door.

"So, I'll see you first thing in the morning mowing the grass."

"Yeah, whatever. I'll do it when I get up. Don't bug me about
it. Bye." I slam the front door to let her know I don't appreciate
being bribed just to get some money. I let my body go limp. Clay's
posture is exhausting. I walk around the side of the house to spy on
her through the window. I hope she needed me.

She sits in the living room, smoking a hand-rolled cigarette, in her own world. Her legs are up on the chair, like a kid's. She's listening to a radio program against the privatization of schools. She's fine. Totally normal, like nothing happened.

Clay better come back as his normal self.

I can't keep this up forever. I walk away, looking for more disapproving frontiers to test.

A small flock of white egrets walks around the front yard eating bugs. I walk up to them, expecting them to fly away, but they don't. They peck around me, unafraid, like I'm a horse or a cow. I get into the truck.

Susan looks at me through an opening in the curtains. She's watching me. She didn't let my weirdo behavior slide by. That makes me feel good, more important, more vital.

I sit up straight and wave to her, firmly. Then, I give her a shaka sign.

She hesitates for a second, then waves back and throws a kiss with her hand.

I get a little sad.

23

On crooked branch
chameleon looks like bark,
until he moves.

I stop to get a curry plate lunch at Takamori's in Kailua, an old, cheap outdoor diner sort of place where all the locals eat at least a couple times a week, after the beach or surfing or whatever. Macaroni salad and rice comes with everything for four dollars. I order in perfect pidgin, like I'm possessed. I scarf the curry down, throw away the Styrofoam plate, and drive away up the Pali Highway, which slices a thin path over the jagged, moss-covered peaks of the Koalau mountain range that divides the island. The glimmering lights of Kaneohe and Kailua look peaceful from the lookout. I blast through the tunnels and honk the shrill Japanese horn, to warn leeward Oahu and town I'm coming.

I turn the engine off and glide down the mountain. The tires on the pavement make the noise of how I imagine octopus suction cups sound when they release from the side of a whale. The air is warm, humid from the jungle, and freeing. I raise my arms out beside me, like riding a bike with no hands, and let out a big scream. Independence. I race down the highway till town's in sight.

The tall buildings and Asian neighborhoods of Waikiki and

Honolulu are lit by the last golden sun of the day. Streetlights and porch lights are already turning on. They make the city sparkle below the yellow- and pink-streaked sky.

I let off the clutch and jump-start the truck, something I learned from Clay. I turn and drive up the road into Tantalus, a hillside grouping of big houses, domes, and A-frames canopied by huge old banyan trees and a mess of bright-flowered vines that look like they came from outer space. At the turnout I see the incredible view of Honolulu and Waikiki's silver shiny towers.

I slow down and drive past a group of Hawaiian and Portuguese guys hanging out looking over the city, sitting on the hoods and trunks of a couple classic muscle cars with Hawaiian sovereignty stickers on the back bumpers: Union Jacks and stripes, the Hawaiian flag, with SOVEREIGN printed under it in bold, mean-looking lettering and NO HAWAIIANS, NO ALOHA in black on white backgrounds. They have a red plastic cooler and each of them has a Primo beer in his hands. They look mellow, like they hang out here all the time.

Clay would want to hang out with these dudes, at least see what's up with them and ask how the surf was today.

I can be him. He needs me to fill in for him. I can feel it. The world's not worth being in without Clay. I turn around and race back. I slam on the brakes and slide sideways into the turnoff, almost smashing into one of their cars—a shiny old red Pontiac with a surfboard rack on the top and white letters on the tires.

"Eh, brah, watch it. Don't try act big!" a tall, dark-skinned guy shouts.

"No worries. Howzit?" That was fun to say. I've always wanted to talk like this. I step out and walk over to the guys' cooler and grab a beer.

The guys look at one another, then to me, like I'm crazy, or *lolo*, as they'd put it. "Like beer?" he sarcastically asks.

I act like I didn't hear him. "Howzit? You deaf?" I unscrew the beer and sit on the trunk of a big muscular guy's old Chevy. I look over my shoulder into the car. The seats have leopard-skin covers. "Nice seat covers, brah. Where'd you get 'em, your grandma?"

The guy points to me with his thumb, gives his friend a look like, *Who the fuck is this kook boy?* and tries to grab my beer away.

I hold it tight. Some beer splashes onto my chest. It's cold on my skin.

He pulls harder. His face is strong and tan and he smells like cologne. His eyes are tree-green.

I let go of the beer and look down at his big, tan, rough hand. It's so close to me, I can see his veins and calluses. It looks powerful and experienced at fighting. I look down at my bony, hairless chest in front of his hand and realize that I'm shirtless and skinny. I was fooling myself to think that I looked like Clay, with the body of a surfer, like these guys. I fold my arms around my body and get up and walk to the truck. I drive away without looking back, making my way down to a quiet neighborhood, nearer to town, with a hillside view of Waikiki. I turn off the engine. I'm in the dark under a big banyan tree that covers the road. The houses are low and Japanese. The streetlamps are pink, the color they turn right before they click on for the night.

Two skater boys my age ride down the hill on their boards, with their arms out beside them. One's wearing a Frankenstein mask. They look free and happy.

I duck down so they don't see me. I lie back on the seat. I'm exhausted already. I reach up and pull off the rearview mirror and look at myself through a big crack and sticky beer residue. I switch on the interior dome light with my foot. I broke that too. It's now just a bare bulb that looks like a Christmas tree light.

"Look who it is."

I hear voices that sound like older girls doing an impression of younger girls.

They must recognize the truck. This sucks.

I angle the mirror up so I can see who they are.

It's two girls, walking up to the truck, both around Clay's age and both suntanned and pretty, in that beach-girl slut sort of way. One's wearing loose board shorts and a tiny tank top and sparkly makeup. She looks mean, like she'd turn on you at a moment's notice.

The other one is sweeter, with long blond hair and a pastel tank and shorts. She looks like she'd rather not be here.

I pull my legs into my chest and slide my hand over to lock the door. In the mirror, I watch them walk up to the window.

"Hey, Clay. What are you doing in there?" They knock on the glass.

I close my eyes and concentrate on Clay and try to remember how he thinks and talks. "Leave me alone." That sounded too much like me. I wasn't devoted enough to Clay. I have to forget myself. He'd wanna hang out. I roll down the window a crack. "So, what's up, girls?"

"We're going to a party in Port Lock. Can you give us a ride?"

I have to be Clay for these girls. They won't give me the time of day if I'm my normal self-conscious self. I close my eyes and concentrate. I could fuck these girls if I wanted to. I can play these chicks like I'm a stud boy.

Clay's possessing me. This feels excellent.

"What are you doing in there, jerking off?" The blond one snickers.

"Yeah, and I'm about to shoot a huge load, so shut up."

"I wanna help." The blond takes on a flirty tone and smiles at her friend.

"Gross, Andrea," the other one says.

I sit up, lunging forward into view. "You wish."

They jump back at least three feet. "Who the fuck are you?"

"Clay's friend, and I'll assume you are two of his long list of sluts."

"Fuck you."

"No, thanks." I lean back, put my arm up on the seat, and flex my chest and look down at my dick in Clay's shorts. It turns me on. I feel like I've grasped his sex appeal, his confidence, his power. I wink at the blond one, Andrea. "So, you wanna ride or what?"

"Sure," she says without hesitation. What a whore. What a sellout. "Come on, Courtney." She looks at me with a smile, then whispers in the other girl's ear.

I reach over and push the passenger-side door open and start the truck. "Coming or what, ladies?" I press the accelerator hard, revving the engine. It sounds tough.

"Come on." Andrea gets in and pulls on Courtney's arm.

Courtney rips her arm away and looks up the road. "Where's Clay, anyway?" She looks into the truck like she's scared.

"Courtney. Come on!"

"Come on!" I imitate Andrea's voice.

Courtney gets in and I peel out. I hope they can smell my animal sweat and dick and balls.

"So, I'm Andrea," she says all flirty. "You're Clay's friend?"

"Yeah, we're bros. Sam's the name."

She reaches over to me, like she wants to shake hands.

I peck her on the cheek as I turn a sharp corner without slowing down.

She gets thrown up against me. Her bare leg touches mine. She moves it away quickly and glances at Courtney.

Courtney stares straight ahead with a bitchy look on her face, holding on to the door handle to steady herself.

Andrea presses her leg back against mine ever so slightly.

I shift into fourth gear and reach down and run my fingers softly along the top of her leg.

She giggles and checks on Courtney again to make sure she doesn't notice.

I have to do what Andrea wants—fulfill my part—even though I don't mean it. I tickle her thigh and scrape down her kneecap with my fingernails.

She pushes my hand up, like she doesn't like it. Yeah, right. "How old are you?" she asks.

"Sixteen, why?"

"You look so *young*."

"You wouldn't say that if you saw my dick." I wink.

Courtney looks out the window with a look on her face like she just tasted battery acid.

Andrea looks at me and makes a little smile that's supposed to be sexy.

I smile back to make her think I'm into her and gently slide my hand back onto her thigh.

She spreads her legs a little and settles down into the seat. She's totally into it.

I can't believe she buys my act. Surfer-boys have it easy with girls. "How old are *you*?" I delicately rub her leg.

"Eighteen." She tries to look cute and pushes her hair back behind her shoulders.

"Cool." That's enough conversation. She's ready for the grand finale: my *scène de la crème*. I hold my breath and concentrate, then open my hand on her leg and grab her crotch.

"What the fuck? Get off me!" She closes her legs quickly and traps my hand between them. She looks at Courtney, like she's supposed to save her.

"Then let go, Medusa." I pull my hand from the hot area between her legs.

"You're disgusting. Stop the car!" She looks like she's having a bad trip.

I scream a coyote call and speed up, squealing the tires.

"Oh, my God." Courtney does a dramatic Hail Mary thing on her chest.

I build up speed on the H-1 freeway and turn up Clay's punk rock. "So, you wanna help me jerk off?" I reach down to my surf shorts and untie the strings on top and rip apart the Velcro far enough to see my pubic hair. "What'd you expect, getting into the car with a stranger?"

"Slap the fucker, Andrea."

Andrea slaps me on the cheek. It stings like crazy.

"Wow, that was hot." I say in a dumb jock-boy surfer tone. I speed down the road out to Port Lock going seventy-five in a twenty-five speed zone, passing houses like a blur.

Andrea grips the dashboard. Her nails dig into the vinyl.

"Is that how'd you'd grip my back while I—?"

"Shut up!" She scoots away from me, toward Courtney as far as she can.

Courtney shoves her back. "You're wrinkling my shorts."

Andrea looks at me and slides back over a little.

I smile at her and skid around a corner.

"Be careful, please?" She sounds genuinely concerned.

"I'll ask you when I want you to talk."

Port Lock. An all-haole, upper-class peninsula behind Diamond Head that doesn't feel at all like Hawaii. It's neater and cleaner and richer than the rest of the island. Everyone I've ever met from Port Lock is snobby, plays soccer, and has blond hair. The occasional guy surfs, but he wouldn't dare surf in a spot dominated by local boys—they'd kick his ass if he tried to act local. In the social-life department, though, since most of the kids here come from big party places like Southern California and have parents who are always away on business on the mainland, it's the party capital of the island.

"So, where is this fuckfest?" I ask.

Andrea points to a cul-de-sac called Poipu Place. She's my slave now, too scared to talk back.

I rip around the corner, on two wheels.

Preppy-looking kids hang out in front of a white modern house with fire torches burning along the driveway. Porsches and BMWs are parked along the street. The whole scene's such a gross '80s cliché.

"We've arrived, my pretties." I slam on the brakes and the truck skids to a halt, nearly hitting a couple squeezing out of the back seat of a Porsche.

A tan guy with a preppy haircut and light-blond highlights flips me off. I secretly think he's kinda cute.

Courtney waves at him. "Hi."

Andrea hides her face in her hands. "Oh, my God, that's Daniel."

I flip on the high beams. "Daniel! Andrea here wants you. She just told me."

Courtney accidentally laughs.

Andrea sinks down in the seat. She's embarrassed to be seen with me. Her look turns into sadness, then to anger. They jump out, embarrassed.

I ruined their entrance. I zoom down the street to park. I run my fingers through my hair, take a deep breath, and walk to the house. I see myself in the glass of the front door. I don't have a shirt or shoes, and Clay's dirty blue surf shorts hang obscenely low off my hipbones. I shove the big wood door open, and a blast of cold fake-feeling air comes at me, like it's being filtered by a purification system. It's totally dehumanizing. It's such a perfect night outside—bright stars, warm trade winds, yellow moon—and these fuckers have the air-conditioning on full blast. I get a chill up my spine, and all the tiny blond hairs on my arms stick up and my nipples get hard. The tile feels freezing on my bare feet. I feel my balls and dick shrink in the artificial coolness.

A couple girls turn and look at me for a second, then light up a joint.

A blond guy wearing a vest checks me out. "Who are you?"

"Clay Anderson's brah. He invited me." I talk in a pidgin accent. "It's Sam." I give him a shaka sign.

All these Port Lock guys are totally intimidated by Clay and his bros and the locals. "OK, brah. No worries. Like beer?" He tries to speak local talk with me and points at the drink table.

His tanned friend wearing surf shorts that have never been used for surfing comes over and nods at me.

I flex my bicep and smile at him.

He smiles back and pours a drink for himself.

Everyone's buying my act.

A table is set up in the entry with all kinds of alcohol—wine, vodka, mixers, beer, real glasses, even some sick-looking pâté. There's no keg, no junk food, no plastic cups and spilled drinks or loud anarchistic music with lyrics about not fitting in and hating the status quo. There's nothing to make me feel comfortable here, which helps my act. This isn't a party; this is adult dress-up, and all these fuckers are training to be good capitalists.

I pour a big gulp of Scotch into a wineglass and spill some coke on top of it. It makes a stain on the pressed white tablecloth. I down it fast, which burns my throat down to my stomach.

A guy who looks like he's got bronzing lotion on stares at me, offended.

"Eh, brah. Howzit? It's Sam. You no remember me? Out at reef." I gargle through a mouthful of Scotch.

"Oh, yeah. What's up? I'm Trevor." He has no idea who I am, but I know who he is. I've heard about Trevor. Trevor Wilson, the infamous '80s-style coke boy who has parties all the time in his parents' abstract fucking box of a house while they travel the world, exploiting third-world labor to make their stupid aloha-shirt clothing line.

I can't believe I'm here. It's like Darwin said: survival of the fittest. It's always the scrappiest species that prevail. Coyotes and spiders and rats and people like me.

These passive capitalists are on the way to extinction. They'll be too busy watching TV, shopping, and paying their maids in these huge air-conditioned houses to notice when Diamond Head erupts again. They can't even see that I think this party is a joke, that I don't belong here, that I'm dangerous. All I have to do is be confident, and I've got power I've never had before.

I spot Tammy. *Shit.* My ears ring and I start sweating. I duck down and run into a dark hall. What's she doing here? She can't be here. She knows me. She knows my personality and how I behave. She'll see through my act and tell people, and I'll end up with a broken arm.

I spy on her from around a corner.

She's surrounded by what look to be her closest friends.

I rub my feet on the carpet till static electricity builds up. I want to get as amped-up as possible. The Chinese believe we all have an electric energy field that gives us power. I want to shoot a bolt at Tammy and knock her to the floor.

Tammy says hi to the girls I drove here, Andrea and Courtney.

Andrea uses huge gestures describing how she had to hold on when I flew around corners.

Tammy's my poison. She can beam Clay out of me.

Courtney waves a couple muscled pretty boys over, and they talk about something—me, I think. They're going to find me and "ask" me to leave with their Republican tact unless I do something.

I dive down below a dark wood table and crawl to the stairs. I leap up them, not looking back. I run into the security of a dark hallway and walk out on a deck above the front door. Instantly, I feel different. The air is soft, warm, and moist compared to the dry temperature-regulated environment inside. I feel my pores and lungs open up. I take a deep breath and look up to the stars.

They just float there, still and permanent. They'll be the same tomorrow no matter what I do.

I can do this, even with that bitch Tammy here.

A couple pickups drive up in a row, like a convoy of military vehicles.

Cool. Some of Clay's bros and the local boys. They always crash these parties.

Manny gets out of the first truck and opens the door for his girl, all gentleman-like. "Like drink, Leilani?" He acts all official with her. It's cute.

I sneak down the hall to the top of the stairs and crouch down so I can see the front door.

The local guys and their girlfriends walk into the house. Ten or so guys jump out of the back of a pickup right outside the front door and say their typical greetings. "Eh, brah."

"Where's the sistahs?"

Their girlfriends, beautiful girls with long black shiny hair and strong pretty faces, smile and walk in. One fixes the plumeria behind her friend's ear. "Aloha. Hi, Charlene. How's it going?"

Trevor walks up to them, all puffed up and proud, but he backs off when he sees the locals. He can't really tell them not to be here. They're the real Hawaii. There's an unwritten law that you don't fuck with them. He stands aside, overwhelmed by their boisterous island charisma and connection to the waves and nature and the *mana* of the island. They bring the aloha spirit into the house with them, without even trying.

I love watching the Port Lock kids get walked over by Clay's friends. I lift a glass that someone left on the top of the stairs and smell the purple contents. Red wine. Should work fine. I swirl it around, then swallow it. I run down the hall to explore.

I pick a door and open it.

A naked girl rides a naked guy on a huge bed with pink pillows. His legs are spread far apart, and his balls are smashed under her bouncing up and down.

"Go get 'er, brah." I slam the door and try another. I feel like a detective. I open it. I think it's the parents' room. There's a big bed overlooking windows and double doors leading out to a deck with a view of the ocean. I go to the medicine cabinet to look for narcotics.

Rich people always have codeine, Valium, or at least some sort of back-pain pills.

I find a plastic bottle of Valium and gobble down three. I look in the mirror. I look like a wild animal. I flex my arm muscles and tighten my stomach so I can see the rows of individual bulges. I splash water on myself. I look confident and cool, strong and sexy.

I go over to the closet and open the door.

It's bigger than my bedroom and full of ridiculous things that have no use. On one side, there are rows and rows of dresses and women's pants and suits in bland businesswoman shades of gray and brown and black. Boring.

I turn around to look at the dad's side. It's all dark-blue suits, a rack of ties, pants. Oh, fuck, a full-on blue Naval uniform, with tons of pins and medals tacked on. I take the clear plastic off it and hold it out in front of me. *He must have done some evil things to get all these awards. He's definitely a fascist. These are Vietnam awards. He killed babies and farm workers for these. He occupied lands that weren't his, leading a troop of stupid grunt boys. It's almost like staring at an original Nazi flag or something.*

I have to put it on. I pull off my shorts and grab the uniform off the hanger. I step into the pants. They're too big, so I find a belt to hold them up, then put on the jacket with no shirt underneath. I place the hat on carefully as a finishing touch and walk over to the mirror.

The Valium combined with the Scotch is soothing my muscles and relaxing my spine.

I stand up straight, push my chest and dick out, my shoulders back. The broad shoulders of the suit make me look big and muscular. I look like a dictator. This is my island nation. This feels real. This is my calling. I should be in power. I can rule firmly, effectively, and fairly, although fairness doesn't matter here with all these fuck-ups around. I bring my arm up, drawing sharp angles in the air, and salute myself in the mirror. "I do solemnly swear to be true to the rules and jurisdiction of the island of Sam. May God help us all." I walk down the hall and stop at the top of the stairs. I take a deep breath and hold my arms straight down my sides. I lower my voice and practice a German accent. "Excuse me, everyone, excuse me." I clear my throat and yell. "Excuse me, my people!"

No one looks up, but a couple tan guys laugh at me.

"Shut the fuck up! I have an announcement to make. I won't be ignored!"

The party goes dead silent, and everyone looks up at me. I feel so whacked I might pass out. I don't see Tammy. *Maybe she left.* I hold my chin up and take a deep breath. I try to harness power from the room. I'm the center of everyone's existence. I'm a dictator. "Clay Anderson doesn't give a shit about Tammy Black." I hear a gasp, I think, but it could be in my buzzed-out head. I avoid looking at the faces of the people watching me. It's a power trick I learned about Hitler in school—never let them have eye contact.

Tammy walks in from another room and immediately looks straight up at me. Her face mangles up on itself. She stares at me like I'm a rabid dog with poisonous drool hanging out of my mouth.

My body tightens. My hands start shaking. I imagine her coming up here and hitting me, but she stands perfectly still, holding a wineglass by its stem. Her black dress makes her look like an evil seductress.

I feel all my confidence, all my power and potential fall away from me.

She's the one person I can't fool.

I've seen her control Clay, tell him what to do, make him repress himself.

She beams the confidence out of my body.

In a flash, I see this situation from outside myself. I'm skinny, shirtless, barefoot, dirty as fuck, lacking sleep, hungry, and dressed in a stupid Navy uniform. The jacket's shoulders are too big and look clownish. The hat makes my head look small and shrunken. The sleeves are too long, hanging over my hands. I look like a young kid dressed up in his father's clothes. I'm pathetic. I'm a delusional psychopathic liar. I stand out like a homeless guy at a charity gala.

"Clay's my boyfriend. Right now he's on the Na Pali coast on a Native American dream quest. When he comes back, he won't be the same person…" I feel faint. "He's…not interested in your shit and…he even has my name tattooed on his arm…" Suddenly, I can't think of anything else good to say. This is fucking disgraceful.

Manny runs at me with his arms out.

I fall forward down the stairs, not gracefully and athletically, like Clay would fall, but dramatically sloppy. I'm outside of my body. I feel myself land in Manny's strong arms. My Navy hat tumbles down the stairs.

Tammy's voice: "Drop him, you dick!"

24

Eyes on falling leaves,
I get lost in the patterns
of bright red and orange.

I wake up on the floor. I'm sweaty, and I have no idea whose fucking room I'm lying in. My chest has lines on it from the grass floor mats. A tropical leaf–patterned sheet lies crumpled in a ball at my feet. I stand up. My head throbs with a dull headache. My muscles are sore.

Bamboo shades hang crooked, halfway covering the window. A pile of surf magazines lies on the floor by the bed. On the desk, there's a framed photo of a pretty, dark-haired girl with flowers in her hair and a puka shell necklace around her neck.

I walk to the window, stubbing my toe on a surfboard leaning against the wall. The board falls sideways and slams on the floor. It makes a loud, hollow-sounding bang and leaves a waxy line on the wall. I try to rub it off with a dirty sock, but it just makes the scrape more obvious. I try to put the board back but it falls again and makes an even louder thud.

I look out the window. The house is in a grove of banyan trees that block out the sun. The trees have hundreds of complicated trunks and roots hanging off the branches, some reaching the ground forming new trunks. They look haunted. A blue plastic tent covers some lawn chairs and a couple old couches and tables made from old phone-wire spools.

I hear the voices of Hawaiian boys speaking pidgin. I duck down under the window.

Did someone take me hostage?

Guys that speak pidgin hate me. I don't belong here. I'm a white kid. A fucking haole. Why did Europeans ever invade the islands? Native people hate Europeans, and I know why. They bring their suitcases of money and their machines and arrogance and religions and force them on the locals.

I should have locked myself in my room last night and shut the fuck up, maybe smoked a joint, or called someone normal, like Jared. I pace the perimeter of the room. I'm thirsty as fuck. I have to piss. I need out of here. I need a phone. I lean down to see under the bed. Only some shoes and an all-girl porn magazine. I open it part way and see a naked girl licking another girl's nipple. I check a row of shelves. There's a big square box covered with a Hawaiian tapa-printed cloth thrown over it and some college-looking books. *Business 214: A Better Way to Do Business in a Multicultural Environment.* A notebook with nothing written on the pages. A couple of glass dolphin figurines that look out of place, dried leis, and a framed photo of a young girl doing hula at some contest. I take the tapa fabric off the box to see what's underneath.

A bright green lizard sits under a gnarled piece of driftwood, inside a cage carpeted with green Astroturf. His eyes turn in their shallow sockets, almost a full 180, facing me. *Fuck, it's Eddy. I'm at Manny's house.*

"Eddy!"

I wanna pick him up and kiss and hug him. "Eddy, how are you, man?" I stare at him through the glass. "Don't you recognize me?" I reach in the cage to pet him, and he starts doing these miniature lizard push-ups. "I'm Clay's boy, Sam. You've seen us do it." I pull out an old telephone half buried underneath some clothes on the shelf below Eddy. I pick up the receiver. The comforting dial tone buzzes in my ear. It's one sound that's always a constant, no matter where you are in America: in a prison, at a pay phone on the beach, or in a mansion. I dial Clay's number.

I know what he's doing if he heard about last night—screaming and punching his walls and door in, throwing his surfboard and shoes through his window.

I listen to the high-pitched ringing. Nothing. I count until the answering machine picks up. I hang up.

I open the door and stick my head out to look down the hall. I see Manny's mom in the kitchen standing over a deep fryer. I smell sweet bread and sugar.

She looks up at me and smiles, like I'm just one of Manny's friends, a normal person. Little does she know.

I nod to her, lifting my chin up and sort of saying *hey* with my eyes, imitating what all the surfers do, and run for cover in his room. I lock the door and let the bamboo shade down as slow as I can, so he won't notice my movement from outside. I find Manny's shirt drawer and look through it.

I take a yellow Castle High School T-shirt and slide it on. It's way too big and it smells like a mixture of laundry soap and weird cologne. I find Clay's keys on Manny's dresser next to my wallet and a twenty-dollar bill.

Manny must have emptied my pockets before he put me to bed.

I hold my breath and walk out and into the kitchen. The floorboards creak under my feet.

His mom sits at the kitchen table reading some kind of newsletter.

"Eh, little brah." She looks up at the clock.

I follow her gaze. It's 2:30. "Hey."

"You Clay's friend. I'm Ana, Manny's mom. Like *malasadas?*"

"No, thanks, I'm late for something."

She's slow-paced and mellow, cooking inside while her son and his future wife have fun in the backyard. "I tell Manny you had to go." She winks at me.

"Bye." I charge through the front screen door.

Clay's truck is parked on the grass.

I open the door and almost gasp.

The rearview mirror is glued back on. Clay's surf shorts are folded on the passenger seat with a package of fins on top, neatly, like my mom would set them on my bed. Clay's pickup has been vacuumed and polished. The scents of Windex and Armor All make me sad. This was the only place I know of that contained all the things that embodied the way I felt about Clay and how he felt about me.

I turn the radio on and drive east toward Kaneohe and Clay's house. I pull into the driveway, nervous and sweating. I'm scared the house won't feel familiar. I scan from one end to the other, trying to pick up on small changes so the rejection won't hit me all at once.

Clay's skate shoes and Susan's gardening slippers sit by the front door. There's a trail of sand leading to the carport where he leaves his surfboard, but no water from recent surfing.

Susan's gardening tools are out, sitting by a half-tilled flower bed. Her car is gone.

I walk up to the door. It's open. I walk inside quietly.

Clay's shoes that he wore on the camping trip are sitting in the entry, coated with orange dirt, and his shirt's flung on the ground beside them. I pick his shirt up and press it to my face. It smells strong, like he was nervous or pissed off, or possibly worried, or turned on. I need more evidence.

The phone rings. I stand by the answering machine and watch the red light blink. It activates. "Hey, if you wanna talk to me or

Susan, leave a message, but don't make it too long 'cause you suck. Aloha." It beeps and the tape rewinds.

"Hey, Clay. Howzit? It's Manny-boy. You back yet? I got some pretty interesting news about your little brah, Sam. Call me, braddah. I'll be at Leilani's later today. Laterz."

The PLAY button starts to flash.

I tiptoe down the hall to see if anyone's home. Clay might be sleeping. His room's illuminated with soft afternoon light filtered through the trees. I don't see him, but I hear a surfing contest on TV.

I run back out to the answering machine and press DELETE. It rewinds Manny's voice and the light goes out.

"Hey."

I jump and turn around.

Clay stands perfectly still, watching me.

"Fuck, you scared me."

"Not half as much as you scare me."

He knows, and he doesn't understand. This is my worst nightmare. He doesn't appreciate what I was trying to do for him. He doesn't get how scared and sad I was, how much I'd love for everyone to just know about us and get over it already.

"Why don't you just erase my whole fucking life?" He struts down the hall into his mom's room.

I follow him, stopping in the doorway. "Why are you being like this?"

He plops down on his mom's bed. "You know why."

"You should have called me. I was waiting to pick you up. I have the truck."

He takes a deep sigh and stares at the television, at a stocky, muscular Balinese surfer doing his run. Then he freaks out. "Take the truck! Go live in my room! Have all my shit! Take my mom! Just get the fuck away from me!" He stands up and walks toward me.

I don't know if he's going to kiss me, hug me, kill me, or punch me.
He pushes me hard and slams the door shut in my face.

I shout through the door, "I know what you're thinking… you're just—"

He pulls the door open violently and stands in the opening like a dog poised to attack. "If you know what I'm thinking, you know that I have no fucking interest in seeing you."

How'd he hear about last night? Manny didn't tell him yet. Maybe Tammy and her friends…

"I don't think that many people even heard me."

"Are you fucking crazy? The whole island heard. You fucked up my life forever!" His face goes from pure anger to despair. He sits on the bed and retreats into the surfing contest. A tan, muscular boy gets thrown off his board like a doll. He's taken underwater into the power and depth of the wave.

Tears fill Clay's eyes. He covers his face to hide them from me. "I don't know what to do. Never leave my house?" His anger builds again. "I can't go surfing or to Kailua or anywhere! I'm fucking trapped here…with you!"

"I did it for us."

"So I'm the laughing stock of Oahu? So I'm left with you, and everyone else hates me?"

I don't know what to do. I stare at my name in his tattoo. "I'm sorry. I love you. You said you loved me."

"I just said that to fuck with you. I don't love you. Leave. Get the fuck out of here."

I stand in the doorway, afraid to leave and afraid to stay. "Your truck's clean."

"Fuck off!"

I kick the wall as hard as I can. "You're a fucking liar!"

A tan, handsome guy on TV rides a perfect wave, smoothly and stealthily, without a worry on his mind.

I throw myself on the floor. I want to feel pain so this situation has some substance, some reality outside my mind. I get up and fling myself to the floor again. I land too well to hurt myself. I learned how to fall without injury from Clay's dumb karate lessons, when I thought everything he could teach me was the coolest. "Clay!" I scream, like a military drill sergeant.

He pokes his head out of the sheet, his face wet from crying.

"Look me in the eye."

"What?" He sits up forcefully.

"I hope you die." I run out of the room. I'll find someone better than him. I'll fulfill who he thinks I am. I'll lie and make up shit and ruin lives getting what I want. Tears run down my face. I can't stop them. "Fuck!" I run down the hall to the front door. I spot my backpack by the door, so I strap it on while I'm running.

"Sam!" His mom pulls in the driveway as I'm running out the door.

I take off on my bike that's been stashed in Clay's carport for weeks. It's creaky and dusty. It's from an abandoned part of my life that I completely stopped living when Clay took over. I take off down the street without looking back. I ride down the hill on my bike away from his house.

I ride my bike down the long hill to my neighborhood and turn in by the HAIKU VILLAGE sign. I ride up to my front yard. My front wheel catches on the curb and I fly forward and crash on my head in the grass. My bike lands on top of me and a pedal scrapes my calf, making it bleed and sting.

I can't get up. There's no reason to go inside, no reason for shelter. Nothing could make me feel better or worse. This is the bottom. "I fucking hate you, you liar fucker shithead dumb-ass!" I throw my bike off my legs and stand up. I get dizzy, and a wave of sadness almost knocks me over. Tears drip on my shoes. I'm scared to go into my room. I don't know what I'll find. I climb in through the window and jump on my bed and fall back, out of breath. The room's humid and stuffy, and the door's closed. There aren't any phone messages on my dresser, like there used to be: no signs of life.

The rest of the world forgot that I exist while I was out trying to tame the wild boy, something I never wanted to do anyway.

I could have died, and even my parents would have taken a week or two to notice. I hate myself. I roll off my bed and hit the floor. It's too hard being me. I can't stop crying. I want Clay to come over, but I know he won't.

25

Monster swelling waves
rock my small kayak and throw
me in the current.

Thirty-two days pass and Clay's absence is everywhere: in my muggy room, on the streets of Kailua, at crowded Lanikai beach, at the cheap burrito place, and at Board of Hawaii, where I peer inside the window looking for him through taped-up punk show fliers.

My parents finally got over me disappearing for three days. *Disappearing* is their word. To me, camping with Clay was way stranger than disappearing. It was another dimension. School's been delayed till November because of this parents' group that found out about some crumbling asbestos in the building's ceiling. The workers need that long to clean it out, so we're off for another month and a half. I'm glad school's starting late, since I'm unable to concentrate on what good, if any, it's doing for me. I don't know what the point of living is, either. It's a new feeling and it's hard-core scary. At least I can write about it. It gives me something to be miserable about, and writers need that.

I finally fix my board and throw the one I stole from Clay's house into my closet. I throw the new stupid birthday-boy board out the window, strap on my pack, and jump out after it, practically falling on my face. I speed over to skate at the elementary school in Keolu Hills, a basketball court with hand railings and stairs, to try to find evidence of my life before Clay. I can't find the energy to ollie, so I stand around by the steps holding my board and watching the other guys rail-slide like it's simple.

They're shirtless and tan, and they move through the air with grace. They look sexy, some of them almost perfect, but I can't like them the way I like Clay. These dudes are children.

Maybe they're too young, and I'm too grown-up now, even though we're the same age. I'm sophisticated and a writer, and they've never even read a haiku. They're naive about how complicated relationships with girlfriends could possibly be, and I've gone through it all with another boy. I jump on my board and glide over to this shady corner to hang out in this place where I'm supposed to belong. All tired and smelly and sweaty, I can't be bothered to act like I really care about being any better of a skater than I was at age twelve—I just don't care about it as much, maybe because now I'm more advanced than just needing physical activity to define me. I sit down on my board and take my pack off. I get hot in the sun, so I take my shirt off and lean back on the metal chain-link fence, which feels cool on my sweaty back. A haiku comes to me. *On my chest, salty sweat drying, replenishing tear supply.* Someone pokes my shoulder, and I twist around and see Clay standing there under a tree looking sort of bad, almost gruesome—dark circles under his eyes, black sweatshirt on a hot late-summer day, and scabby, deep scrapes on one of his cheeks. I can't believe it's him. He's like a beat-up ghost remnant of Clay, reminding me how stupid I am for loving him in the first place. He leans down and looks at my board. "Finally put the wheels and trucks on that I gave you, huh?"

"What happened to you?"

"I got into a fight with this gnarly dreadlock dude on the North Shore. I kicked his ass." He motions punching into the air like some stupid ego touch-boy.

237

"Oh." I'm truly not interested in his stupid surfer-boy fights, but I want to hug him and tell him everything will be fine. That's out of the question, though, since there's chain-link between us. I think he made it this way on purpose.

"Listen…I want you to meet me at the beach tomorrow. I want to talk to you. I got to get some shit off my chest."

"Like what?"

"Just come, man." He starts walking away just as another skater my age comes gliding up to sit down and drink his green tea in a can.

"*Sayonara, kyoodia,*" I whisper. He taught me that Japanese and I'll never forget it. *Goodbye, brother.*

The wind is strong today, but it's sunny outside and I can't help but be excited about seeing Clay in the perfect golden light on the beach. I hope he'll be wearing his low-hanging flowered surf shorts and no shirt. I hope he'll take me into his sexy wolf-boy arms and wrestle me to the ground and consume me so I can forget about all the bad shit between us. I decide to walk to the beach so I can appreciate every moment of going to see Clay without rushing through this important moment. As I round the curve into Lanikai, a neighborhood that overlooks the Mokaluas, two small triangle-shaped islands, a haiku comes into my mind, mostly out of feeling hopeful about Clay. *Distant islands, enveloped by warm ocean, I'm not that far away.* I feel sort of stupid because I've hardly ever come up with anything so fucking lame. I'll never repeat it to anyone. I'm glad I don't have my pack with my notebook in it, because then I'd feel tempted to write it down.

I round the corner and see the right-of-way to the beach looming in front of me. Clay's truck is parked right outside it, looking confrontational and sexy as always. It almost scares me as I walk by, analyzing its aggressive lines; its carefree, crooked parking spot with its tail hanging out into the road.

A car honks behind me, a high-pitched Japanese car horn. I turn around.

It's Kendra in her old Honda hatchback. She looks like a Japanese superhero, with her black hair back behind a pink head-band. She pulls up beside me, and I wonder if she could hear me thinking my lame, hopeful haiku. "Hey, Sammy. Going to the beach?"

"Yeah. I'm supposed to meet Clay there. We're sort of not talking or whatever, but he wants me to meet him for some reason."

"Wait for me." She parks on the grass in front of Clay's truck and walks over to me, holding a weird wicker beach-bag thing. She looks a little concerned. "Listen to this, Sam." She pulls a notebook from the bag. Oh, God, I'm forever condemned now to hearing her sentimental love poems. She clears her throat while walking down the right-of-way. "Love is scary, gnarly wood that makes many strong men flee. Careful of the wolves that howl when love is hoisted high on a tree."

"That's good," I say. "I like it more than that other one."

"I wrote that this morning. I heard about what you did, Sammy. Jared told me." She closes her book and shoves it back in her bag.

Now I really feel stupid. "Yeah, I was fucked-up. I don't know. That's why Clay's pissed."

"You're brave to show up. I wouldn't be here."

"You don't know him like I know him."

"Maybe, but I've seen him kick a big Samoan guy's ass." She stops in a shady spot.

"Then why are you here?"

"All my friends are here. Clay's here."

We'll end up in some *From Here to Eternity* embrace on the beach. "OK, well, stop by and say hey later. I'm gonna go find Clay."

I hold my breath and walk down into the sunlight. When I step out onto the beach, it's like walking into a party. A big group of kids are partying, drinking beer out of one of those Styrofoam coolers that gives me the chills to touch. The sound of the lid coming off and rubbing onto the rim makes me want to curl up into a ball on the ground. I look both ways for Clay and start walking to the right, where he usually hangs out if he comes here to swim in the late afternoon and where, before me, he used to party with Tammy and all of her stupid girlfriends and his macho crew of illiterate Kailua boys who can talk for hours about nothing. I walk a couple houses down the beach, and Clay comes walking up, sort of strutting.

Kendra walks by with her big bag. "Hey, Clay. How's the waves today?"

"Not bad."

She looks at me, then at Clay, and walks down the beach to her group of friends. I don't know how she hangs out with them. She's so much cooler than they are.

I look at Clay, who's watching Kendra walk away. "Hey."

He barely looks at me.

I feel like I'm an embarrassment. I'm an embarrassment on the Travel Channel's World's Best Beach five years in a row. Now, that's an accomplishment.

"You showed." He's holding a beer, and I can tell he's fucked-up.

"Why wouldn't I?"

"You don't know?" He takes a big gulp of beer.

"What'd you mean, Clay? I miss you." That took so much fucking guts to say I feel like I'm going to hurl.

He cringes—like, literally—and instantly, I feel like I should run away down the beach, run to my house, go to my room, buy a plane ticket to somewhere like San Francisco, and never say goodbye to anyone I ever knew here. "Come over here, man."

"OK…" I follow him down the beach toward the group of kids he's hanging out with, but he walks in front of me like I'm a fucking dog or something. He's taunting me, and I know it's pathetic that a part of me thinks that he's going to lead me somewhere private to kiss and make up. As we get closer, I see Tammy and her friends, and these dudes I used to always see Clay hanging out with—these local boys, Portuguese and Hawaiians and haoles who think they're not. They're all surfers—not the cool, spiritual kind, but the serious, macho, alcoholic ones, the ones that make the beach stressful for anyone who's not one of their stupid brotherhood of lameness. "Clay?"

He throws his beer can down and gives me the meanest look I've ever seen. His lips are snarled up, his eyes look swollen and intense, his muscles are fully tensed. "Fuck you."

I feel like I've been stabbed in the chest. I start to walk away.

"Come here!"

"Fuck, no."

"Come here, please." His voice softens.

I turn around and see my name tattooed on his shoulder muscle. I look away as fast as I can, but I know he saw my expression change when I saw it. "What?" I say.

And then it happens. He punches me in the face so hard, I don't know where I am. I feel heat on my eye and nose and hot wetness—blood pouring out of my nose. My eye swells instantly as I fall backwards onto the sand.

He takes a step over to me and I look past him and see the top of the palm trees in the sun. He kicks me in the ribs and I lose my breath. I can't breathe. I can't open my eyes. As I gasp for air, I enter another world: truth. I hold my ribs and sob. I try to stand up and fall back on my hands, hurting my wrist. I try again and balance enough to fall forward into a step and then another one till I realize I'm running—running away from Clay, running away for my life, and fuck, is that scary. My eye and nose throb as I run. With every step, a rush of sorrow flows out my eyes and nose. I was never who I thought I was. He was never Clay. I was never Sam. Everything is nothing. I'm so fucking stupid. Everything I always thought I wanted is wrong. But now, I'm just running, bleeding, sweating, crying as far as I can till something looks familiar again. Behind me, I hear Kendra screaming.

"God damn it, Clay! What's your problem?"

I look back while I'm running away.

Kendra runs past Clay behind me, flipping him off as she goes.

I go into superdrive idiot skater-boy speed and practically dive down the right-of-way to the road. I run out in front of a car and duck down behind a big flowering bush.

Kendra runs out into the street, out of breath, and looks both directions until she sees me. "Sammy!" She leans down, scared and pissed off.

I ball up, silent, my chest rising and falling fast, and my face stinging and throbbing like hell. I can't face her right now. I can't even face myself.

I examine my black eye and swollen nose in the mirror on the back of my bedroom door, which is now free of haikus. I ripped them all down because they remind me of Clay. I've avoided my parents seeing my injuries over the last three days by wearing sunglasses and only risking walking past them when it's dark. I don't really think they give a shit anymore, anyway. I left them behind for Clay as well as everyone else in my stupid little life. Only I didn't know how stupid and little it was before I was forced to look at every element of it and examine exactly who cares about me and who wouldn't even notice if I died. Most people are in the "don't care" category. Jared still likes me, I'm sure, but I fucked him over for Clay. He's got his own thing going on anyway, and I know his parents think I'm a bad influence or whatever after-school special phrase they'd use to convey that I'm the one who buys the drugs, skips the classes, and doesn't want to grow up to support the capitalist system, like every other young fascist around here. I sit down on my bed and hold my phone, like someone's actually going to call. I dial Jared's house. The answering machine answers. I hang up. I dial Clay's number and start to sweat as it rings.

"Hello?" his mom answers.

"Uh…is Clay there?" I ask in a dumb, deep tone.

"No, Sam. He's out surfing. Do you want me to tell him you called?"

"No, please don't. Tell him to fuck off." I hang up quickly, already feeling stupid about doing that to his mom. God, I'm a stupid prick. I roll off my bed onto the floor, which makes blood rush into the swollen areas of my face. I lie there, feeling the strange sensation of my eye and nose throbbing like a pulse. My face feels hot. A thin film of sweat coats my entire body. I never felt this alone before. I never knew this feeling existed, even though I complained constantly about feeling lonely. This is something different; this is deeper, and I'm not sure I can escape it. I reach for the thick, messy blue file folder of haikus I wrote over the last couple of months.

I look through all of them—most are hopeful and about nature and the weather and the pure beauty of Clay's body and face and spirit and my spirit under the lame spell of him and me feeling horny in nature and wanting to do it outdoors like rabbits and the one simple leaf that falls and the one spring blossom that lasts only minutes and how scared I am that I'm a part of this vast system that renders everything almost meaningless. Well, I sure as hell am part of it, because whatever stupid thing I thought Clay had, it was as good as nothing. It was an illusion, not that everything isn't, I guess. We just believe what we want to, no matter what the signs and the earth and our friends and parents are saying from the outside. We just veer into danger like a drunk driver on our own blind paths of least resistance, steering toward tragedy, heartbreak, and being totally alone so that no matter how hard we scream, no one will care. We're able to ignore everything we've ever learned and just abandon our intuition and careen into the face of hell.

I fall asleep, then wake up just as it's getting dark outside. It's cooled down, so I feel like I can cry and the tears will evaporate, instead of just running down my cheeks and dripping off my chin, which has ten new hairs, onto my smooth bony chest. I load my black backpack with my notebooks and all the folders of all my haikus about Clay and the time we spent together and jump out my window. I grab my board from by the front door and jump on it and glide down the smooth black asphalt. As I push off and glide, I almost feel all right for a second. I love crying right now. The cool evening air makes my T-shirt flap across my chest and dries the tears as they flow. I skate down the main street, and there are hardly any cars since it's Sunday evening, and I hardly think till I'm walking, carrying my board, up the little hill that leads up to the old stone marker at Lanikai, where Clay hit me. As I walk out through the right-of-way onto the beach, the last of the Sunday beach crowd is going home to have dinner with their families. It's getting dark now, and I walk down the beach to try and see if there are still indentations in the sand where I fell after the punch. I can't find any evidence—today was too crowded—and the tide is coming up, erasing the weekend's footprints and sand castles and complex roadway systems designed by younger boys who don't know the pain I know. I sit down for a while and read my haikus, especially the ones that really conform to the formula of five, seven, and five syllables, when I cared about sticking to the formula, when I thought some sort of formula existed and things in life made sense. *His beautiful lips, I kiss and in return, I get a boner. I look in his eyes, my heart races, I get hard, I really love him. The boy I love has perfect imperfection. Am I his equal?* I read till it's too dark to read. I walk up into the yard of a big house to look for a kayak or some kind of canoe that I can steal to take a cruise around, maybe out to the Mokes if the waves aren't breaking over the reef. I sneak up into the dark yard and look under the house, where most people keep their canoes, and there they are—five or six of them in a row. I drag the smallest kayak out by the rope attached to the front of it and shove it into the gentle water and hop on with my backpack. I paddle out as fast as I can, just in case the people who live in the big house heard me. I stop paddling once I'm as far out as the first coral heads, and I lean back and stare into the stars. I see my favorite constellation—the Seven Sisters of Pleiades—seven bright bluish-white stars in a cluster that have always drawn my eyes to them, maybe because they're not lonely stars in space; they're together, and each one has six sisters to talk with about problems. I sit up and feel sort of dizzy from my black eye and swollen nose. I'm in the blackness that I usually only stare at from shore. It's comforting, and I always thought it would scare me. It doesn't at all. Maybe Clay made me stronger, braver. How could I not be braver now? I fought for every word I ever said around him.

I take my beat-up, sticker-coated file folder of Clay haikus out of my backpack and watch the papers flap in the breeze. If I didn't hold onto them, they'd blow away, skip across the surface of the ocean till the water weighed them down. I open the folder and let them fly. A gust blows like nature is again on my side, helping me. Months of haikus scatter into the ocean. As the last gets pulled away, I lie back and stare at Pleiades. The salt of my tears stings my swollen nose. I sit up and look for my haikus in the dark-blue water. The last of them sinks, waterlogged, into the ocean and begins its gradual process of decomposition, returning to dirt or scum or biological matter till the words are meaningless, which I guess they always were.

I paddle out even farther till the shore looks like a double string of white lights—the real lights and the reflections on the water. I squint and the island looks so small, so insignificant in this huge universe. I'm a tiny piece of dust—God, I never wanted to think that. I'm not some hippie Hawaii boy, but fuck, I'm small and I know it.

Acknowledgments

Very special thanks to John Rechy for golden advice and inspiration.

Aloha to Terri Fabris and Kim Fay, without whom this novel would not exist.